C000067162

Delia Jarrett-Macauley, the youngest daughter of Sierra Leonean parents, was born in Hertfordshire and now lives in London. She has taught at the universities of Kent and London and is the author of *The Life of Una Marson, 1905–1965*. This is her first novel.

Moses, Citizen & Me

DELIA JARRETT-MACAULEY

Granta Books

London

Granta Publications, 2/3 Hanover Yard, Noel Road, London N1 8BE

First published in Great Britain by Granta Books 2005

Copyright © Delia Jarrett-Macauley, 2005

Grateful acknowledgement is made to the following for permission to
reprint previously published material: 'I Hate You Then I Love You',
words and music by Tony Renis, Norman Newell, Alberto Testa,
Manuel De Falla and Fabio Testa (copyright © 1997 Peer Edizioni
Musicali/Tony Renis Music Publishing Corporation; Peermusic (UK)
Limited (26.67%)/Chester Music Limited (16.66%)/Universal/MCA
Music Limited (33.34%)/Copyright Control (23.33%); all rights
reserved; international copyright secured; PENGUIN is a registered
trademark of United Biscuits (UK) Limited, used with permission).
'Laidu', words and music by Rokia Traore, published by Editions Label
Bleu, represented by Reverb 2 Music Ltd, Reverb House, Bennett
Street, London, W4 2AH; reproduced by permission of the publisher.

Delia Jarrett-Macauley has asserted her moral right under the Copyright,
Designs and Patents Act, 1988, to be identified as the author of this work.

All rights reserved. No reproduction, copy or transmissions of this publication may be made without permission. No paragraph of this publication
may be reproduced, copied or transmitted save with written permission or
in accordance with the provisions of the Copyright Act 1956 (as amended).
Any person who does any unauthorized act in relation to this publication
may be liable to criminal prosecution and civil claims for damages.

A CIP catalogue record for this book is available from the British Library.

1 3 5 7 9 10 8 6 4 2

Typeset by M Rules
Printed and bound in Italy by Legoprint

To the memory of Cassius George Macauley

'Because it became hard for me to be a human being does not mean that I have become a monster.'

'At the Mind's Limits', Jean Amery

Prologue

The place is not like everywhere. Normally as you walk through the city, from Kissy by the harbour up to Murray Town at the top, you can hear various greetings; some say 'Indireh', others 'Buwa', occasionally you might get a 'Bonjour', and many people just say: 'Mornin, ma.' It is a city where everyone speaks at least two languages, and meeting and greeting is not necessarily a quick and simple thing. That is how different people have lived together there for a long, long time. But war came, and greeting near-strangers became a fool's pastime.

Vultures appeared in the skies, croaked and exited to hover with other gods. Darkness, when it descended, kissed away the orange-purple light of the villages and the silver sheen of the seashore. Now it was blackness for true. This was the end of an era for the people of the city, now passing each other with bowed heads and despairing glances along the roads. And it was the end of an era for the hapless niece of an old man, who was now flying 'home' from London.

Freetown would never be the same again. At the earliest sign of trouble foreigners said it was none of their business and secreted their accounts away. Planes left on one-way excursions. People stayed in their homes if they could, if they wanted to. Homes were ransacked, torn down and burnt. Former government ministers stole stale bread. Families did not know themselves, who was a friend, who was not. Who has gone over? Who is safe?

They heard The News and knew it was their stinking news: chapels looted, icons destroyed, imam burnt alive, loss of reason, loss of life.

The friends of the old man, Moses, could not speak the unspeakable. But eventually they whispered that it was indeed Citizen, Moses' grandson, who one dazzling morning that March had led them to the mangrove swamp to show what 'the big soldier man' had made him do. There he pointed to a bulky shape, twisted and distorted, strange in colour and horrific to smell.

It was a woman. Her hands were tied behind her back and her legs were bound together. There were several bullets in her back. It was Adele, his own grandmother.

One

It was late November, crisp and chilly, but I was dressed
lightly and wore no tights, to avoid discomfort on the flight.
I had arrived at the airport in good time, no thanks to the
minicab driver who sat in the traffic on Lavender Hill, stub-
bornly refusing to U-turn.

Heathrow Terminal Four, at nine in the morning,
thronged with the usual traveller types: the bleary-eyed, the
over-excited, the always-at-ease cosmopolitans – all milled
about in the open spaces and filed into rows for check-in.
There was a steady hum of voices above the intermittent
announcements. I had scrutinized the boards for the flight
and, dragging my huge suitcase, I went to stand in line for
processing.

Looking around I felt relieved at the sameness of the line.
A few trunks and suitcases as big as coffins were stacked on
top of trolleys, smaller cases with the last-minute purchases
that would try to pass as hand luggage. There was much
sighing and shuffling from adults, while the children sat on
available bags or gripped the trolleys for their last few minutes in England. The line was almost completely made up of
black people, except for an Irishman who had hoisted his
small son on to his shoulders and was receiving a commentary
from above. The African woman in front had an old brown
suitcase with a metal lock and string tied around it; it must
have been more than forty years old, with labels on it still,

pock-marked with stains. Her daughter, about five years old, was holding the hand luggage, shoppers in white, blue and red plastic, and had a Winnie the Pooh rucksack on her back. We exchanged smiles. I helped her lean the shoppers against the larger cases, and out of Winnie the Pooh's belly she pulled an African doll whose face was friendly but squashed from oversleep.

An airport terminal is a place of infinite outcome. The unencumbered observer can watch thousands of passengers moving towards some half-planned ending, like balls being pocketed by the amateur snooker player.

When I finally reached the desk I put down my ticket and passport with a quick, 'Window seat if you have one left?' and hurled the case on to the luggage belt.

'This is the queue for the Ghana flight. You need forty-two further down.' A red-painted fingernail pointed along the hall and I looked after it, aghast.

'Are you sure? Can't you just . . .'

My daydreaming vanished and I forced myself to focus. It was so easy for me to become lost in other people's private dramas, I realized that I was holding back from entering my own journey. My companions were undoubtedly on vacation. Had I stayed in that first queue, perhaps changed my ticket, I could have found myself in a peaceful part of West Africa. With just one flex of the credit card . . . Certainly I needed a holiday, and my appearance – pink T-shirt, linen jacket, sandals – was that of a typical holidaymaker; but that was not the reason for my journey.

I had received a call from my uncle's neighbour in Sierra Leone asking me to visit, if I possibly could. 'Sorry to be the bearer of bad news but your Auntie Adele is dead. Your uncle needs his family by him at this time. Will you come?'

I did not mean to say yes so promptly, did not want to be fetching pen and paper to write down a list of things to bring. So why did I? Instinct or bad instinct. When I was a girl my uncle had always meant so much to me. But that was when we were still speaking, before I grew up and began to find my own way.

Soon I was in the correct line, still dragging my large blue suitcase, wobbling towards the desk. Every few minutes I looked up to check, yes, the number of the flight was the same as the number on the ticket.

Less than two hours later I was parked in my window seat, being lifted through the clouds into sunlight. The plane was packed: everybody who was anybody in development was heading there. I was not ready to talk, but content to look out at the clouds, snooze and balance the drinking of Chardonnay, lukewarm tea and water.

What was I flying towards? During a decade of internecine bitterness, hope of settlements had disappeared, reappeared with international interventions and disappeared again. But things were better now, and the country was emerging from the worst of its troubles.

I should make something clear. I have never been good at West African politics. I know that had I been there I would have interpreted the conflict differently. Later I felt that others, too, knew this about me, though would not say it out loud. But there is not always time to understand things fully before becoming involved. Hindsight is a luxury. Most people in England well understood that this had been one of the most vicious civil wars of our time – the images in the newspapers and on television were shocking enough – yet it was a world away and they were not a part of it. That kind of choice was not open to me now. Freetown, Sierra Leone, was not on my local map. I could not get there on foot, yet it was imprinted on my life, war or not.

Even without my thoughts of the war, the journey would have been significant. This was a reunion with Uncle Moses after a separation of more than twenty years, a long and painful silence.

For days before my departure from London, I had made numerous trips to more distant relatives and friends who wanted me to carry gifts. One suitcase alone was devoted to black patent-leather shoes, in a variety of styles and assorted sizes from six to ten. I had stockings, tights, medicines, shampoo for half a nation, hair oil and electric pressing combs . . . I had sardines and tins of meat. People had warned me that stocks were low: everyone was just managing, sharing whatever they had with friends and neighbours. 'It's not easy to get rice even. Bring rice.' I took rice. The night before I was due to travel I lassooed the last one-kilo packet of long-grain to my shoe bag and popped it into the hand luggage – an emergency supply of staple food, in case my suitcase went missing.

I curled up more tightly in my seat and slept.

The jeep ride from the airport seemed endless. We shuddered along the roads and, following the driver's instructions, made no sudden moves at the checkpoints, keeping our heads down.

We drove north through what seemed evacuated commercial quarters, past weeping buildings: schools, banks, stores, government offices. Once, the jeep jolted to a halt. On my right was a school outside which traders were selling various wares; to my left stretched a line of handsome young men bisected by a line of others whose limbs had been chopped off.

When we reached a residential part of the town, about a quarter of a mile from my uncle Moses' house, I begged the driver to let me down so that I could walk a bit. He followed behind with my things, though he was puzzled at such independence. I felt strong, and contact with the ground was good after hours of sitting. It was a beautiful morning – sunlight softened with a bluey haze. The Atlantic breeze often gave this coastline an advantage, nevertheless sweat was beginning to snake on my skin in intrusive rivulets.

The wooden house next to Uncle Moses' was all ramshackle. Outside in the yard were pots, girls' clothes and a brown-and-white striped mattress. There was no one about, but a chicken came to look. In imitation of the bird, I stretched my neck forward, but as the neighbours were not there I moved on up the hill. It should be only another two minutes. I was there in ten.

A long path led to the yard of the house, since it was built well away from the road. As I walked up the path, I could see a young boy hanging about outside the house. I knew that must be Citizen.

He wandered around the tree, looking down at the dusty ground as though searching for some precious item. He could not find it. He idled back to the house and settled in one spot. When I reached the wooden two-storey with its faded blue paint, Citizen was framed as an expectant host. Perched high on the balustrade, arms akimbo, he was munching on some tobacco like a Cuban plantation worker more than twice his age. He looked more burnt and more punished than any plantation worker ever did. His eyes were red. His short hair was unclean; his cheekbones stood out prominently and suggested poise. I drew back. Then this eight-year-old boy in his torn shirt looked up and stared at me.

His colouring was mine. But his spirit was so far removed from anything I had ever met that I nearly wept. Suddenly, I felt panic, separate and afraid. Then from somewhere inside I recalled a poem (or was it a prayer?): *I've been longing to see you, I'm so glad to see you.* I turned to look at him more closely and share a smile, but Citizen had already moved away.

*

Three days later.

It is essential to take this slowly. I don't know whether other people were standing or watching me. I remember only the squawk that came out of my mouth: animal anguish. Anita, the next-door neighbour, was holding my hand. A glass was at my lips. Water touched my tongue, hot and frenzied, and fell on to my blouse. Out of the moment, so much wordless feeling, so much horror, so much nothingness. Gradually, I felt myself turn from stone into a climber on a hard rock surface who just dares to look down between parted legs and witness the passing of ghosts.

Anita was coming towards me again, gliding, her movements liquid. She poured herself into a shape of love and wrapped it around my tense body. My feet were cold, so cold they were dying, and speech had deserted me. I remember thinking stupidly that I knew how to speak and how to move my limbs. I had done both for thirty-nine years. If I tried now . . . I put all my energies behind both actions, raised my hands to my eyes and cried. The wetness on my cheeks reassured me. At least sorrow could be managed.

She spoke my name. 'Julia, Julia.'

'Yes.'

'It was me who called you. Blame me. It was me who called and asked you to come.' She had let me come without knowing what I was flying into: that Adele had been killed by her own young grandson, Citizen.

Had I known, would I have made the journey? Could anything have prepared me for this?

Small pink apples lay on the white plate and I ate one. I asked Citizen whether he would like one too. He did not answer. I didn't know if he had heard me. Then I realized I had been whispering. I was afraid of him; not because he was dangerous but because I didn't know him at all, did not know how I could reach his mind. In the three days I had been there, I had not spent much time alone with him, so had no way of knowing what he was thinking, what he liked, what he wanted, or what he would do next. I looked out into the yard but I wasn't seeing clearly. He was looking there too. A bird fluttered around looking for grain. It passed by, calling us to come and see the extent of its hunger. It flew into the tree and down again. Citizen meticulously followed its movements. Concluding that there was no grain to be found, no compassion on offer, the bird flew away.

Again silence cut between us. Citizen sat watching the space where the hungry bird had been, all energies concentrated in his stare.

I tried again, this time in a clearer voice: 'Do you want one?'

This time he did reply. He said, 'No.'

The photography studio was as big as the neighbour's house. It had more furniture than the neighbour's house. It was easy to tell that it was both a shrine and a workplace. Separating the studio from a small back room was a curtain made from an old African lappa in the deepest blue, the tint of God's soul. Around the studio walls there were some dark wooden shelving and photographs dating back to 1890. One of the photographs was a daguerreotype that showed a young man holding a camera, with a grin on his face. Underneath, plastered crudely on the wall, was a strip of paper reading: 'Decker's son (JP) about 1912'. The next picture was of a young man and his sister – Uncle Moses and my mother – posed in front of the Methodist church. From the hatstand at one end of the room a stethoscope dangled. In the far corner was a long table covered carelessly with a crocheted runner. Peanut shells and skins feathered the cloth; some had floated down to the floor. There lay an overturned stool, a camera case and three black-and-white photographs, their edges curling like tissue paper.

On the floor lies the old man, Moses. He has cried himself into the shape of a foetus. When he wakes in the morning, he will remember they said Adele is dead. Then he will remember how. He will return to the shape of a foetus in vain. He has slept enough.

He could not keep out the sounds of the morning: the hens going about their business, the birds in flight. His people. But more than the sounds outside, he could not remember hearing his wife. Her silence filled the studio. Her face filled him.

When in his sleep he reaches out to her, the River Rokel will wash over its banks. When in his sleep he twitches and releases her, a crevice in a diamond will choose to be luminous.

We were lucky. The whole of Uncle Moses' house was still standing, with the exception of the servants' quarters at the back and the old washroom. One day those had been blown down. His neighbours were not so fortunate: their whole lean-to was knocked down and burnt. Anita had just managed to get out in time. She had saved the hard brown-and-white striped mattress. She also had one big pot because at the time she had been cooking.

She laughed with me and said, 'I just tasted the soup when *bham*, the wall fell down. I did not know what I was doing, I just lift the pot from the stove and rush out. Next thing the other sides just fall down, *bham*, *bham*! That's it – end of the house.'

But she had a house again now. It was wooden and had three sides. When things improved, she told me, they would get a fourth.

We were lucky. It was a cool morning and the elements were moving inside us. With the coolness came the restlessness of waves. It felt as though they were looking for answers and, finding none, fell back into silence. When I saw Uncle Moses he seemed somehow calmer than he had when I first arrived, and his voice was stronger.

'You sleep all right?'

'Yes,' I lied. 'Fine, just fine.'

There was comfort in the familiar. The kitchen, more than the other rooms in the house, looked the same as I remembered. Its table was spread with a clean thick plastic cloth; half a dozen copies of *Good Housekeeping* magazine from the 1960s and Adele's cookery books lined a shelf above the stove, where pudding moulds, wooden spoons in a jug and the flowery blue serving dishes also sat.

'Don't know how I can begin to tell you,' he said.

I did not know either. I wanted to give up before he had even started. I pulled one of the chairs to the table where he sat picking at some bread without spread of any kind. He nibbled and took sips of tea, mashed it in his mouth, and repeated this again and again. I joined him, and so for some time the two of us sat mashing bread in hot tea, like two toothless old people.

It was something we had in common: the love of a good strong cup in the morning. In this, at least, I had done something positive by bringing tea bags; as Anita had told me, during the war Uncle Moses had reused the tea until there was no trace of flavour left.

In the three days we had not said anything much. It seemed enough to be coming through this in silent company, a hushed post-mortem. When I first set eyes on him, my fingers had trembled, my teeth had chattered. He had come close to me, towering over my nervous frame, but had not touched me. He had gazed down at my luggage as though it irritated his eyes and his spirit, like bounty offered too late. He had looked at his watch. It had stopped. He had shaken it.

11

'It does not work well,' he had said.

Those had been his first words to me in nearly twenty years. He had flicked the face of the watch with his fingers and, I assumed, it had started to tick again. It had been time for him to go into his studio. He had left me standing alone in the kitchen. That had been the worst moment. Everything in the kitchen reminded me of better times: family togetherness, laughter and plenty. Alone I had carried my cases up the stairs.

Citizen had not slept in the house that night. In the morning he had been sitting under the tree. Uncle Moses had seen him there and, as soon as Citizen had come into the kitchen, left for his studio. Citizen had lingered at the door. His hands had been cupped over an object at which he peeped occasionally. After a while he had pulled his hand back and revealed a feathered carcass lying on his palm. He had hesitated a moment to make sure I was not watching, then lifted the carcass to his nose and sniffed it. Did he know how the dead bird should smell? He had placed the carcass on the kitchen table, opened a drawer and taken out a large cooking spoon. He had gone back into the yard and with the spoon began digging by the tree. Meanwhile, Uncle Moses had come back in. His gaze had registered the little carcass, the boy outside and me just as one might unpleasant memories, with weariness but no particular surprise, and he had returned to his studio with a glass of water. He had not witnessed Citizen's return to the kitchen, his cradling the bird, his burying it under the tree.

On the third morning Uncle Moses broke that merciless cold with words and phrases he had probably been honing since my arrival.

'That morning . . . that morning, you should have heard the *BAP, BAP* in the street. The shouting and noise. I rushed to Anita dem and told them to come here.'

He spoke quietly: 'I said, "Let us all stay in this house together."' The eyes that looked at mine were dry, not reddened with grief, but glazed and weary.

He told of how the coup had begun and later we both heaped curses on all the incompetents who had ever been in power, everyone we could name. We blamed international relations. We did Third Worldism. We did rich, poor. We fast-forwarded to talk of food shortages, and how Britain figured in the international community; I blustered about questions in Parliament and how things were going to improve. But we did not go near Adele.

Could her death have been averted?

We backed away from that moment again and again. I felt the sickness of relief, something I did not dare admit – I was alive. *No one is going to get me.*

We stayed where we were, in the margins of truth.

Uncle Moses' father, the country's leading pharmacist, had seen to it that we had a good beginning. He had had a shop on the corner of Pademba Road in the 1930s, close to Cotton Tree. From his father, Moses had inherited chemistry bottles, three white linen coats purchased in London in 1936 and the spread-out nose that appeared on our side of the family. He drew from his mother, my maternal grandmother, a more chilling history, for she had not raised him.

My mother had often repeated the story of how Grandma Sara, a slender gracious woman with vivid eyes, was kind enough to hand her only son over to the sister who had no children. It was just after the end of the First World War when money was a bit short for his parents. Moses used to talk about the day his mother left him with his aunt. For years he was a little bit afraid of his aunt even although she was not unkind, and on visits home he would look around to see if things had 'picked up' enough for him to be allowed back. Things never did 'pick up'. Moses began to see how devoted his mother had become to her firstborn and how she would look intently at her daughter's face for hours, for fear of missing a change in it. Suddenly, the little girl's face would change, arrange itself differently, reveal something new, sometimes achingly so. Her mother watched every change and relished the bond with her daughter. Moses created his own private world and while his sister was full of maternal adoration, he went hungry.

It seemed to me there was something unnaturally cruel about the way Moses had been treated. Perhaps I imagined it, but then wasn't it cruel that one who had felt abandoned should be expected to rescue?

Uncle Moses and I had a good history. It had begun with occasional weekend visits to our house in England when I was a girl. He stayed one whole summer and, if I remember rightly, that summer turned into autumn and he was still with us at Christmas. I was seven that year.

'There are things I want to know,' he was saying to me, 'and many things I have to tell. But who is going to listen?' He paused and swallowed hard, seeming to spiral into memory. He couldn't find the words, though his thoughts changed the arrangement of his face.

I pushed back my chair and came round to his side of the table. I leant his head against me and closed my eyes. I saw words spread out before me and spoke them:

'She was a good woman.' Moments later I was back in my seat.

He lowered his eyes and remained silent; then in a whisper:

'She's still with me, every day.'

A little later that afternoon, back in my bedroom, which looked out on the yard with its elegant plane tree, I took in the view beyond: the sea, the mountains and the sun in crimson reds and gold. All three features blended into a perfect vignette, then separated once more.

I gazed out at the scattered roofs of Freetown, a city of browns and tans, earth colours fixed by the sun. The dwellings ranged from huge brick mansions, executive and professional homes to wooden houses with tin-pan roofs, shelters, huddles, pavements.

Looking down, I saw that Citizen had turned up. He was ramming himself against the plane tree. I could not make out what he was trying to do. Was he rubbing his back on the tree trunk for comfort, or, like a beast, scratching himself against its tough bark? He pushed hard against the tree's elegance as though he were trying to destroy it.

He came and went as he pleased, like an independent adult. We had seen nothing of him since the day before. Indeed, I had assumed he had run away, out of our lives again – he was out of our conversations already. I could not get Uncle Moses to say anything at all about him, not even to mention his name. Futilely I tried to bring him back into our life but I was too clumsy. It was as though each time you try to pour a drink, it spills.

Getting closer to Citizen had so far proved impossible. Without much knowledge of what he had been through, I saw this wretched child soldier as confused and confusing. Was there any bridge back to normal childhood?

Around four o'clock, something impelled me to leave the room. I went into the yard and looked at the plane tree, its branches spreading shamelessly up to the sky. It was the bark that showed me the story of that afternoon. Citizen had marked it using a twig to indicate his current height, measuring himself to see if he had grown beyond the other markings that were surely his own. The top mark, today's height, was about three feet six inches from the ground. Needlessly I questioned the tree: 'Tell me, has Citizen grown since the beginning of the war?'

Sierra Leone is the land of gold and diamonds. This Sierra Leone is a land of mountains and rivers that hold diamonds, colour and the sun in their memory, the home of descendants of struggle, free and freed, settlers and migrants: a new Jerusalem. Palm-wine merchants, craftsmen and doctors, market women and bankers, Temne, Mende, Creole people, all lived side by side. Once the palm trees saw them all, bowed down to all. But now under the bullet-splattered rubbish lying on the roads are the trinkets and plates, rugs and dolls of these belittled ancestors. Where is their gold now? Breeding hate like maggots. Where are their diamonds now? Some are alive; some are out partying. They are underground like hundreds of water rats with long tails and anxious eyes. If an inspector comes and puts the light on they will scatter into cracks in walls, dive into the River Rokel, into bog wastes and gardens. If the light does not go on, they will continue as they have for decades — hard, abrasive, cold.

The next evening, Uncle Moses and I sat and talked until about eleven. There was light, following the long power cuts, but we were sparing of electricity and had come to enjoy our candlelight. We balanced our drinks on the arms of the sofa, which had extra sleeves to protect the fabric, although these were already wearing through. The rest of the house was dark and quiet. Citizen had run off earlier in the day, taking the pot of rice I had left out on the side.

'Well,' Uncle Moses began, 'what do you think of Citizen? He's a ruined boy, isn't he?'

'He's damaged by all this, I'm sure; and, well, yes, lost, very lost.'

'We all are,' his voice continued, 'but he needs care. Someone who would care; someone like you.'

There was a pause before I answered: 'Oh, does he? I

thought he'd need people here; people who understand what's happened to boys like him, what they've been through.'

'Maybe.'

'I don't know. I just assumed this environment would be best. Surely he needs something familiar; something as close to home as possible?'

'Of course, it would be hard to like him. I don't blame you for feeling like that.'

I did not answer. I turned to face the window against which it was raining hard. Citizen was somewhere out there, 'roughing it', we would say. I took comfort from the sound of the rain; hard water spitting hard on the glass released my tension. My eyes were still averted but I sensed my uncle's stare.

'I can't see what I could do with a child like him,' I said. 'As a matter of fact I have a horror of . . .' My voice trailed off but Uncle Moses came to my rescue:

'Well, your just being here is a blessing to me.'

I was thinking about the first time I had come to this country – no, even before I arrived here, dipping my toe in Dakar, a foretaste of what was to come. *The boat sweeps into harbour, the sun pampers us, down the ramp I run into the bustling market street, cotton frock in camomile with bow undone, bounding into the African sunshine, warm beyond the compass of imagining. It is not the colours that strike me first, nor the compelling smells of fruits but how the black faces shine back at mine, smile and look with joy at me. And I look all around, turn and run back again, eager to be sure that what I think I am seeing is real and for true, run into my mother's arms and cry out: 'Oh, Mummy, Mummy, all the people are black here.' And for this she loves me and says, 'Yes, my dear, this is Africa.'*

'I'm glad I'm here,' I said now.

'Yes, you are welcome to stay as long as you wish. But of course I want you to get on and do whatever you wish to do

17

with your life. You know that, don't you? I know I told you long ago to come home and make us proud, but you never answered me.'

He meant that I had turned my back then and was doing it again now.

'I am sure you must be doing well. You don't need to be held back. Don't be like me at your age, always holding back. Plan what you want and get on with it. Make things work in England. After all, that is your home, isn't it?'

'Oh, yes,' I said. 'England is my home.'

That night, lying in a clean bed with a white cotton sheet covering me, I could not sleep in spite of myself. I wanted to be up and doing, to regain a sense of control, to banish from my mind his despairing glances and be rid of the images of men, women and children on sticks, waiting for limbs. I wanted to be busy, but busyness was not what anyone here was good at. Instead there was a permanent tension, which engulfed me too along with the encroaching darkness.

At midnight, still wide awake, I heard movement on the stairs and left my room to find Anita, Uncle Moses' neighbour, standing in the shadowy corridor with Citizen in her arms. He was fast asleep. His clothes were wet but his legs looked dry and patchy from rain. He snored softly, oblivious to the trouble she was taking; his head had fallen against her breast.

'He was just in the yard with his rice pot,' Anita offered. 'I left it down there.' She nodded towards the kitchen.

The concerned mother held him close, rubbed his hand and carried him to bed. Three steps and I was with them, watching as her bronzed arms eased him under the sheet. Standing by the door, I felt that Citizen belonged with her, but said nothing. The look of concentration on her face as she tucked him in was that of a woman who was comfortable with moving children's bodies whenever required. For twenty years she had done this and in twenty years' time she would be the same, confident and dextrous. Although we must be almost the same age, I did not feel her equal.

Citizen was in deep sleep, the cool white sheet wrapped around his tiny body. She tiptoed from the room. Glancing back, I sensed an older woman bending over the bed and smelt the air filled with the scent of freshly peeled oranges.

Downstairs, Anita pulled her dress over her head and hung it up in the kitchen. Then, standing in her underwear and without any fuss, she put the rice pot to soak, scraping the remains out first. She looked into the cupboard for something to drink, brought out a bottle that could have been brandy, took two small glasses and poured for us both.

'Drink it down fast.'

Obediently I gulped. It tasted more acrid than brandy and was unfamiliar, but my head cleared and I immediately felt more relaxed.

'Good,' said Anita, though I had not commented on my changing state. 'Now let's talk about Uncle. What are you going to do about him?'

She lit a small white candle, which had already burnt halfway down its length, and turned towards me. I looked at the wall and saw my uncle shift through the years from our first meeting to now. His large frame was illuminated as he sat between us like a hospital patient awaiting a diagnosis. Anita threw a quick glance at the empty chair between us as if to say: 'We've been expecting you, Uncle.' Then her dark eyes were back on me and she clasped her hands, waiting.

'Citizen did not start like that. When they first brought him, it was Elizabeth, my big daughter, who went down there and brought him. When Mr Moses see him, how the water fell from his eyes. He said, "Yes, yes, let the boy come." But now I worry. It is too much for him. Most people will not even let a child like Citizen near their house after what he's done. They cannot stand the sight of them. They believe they are little devils. Bad bush.'

'Well, that's understandable. But in fact Citizen is hardly ever here. He must feel he can't stay here.'

'They look and feel it cannot be. Who wants a child who only knows how to kill? What kind of nightmare is that? What kind, eh? If they keep these children here, is like keeping something bad in the blood. Something rotten, isn't it?'

'Since I've been here I don't think they've seen each other. Citizen is always running away and Uncle stays in the studio keeping busy, I think, or at any rate out of the way.'

She carefully repositioned the candle that was beginning to drop its wax.

'Yes, he's been busy. To look at Mr Moses you wouldn't think he's seen so much, but he knows things, really he knows.' She paused and looked hard at me. Was she beginning to make sense?

She went on. 'They know that when a boy has killed family nobody will want him, except somebody distant, somebody from far away.'

I was nodding as she spoke. This encouraged her.

'Maybe it wasn't your plan, but you could help them, both of them. Did you know that?'

I nodded again. I had been trying not to know it, but it was there as a fact. I said: 'I have been trying to understand what has happened here. Please give me time.'

Dawn was up before me, a more delicate and pleasing light than the day before. Anita, as always, was out with her daughters. On most days I saw them in the yard together. They reorganized their few belongings with the seriousness of highly paid interior designers. The youngest, a nine-year-old called Sara, had a bicycle that had evidently been bright yellow when new, although the paint had rubbed off in most places. She rode in circles and then turned the bicycle over a small mound, just like the boys in Brixton. I smiled to myself.

Anita steeped the tea in the large blue jug that held enough water for us all and closed the space between our night thoughts and the arriving day. I was trying not to think, *This is when you would be getting dressed for work. This is when you would be rushing for the train, knowing more or less what the day might bring.* While we sat and waited for the stewed tea, her eldest daughter, Elizabeth, came to join us. She was no longer a girl but a young woman – twenty years old – whom I promised to welcome to London whenever it took her fancy. She was warming to the idea and with a light-hearted laugh asked me some questions. The idea of London was constantly there in our war-torn yard, like the ticking of a clock.

'Will I be able to sell my designs there? Do they have this kind of thing already? Is it easy to get into television? Do Africans work at the BBC too? How much did you say a house costs?'

Elizabeth wanted to design clothes and jewellery and was both intrigued and excited that 'ethnic' arts were fashionable in London. Not only did she envisage her clothes doing well on the catwalk and in the high street, she also fancied trying costume design for television and film. Her life plan was sorted.

Anita looked on anxiously as we spoke about London. Perhaps I should have invited her as well as Elizabeth, but I did not, imagining that she would not want to leave here. Besides, her youngest child was not yet a teenager: she needed her. But did the mother resent my suggestions for the daughter? Having drunk her tea, she was working her way through a pile of beans: pulses that had to be picked over so that the bad could be discarded.

'What an exciting life you have!' she exclaimed, putting a full stop to our chattering. So the natural order of things was restored and the possibility of misunderstandings avoided.

Then, she asked, 'Where is Citizen now?'

'He's still sleeping upstairs.'

'Well, let's leave him to sleep. And Mister Moses? Is he still resting?'

I shrugged.

'Mister Moses! Mister Moses! Mister Moses! Mister Moses!'

She gave a concerned glance towards his house and stood up. Her voice became louder and louder. She might have been summoning the saviour of a people. When you call out for someone in that way, no matter where they are, no matter what they are doing, they will come to you. A more obdurate old man might have ignored her insistent calling, but my uncle appeared dutifully before his neighbour within moments. He accepted the mug of tea Anita had waiting, raised it to his lips but did not drink, though the beverage must have been cool enough, returning it instead to the ground by his feet.

Anita chattered about her plans for the day. I suggested that we might visit the ex-child soldiers' camp at Doria to which Citizen had been returned by his rescuers. I hoped it would help me understand Citizen better. But the request elicited a small, tremulous glance from Uncle Moses who, more often than not, stared fixedly into the distance, not trusting that I would be kind.

At seventy-six years old, my uncle was lost, his spirit troubled, his manly frame stooping, his toenails hardened and yellow. The image of him as I had known him years before came to mind. The man sitting opposite me, the man whom I had always called Uncle Moses, had me at a disadvantage, for he had known me as a child, longing to climb on to his knee, to play, to look splendid in his eyes. How was I to take this reversal of need?

A house where nothing melts or yields; a garden long and narrow, full of strong perennials and pink and yellow roses growing abundantly along the side of the lawn, their perfume filling the air.

Our black cat, Jinx, walked out on to the lawn, gave his bones a stretch and crumbled into an afternoon of relaxation. We children, quick and black, darted into laughter, darted into quarrels and tumbled into play. Our life was all in primary colours: we rushed out of the Wendy house, it was yellow and red. We piled stones in front of it to make an outside stove and planted a pot on top with tomato-flavoured rice and lettuce.

My older sister and I, two years apart, were partners in crime, lifting one-penny Cadbury's chocolate bars in purple and silver foil from the corner shop, then instantly returning them when guilt upset us. Our first successful break-and-entry had been our neighbour's larder and we did the job one Saturday afternoon because there was no pudding. For some reason lunch had been rushed, the burgundy-rimmed white plates were still on the table and our elder cousin was reading. She was not one of us, but another species who, when sniffed from under the dining table, seemed an extra-large, alien female with stockings and weeds growing between her legs. For the job, I acted as decoy, setting up an elaborately noisy game of hopscotch on the pathway, while my sister flattened her rounded body against the side of the house, stepped on the heavy metallic bin outside the larder window and pushed it up until she was in. Within three minutes she was back, a pink cake in each hand. Dusty from muck on the window sill, she offered the booty: 'I didn't see anything else we could eat right now.'

That was the summer Uncle Moses came to stay. He had a
car that looked like a bumblebee and made gruff noises on
the road. When he pulled up we could hear the bee from the
back of the house.

At the far end of the garden stood an air-raid shelter.
During his stay Uncle Moses was often down there in the
evenings where, he said, an old African beggar lived who
only came out at night. The beggar had been seen trawling
the dirty water in the air-raid shelter with his fingers, fishing
unsuccessfully for mosquitoes. So, he was starving and in
need of cooked food. Uncle Moses showed me the pewter
mug and the tin plate to prove it. 'Every morning, I pick
them up and take them to the kitchen for washing.'

At night after dinner Uncle Moses would take the plate,
laden with remnants of the meal, down to the end of the
garden, along with 'a small stout'. He was scraggy and bony
like an elderly cockerel, but his hands were large and his fingers strangely fat. When I insisted on seeing the old beggar
man, Uncle Moses promised to lure him out by dancing on
the top of the air-raid shelter and stamping his feet in an
exotic rhythm; but the beggar man never did appear.

'Click your fingers, Uncle Moses,' I encouraged. He tried,
but his stubby fingers would not click, nor would the beggar
man emerge. Beyond the air-raid shelter was a muddy rubbish dump sealed off by willow and nettles all around. The
weeds pressed in on the dump, guarding it for themselves so
we never dared to vie with their authority, but after the non-
appearance of the beggar man, Uncle Moses agreed to go and
investigate this forbidding terrain. He returned with black-
ened leaves and gnarled twigs in one hand. The fingers of his
other hand were closed over the palm. As he opened them, a
ladybird, black and red and beautiful, trailed across it.

He used to wear black cloth trousers that were patched
with sacking on the left leg. I thought he could have given

this pair to the beggar man and bought new ones, but he said he needed them himself for use in the garden and for all the time he spent with me. I liked that: special clothes for being with me. I wondered what my father would have made of that. My father was dead, but two of his ties hung in the wardrobe in the spare room – a silken blue tie with light silver lines and an old tartan one in greys and greens.

I don't know which Christmas it was, but I must have been either six or seven. It was my happiest Christmas ever and the one during which I got to know Uncle Moses much better. It was a strange time, an exciting one. Although I was still a little girl I was discovering that there was more woman in me than before and I was enjoying the order of things, knowing more how to control them. I knew this from the morning when my mother was making the joloff rice. Presents were stacked higgledy-piggledy beneath the tree; neighbours called in for drinks; the sideboard groaned under the weight of cakes, sweets and delicacies.

At the time when lunch was to be served, the pink and tasty joloff rice, topped with fresh green peas, was brought to the table heaped on a large white platter. My mother served me first. But when the contents of the third and what was to be the last spoonful scattered on my plate, my mother observed that a pig's foot was revealed. Quick! She retrieved the pig's foot and returned it to the white serving dish. The pig's foot began to sweat, ready to spring back to me. Just as fast as my mother had reacted, so the piggy flesh jumped out of the serving dish on to my plate. I glared at her. Her eyes needled me. She turned to my cousin and asked her to refill the dish in the kitchen.

All of a sudden I heard Uncle Moses burst out laughing. He laughed and laughed until he was holding his sides: 'Oh,' he said, 'even the pig got the better of you!'

From that day I knew that Christmas was not only about

opening presents, eating turkey and watching *White Christmas*, it was about having a good laugh with Uncle Moses at my mother's expense.

I was never in fragments when he was there, and I became desperate to slide into other worlds whenever he gave me the nod.

One day we went out for the day together in a rented green Beetle because his car was off the road. We chugged along at slow speeds in the city but on the open road the car purred with contentment. It was high summer, over eighty degrees by mid-afternoon. I was cool in my purple printed dress in a shiny fabric and new firm-soled white leather sandals with a criss-cross pattern. Relieved to be able to ditch last term's pair of well-worn plimsolls whose fabric was stiff with whitening, I stretched my feet out with pride. There was no radio to keep us company, so we talked, told jokes, and sometimes I sang a song from my ever-growing repertoire:

'There was I waiting at the church, waiting at the church, waiting at the church, when I found ee'd left me in the lurch, oh, ow it did upset me . . . dum dum.'

Along the lanes the Beetle flew as it took twisting, climbing roads. We travelled away from the city's cement blocks, skyscrapers and looming towers, up past the university fields, beyond the outlying villages where the roads were clear, for us alone.

Stopping much later, Uncle Moses said he wanted to show me something. I jumped out of the car and followed him for about five minutes down a lane and over a staggered step into an open field. It stretched as far as the eye could see and was covered in buttercups. We stood in reverence, breathing in deeply, our eyes watching for the slightest shiver of breeze in the field of yellow. Uncle Moses took out his camera and began to take photos; there was just the occasional whirr of

the camera, then silence again. In the summer heat the buttercups glowed soft, warm and yellow; sometimes a small
breeze blew them sideways. Moses pointed his camera
towards me and I smiled, grinned, pulled faces. *Whirr* went
the camera, then silence again. We returned to the car and
drove to a village where we bought ices – 99s so big they
rolled out of the cones faster than we could lick them.

After a day of such excitement I failed to switch off the
bedroom light when going to bed and this attracted my
mother's attention. Her arm appeared round the door to
switch it off. Then she must have decided to enter. I closed
my eyes, pretending to be asleep. She moved away, looked at
herself in the mirror and patted the back of her head where a
brown comb kept the short curls in place. In the darkness I
was free again to think my unlovely thoughts. My mother
would never understand what a world he brought – my
Uncle Moses – where instead of air there was magic, buttercups and a flying pig's foot.

Of course it could not last for ever. On Sundays, when our
house was usually filled with the voices of African students
talking politics and catching up on news from 'home', my
mother was in the habit of serving everyone food at around
six o'clock in the evening, after which there was happy talk,
laughter and sometimes dancing. One Sunday she had invited
them to come as usual, promising to be 'back very, very soon'.
But she failed to reappear. In her absence a plump Ghanaian
man named Samuel made a long speech about how good it
would be to go home.

'Are you still renting that poky garret from the under-
taker?' He pushed his finger in the face of another student.

'Mmmm.'

'And did he put in that Axminster carpet yet?'

'Not yet.' The man looked frankly embarrassed.

Whenever Samuel paused for breath, he would raise his

cigar to his puckered lips, suck deeply and blow the smoke into the air.

'The time has come for change . . . it's our time now. You say you pay nine-hundred-and-eighty pounds for a house, George, I'm not wasting my money. Accra, here I come.'

He puffed again and all of a sudden Uncle Moses shouted: 'Quit that blasted smoking!' and walked out of the lounge and into the empty kitchen. I followed. The endless smoking was irritating the back of his throat, he complained, and he was very hungry. We searched for food but there was nothing to be had. The larder was empty. Not a biscuit nor a crumb to be seen in the bread bin. The breakfast dishes had been washed but no one had even begun to cook lunch. Frustrated, Uncle Moses returned to his seat and waited.

'I'm not living here in some rented basement, paying through the nose each week when I could be in my own house at home, set up my business and get respect.' Samuel was still talking when, around three in the afternoon, the front door opened.

In came my mother with a new student, Adele, carrying a basket of food. Everyone was polite enough to wait in their seats, although the sense of relief was palpable. In the kitchen food was unpacked: a pot of chicken groundnut stew and boiled rice, a platter of fried plantain, boiled yams, greens, rice bread and cake.

At the call, 'Food's ready!' even Samuel lost interest in Ghanaian life. While we were eating, the house fell silent. Only the scraping of forks on plates and the occasional murmur – 'More salt' – floated into the air.

As the plates were being stacked up, Samuel asked for ginger beer. I ran and fetched a bottle. We drank some, then he resumed his monologue.

Uncle Moses stood up from the brown armchair and went into the kitchen. 'Are you the angel who made this food?' he asked Adele. She smiled. Then he lifted her up at the waist and gave her a twirl in the air. The white-and-yellow striped skirt, nipped at the waist with a thin plastic belt, spun like a merry-go-round top and she laughed. At that moment Adele did not know and Moses did not know, but we all knew that Adele would love Moses and Moses would love Adele.

We didn't see much of either of them after that. Moses would come back from work late at 7 or 7.30 in the evening and would peep round the door of our bedroom, trying to catch us awake, before going out again. He was mostly cheerful; sometimes whistling, sometimes quiet.

And the inevitable happened. He married Adele and they returned home to Freetown.

After he left, I went into the garden and the paths went straight ahead to the air-raid shelter. There was no one. Inside me was a hole that was dark and brown. It was a place I recognized from before but could not yet name. It made me thirsty and tired. It told me that I did not just miss him, I missed myself.

More than thirty years later the gold is on her finger. Her skin hums at his touch. And if he were to leave her side now, she would bristle like a porcupine.

Two

Out in the hallway was an old wooden ladder-back chair that I remembered from my first visit here when I was nine, but it wasn't in the house then. Auntie Adele had had it in the yard. She used to sit there in the mornings, picking leaves and sorting beans in her apron, just as I had seen Anita doing, then tossing the good ones into a wooden bowl at her feet. 'Come and help me pick the beans,' she would ask. Sometimes we didn't want to, sometimes we were keen. One morning when I felt like picking beans I went to find her but she was not there. Instead, her chair in the centre of the yard was being occupied by Eddy. He was their short gap-toothed monkey – he seemed to be about my age. According to Uncle Moses, Eddy had friends, both young and old, all over Freetown. For days he would be on the road visiting his mates and he had developed the knack of hopping on to trucks or even the back of mopeds as they took the corner. This would-be family member had been known to curse the local poda-poda bus drivers for failing to stop for him and loved joining us on outings to Lumley beach and long drives up into the mountains.

So it was not a surprise to me when on our journey to the ex-child soldiers' camp at Doria a monkey who resembled him followed us all the way. He tried to get into the car as we were putting our things inside, but I said, 'No way,' and he immediately understood and withdrew. But as the driver turned the ignition key, the monkey jumped on to the boot. I turned to look at him: 'You're welcome if you can hold on, Eddy.' And he nodded back. When we reached Crossroads, he was still there, following the road with his soft grey eyes. When we turned off the main road and, feeling parched, stopped to drink some water, he was still there. He had some water, cupping his hands quite gracefully to drink and using the occasion to clean some food from his teeth. Finally we arrived at the camp and had to walk up the hill. He jumped down ready to walk too, but I shook my head for him to wait for us. He waited.

A wooden board outside the camp stated that it was a care centre for children affected by the war. Though it did not say it, this also meant ex-child soldiers. As we got out of the car, the air was fresh with sweet-smelling earth after light rain. We climbed the slope to the camp entrance and stood by a wooden gate tied with wire at the top. A sultry-looking guard approached, smoking a cigarette which he threw to the ground as he reached us.

I looked about to see what was familiar. Nothing was. There were no trees and no flowers. I looked up and the sky was without clouds and the sun was hidden from view. I looked down and the ground was solid yellow dirt with no life. I looked ahead and I saw no women. Insects darted around our heads, but there were no birds in sight.

'Morning. What you want?'

We explained our business and within minutes were standing in the middle of a dampened compound that was both very crowded and very quiet. Boys, some of them as young as six years old, were standing in rows. There were hundreds of them, queuing for food as it was well past noon. Hundreds of pairs of eyes turned to look at us, the strangers from the city. There were only a handful of girls, two or three older teenagers who would soon be women.

On a long wooden table at the far end, steam rose from big pots of rice. Mosquitoes hissed. Undeterred, I opened Anita's food basket, unveiling the beans in palm oil, akara, fish in a sauce of tomato and peppers and slices of plantain from which the oil had been carefully drained. We made our offering to the camp volunteers, humble though it was with so many needing food.

'We would like to welcome the two of you here today,' began the priest, formally dressed in a soutane. His slight Irish accent lent a warm precision to the welcome and I smiled.

'I'm really pleased we were able to come.'

'It's good that you've taken the trouble. Yes, oh, yes, to come and see how these children have lived. Yes, oh, yes, to see how we do things here. Yes, it is good.' I nodded. 'And to talk to the other children. Especially to talk to the boys who were with him.'

'Yes, indeed,' I said.

'What is his name again . . . Citizen? Yes, oh, yes, another of our small boys. Oh, yes, quite a small boy.' He sat in a straight-backed chair that reminded me of our church furniture. On the ground by his sandalled feet was a glass of water from which he took small sips as with communion wine. My throat was dry.

A boy walked past. Part of his face was missing; his nose slanted to one side and his teeth chattered by themselves. Another passed as if in a dream; insensitive to the flies that played around his head, he opened his mouth in silent protest, displaying discoloured teeth. At his back, from neck to waistline, a bluish-purple gash festered in the heat. I covered my mouth. Anita, in a gesture of motherly love, followed him and offered plantain. There was no sound from his lips as she fed him. She then thrust her arm into her bag, bringing out a lotion, which she gently rubbed on his face. The boy let out a mighty sigh and looked at her gratefully.

We walked past the remnants of a carpentry workshop. A saw turned hot under the glare of the sun, and measured planks of wood lying on the ground were waiting to be transformed into tables, benches; even a bird's house was on display in the workshop. Two boys clenched their fists ready for a fight, then rolled around in a ball on the ground. Others played and talked in huddles of twos and threes. Their voices rose into the air like starlings greeting the day. The priest led us up to a young girl with a still and comely face. 'This is the girl who brought him to the camp, his little mother, Sally.'

She was standing by a massive wall, not so much a wallflower, more a guerrilla who knew that the structure was protection, one direction from which violence will not come. She clung to her pitch and looked up uncertainly as we approached. Then, sensing friendliness, she relaxed and a smile crept across her face.

'You're Sally, aren't you?' I asked.

She smiled again. A teenager, she was not fat so much as well-rounded and full, with arms that made me think of washerwomen. Sally and I sat opposite one another and said nothing but exchanged thoughts. She told me of how she and Citizen had come to this camp; it had been a Sunday, or she imagined it was from the ringing of church bells. She tailed off to say that she had always gone to church with her family but no longer did and did not know if she would ever again. (Perhaps it was an arrangement with God that no mortal should attempt to alter.)

I asked her where she and Citizen had first met. She explained that they had been in the same unit and, one night, under cover of darkness after their commander had laid himself down on his coat and bare mattress and fallen into drunken slumber, they had run away. At first, it was because they had thought a rescue helicopter was nearby, but even after discovering that this was not the case, they kept going. It was a brave and insane thing to do. They followed a long procession of slow vehicles and crept up the verge to be out of sight of the camp. Then, as the convoy of empty trucks passed, there was total silence. They had waited by the road-side until they felt it was safe to move on. When the black-ness of night was all around, they passed along the verge again, crawling like worms to safety. It was impossible to say how far they had travelled that night, but neither would turn back, not even at the sight of a checkpoint up ahead, where soldiers were stopping people and seizing possessions. Instead, they cut back to a side path leading to a bridge that was still intact. They cowered under the bridge for several hours, drinking the dirty water there, before they made it back to the road. As they were calculating whether they would be able to cross at the checkpoint, a driver spotted them and offered help: he had space at the back of his truck and took them to Doria camp.

I asked Sally if it was only one night they had been on the road. She said many nights. How had they managed? How had it been for them day after day, week after week, to be on the run, with hardly a scrap to eat all day and no one to care for them? To be out in all weathers with no certainty of a roof for the night, to face every road, not knowing whether it would be blocked with soldiers, with guns, with checkpoints, and to have no way of safeguarding life and limb? My whole being was rocked, for I could answer none of this, so I added that I would tell Citizen I had seen her. She said she would like to see him again. Then she asked me a strange question:

'Is he still in this country?'

'Yes, he is in Freetown at his grandfather's home.' *And it is still their country and it is still their home*, I was thinking.

Sally said that the last day she had seen her parents was on

34

25 May 1997. They were up early because her mama, who had been busy planning a conference, needed her husband to give her a lift into town to organize things. He left to get the car but five minutes later, having heard gunshots in the street, was back in the house. They did not know what was happening at first, then they realized it was a coup. There was no point in trying to keep the car; every vehicle was being commandeered. Buildings were set on fire. The whole city was in turmoil. Down at the hotel Bintumani people milled about in their hundreds, trying to get out of the city. The bank governor was there, her staff, schoolteachers, broadcasters, clerks, mothers with babies in arms.

Pressing up against one another's flesh, breathing in each other's exhaled air, they massed into a body of panic. 'Let's try Water Quay!' went a cry, and the pushing began. Guinea would be a sanctuary for weeks or months if need be. They walked faster, until they were running. Sally was just behind her parents. Her mother's blue-striped dress was within inches of her own shoes. She saw the dress. She saw her mother in the dress, and in a minute the crowd swelled and the dress was gone. Sally pushed through the crowd until she saw the familiar fabric again; she kept her gaze focused on it, on the waistband, the hem, the garment she knew well; her mother was within a yard of her own shoes; her mother was two feet away. Then the dress turned and it was not her mother's face but the face of a stranger. The crowd swelled again; the boat heaved upon the black water. A wave thrown up splashed the people waiting below; they pressed forward. Sally rushed towards the boat but a hand grabbed her waist and pulled her into the war. Now she did not know when she last saw her mother's face, or even her mother's dress.

I wanted to sit with her for a while. I could hear the mother's thoughts. She was thinking: *Where is my daughter today? How empty these moments are. Will I ever have the chance again?* I answered the mother's questions: *Even though she is only fourteen, she is no longer a girl but she is beautiful and, yes, you will have the chance to hand on all the gifts.*

Sally told me that when she had first met Citizen she had liked him very much because he reminded her of her little cousin Tommy. She had tried to show him how to read the lines on his palm that told how long he would live and how many children he would have – and she noticed that his hands were surprisingly small. She could not remember how many children Citizen was going to have, but she would have three. Together we admired the lines. To my unspoken question – how was she used in the war? – she did not answer, could not, but I was glad to have seen the lines on her hand.

The priest was back by my side. 'Do you have time to meet some of the boys, my dear?' He guided me away from Sally, holding my elbow as though a dance were about to commence: 'Come and meet one of our youngest and greatest: this is Corporal Kalashnikov.'

And so he manoeuvred me in front of a boy whose very name horrified me.

'Is that your name?'

'Yes, it is, because I did not put my gun down for fifty-six days. That is because I was in charge of all the guns.'

He pointed to an oil drum. He stretched his fingers and one by one cracked the bones in his hands, making me wince again. But at least he was no longer holding a gun and the fingers were nimble and the skin was the smooth brown of fresh coffee beans.

'Yes, he used to live in that oil drum, protecting the guns,' added the priest. 'It took fifty-six days for him to come out and let go of all his guns, so we nicknamed him Corporal Kalashnikov because he was very brave and gave up all the weapons.' He rubbed the boy's noble head. The action seemed to enliven the corporal and loosen his tongue:

'When I first became a soldier I had many jobs to do and I did not like it. I was always tired. I did not want to be a soldier. But then they promoted me and put me in charge of the guns.'

He saluted and his fingers splayed enough to show me he did not know how to salute any better. So much for the corporal's war history. There were no guns now. The empty barrel had a couple of sticks on top. I was thinking it could be a drum, or maybe even a steel pan. It could certainly make music. The melody might be saying: *Today my colours are black, brown and grey; tomorrow they could be red, purple and yellow.* Corporal Kalashnikov could be leading a parade at the Notting Hill Carnival.

I could not bear to see more but the priest was telling us about weaning Corporal Kalashnikov off drugs; he had been in the habit of drinking tea with marijuana and gunpowder mixed in but now he downed pints of water in a day. Inside I felt a hazy dark cloud and guessed I was about to pass out. I made myself concentrate hard.

It was as though I had vomited up everything that had been kept down and now my belly was free and open to take in a different food. My thoughts were with Citizen. I repeated his name to myself, imagined rubbing my hand against his cheek. I had not ever actually touched him but felt sure that would change. I understood much better how things were. This thought gave me some peace and contentment. We thanked the priest for his time and care and made our way back to the car.

Snagged against a nail, the heel of my sandal was coming apart so I was forced into dragging my foot somewhat along the ground. This made me look quite delirious and allowed me to be so. I let go. Eddy the monkey was standing by the car like a valet. We opened the door and, because I was in a gentler mood, I allowed him to sit in the back and look out.

He was company of a sort, a bridge between my awakening self and the children at the camp.

My mind drifted to Sally, her muted voice, her body already a source of pain; to the small boys, selected to bear arms, draped in uniforms made for men and not knowing when their childhood would come to an end. And of course I thought of Citizen; the prospect of seeing him again did not fill me with dread. There are people who claim you and people who remain strange even in ordinary life.

As we drove away from the camp I heard the children's voices ever louder, filling my head. For the first time in almost two weeks, I searched for a way to build a relationship with Citizen. The wind whistled through the vehicle. I moved closer to him; I moved closer to myself, into a narrow space where every emotion was restored to its full essence. A bump in the road, and I went deeper into the contradictions of war. *Who is safeguarding the future for the children, for the purity that is the whites of their eyes and the citrus sharpness of their adolescent discoveries?* I kept my thoughts from Anita and watched with my monkey companion as the scenery changed but my mood stabilized.

The house felt peaceful, a safe retreat. Citizen was standing by the kitchen table, caressing the small pink apples with his little finger, and pressing his brown flesh against their soft pink. Then he took one of the fruits and bit into it. He did not turn, though he must have heard me entering. He sank into a chair, frowning, but watched as I too reached for a fruit, already forgoing my intention of talking to him. *There is no need to bite this fruit – no sooner has the apple seen your teeth it will melt of its own accord and shower its thin white juices down your throat. Surrender. Wait for me: my timidity will retreat; wait for me: my courage will advance.*

For three hours I lay in my room, my body moist with the

apple's juices, and for three hours life wandered through my limbs slowly and steadily, like nothing I had felt before.

By seven the next morning the sun was scorching. Good-natured Elizabeth was doing the family's washing in a big pan, singing as she worked: '*Poda, poda, cam ker me go!*' in an upbeat rhythm. She looked striking in her green blouse and lappa, a red headtie covering her hair. I watched her broad back as she bent down and took each item out of the tub where it was soaking, and wrung it before plunging it into the pan of fresh warm water. She rubbed with a vengeance and when she was done, she tipped the water over the shrubs in their yard.

The visit to the camp had drained me, so I was happy to relax with a novel, enjoying the cool breeze coming in from the sea. Sara was carrying a bucket of mud and stone to rebuild her fortifications at the other side of the yard.

Moses and Citizen were nowhere to be seen.

Anita called out to the girls: 'Wen una done, cam go market!'

'Yes, Ma.'

Elizabeth was singing a melody she had heard the previous night when out with friends in a nearby bar. I imagined some of them must have been just stirring by now, rubbing sore heads and going to find water. But Elizabeth had taken life gently and had paced herself. Her voice was light and sweet.

'Sing for Auntie that song Samura used to sing for you!' called Anita.

'Which one?'

'You know that one he played his – what's it call again? – balafon along with: *tttta . . . ttta*,' she imitated.

Elizabeth began getting into her rendition, her voice filling the yard. I was surprised at how beautiful it was. It grew big and rounded, like a river in full flow. As if dirt and debris could not stand in its way, it ripped apart the thick crusts of a troubled world. Her fresh voice said, *With you I'll share the joys that life will bring; happiness doesn't always protect us from pain* . . . 'Laidu, Laidu . . .' she sang.

It had taken me almost two weeks to begin to feel fully alive here, as if the very knowledge of the roadblocks, the burnt villages, the bombed bridges had taken me out. Yet here was Elizabeth, who had actually lived through it, singing a Malian love song.

There is something about the sound of a love song, so rounded, full and physical. Unseen, on the other side of a love song is the desiring lover who will sing back.

> With you I'll share the joys that life will bring me
> Happiness does not always protect us
> Near you, I'll share your pain
> Yes, young man, only death can separate us.

Citizen came in from the road and pitched himself next to Sara, who was patting down the newly dug-up earth in a mound. He tried to help, but she threw him a look of such irritation that he retreated a few feet. This yard was her domain and she was busy in it.

When she finished rearranging the earth around one or two small plants, she sat back to admire her handiwork. Citizen decided to approach her again. He sat close to her, not right by her side but close enough to suggest an interest in being friends.

'Nothing to say?' she pressed him. His look said: *I'm sorry, I don't know what to say.*

On the morning of our visit to Doria camp, Anita had asked for a few sheets of the writing paper she had seen me carrying. These, I saw now, had made their way to Sara. She folded the A4 pages in two, pressing down the sides to make them into a book. Alongside the sheets were three crayons scattered by Citizen's feet. He looked on, contemplating her drawings and probably wondering if he might be able to join in. But he didn't ask her any questions, nor did he attempt to take the crayons. Instead he watched. After a long while, feeling some compassion for the silent boy,

'Oh, all right, stay, but you have to sit here and be very quiet,' she conceded.

He sat on the ground right beside her. Sara had finished with her drawings and, seeing she had an audience, began to tell a story about a shell with long ears. In her story the shell could eavesdrop on conversations all over the sea. 'One day,' she said, 'the whales were plotting to take over the waters of the silvery snapper, the best fishes in the world, and the shell listened to their plot and went to tell on them. When the snapper heard this they organized themselves into a brave army and put the biggest, fattest snapper in front. They spread the sea floor with poisonous weeds that the whales could not resist and as the whales became sleepy and drugged from eating the weeds, the snapper laughed in their faces and swam away.'

Without uttering a word, Citizen withdrew and went to sit on a stool on the veranda. He looked out to sea, acting as though he saw and felt nothing. Sara approached him and said a few words, which must have struck a painful chord because when she left he again looked morose.

'What is the matter, little boy?' I called. He whimpered and slumped to the floor. I went to stand by him, reaching out to touch him. Without warning he jumped to his feet, shouting into the air, hitting and punching in a way that suggested combat with several ghostly enemies. Sounds emerged from his lips but nothing we could make sense of, no actual words – just noises and grunts that until that moment had been pinioned beneath his tongue. Alone, he battled, then cautiously straightened, as though in fear of being hit back. Finally he was done and gave up, slumped on the floor.

Released from his nightmarish fight, he was still breathing heavily, emitting a *guff, guff* noise, the sounds of a voiceless or wild creature. Eventually his breathing softened. He had just caught a glimpse of himself, the familiar frayed shorts and dusty top reflected in the window. This mirror, like a giant petal, welcomed him in. He hesitated, uncertain whether to trust it or not, but it neither cracked nor turned against him. It did not introduce terrifying background scenes: corpses on the road, trees burnt black. Seeing his own face Citizen relaxed, his image soothing him – his dark eyes and long curled lashes, his short flat nose. He opened his mouth, watched his own tongue shoot out wordlessly. More than a year since he had been rescued, he was still 'the silent boy'. But the urge to speak must have been there.

A cloud obscured the sun. A greyish darkness crept over the sky and hovered. Then it passed. Again the sky was bright; clouds like artistic imaginings traversed the bright blue. A slight wind blew the line of washing and the scent of freshly clean clothes wafted over to us.

Elizabeth stood and picked up her basin. 'Let me go to the market.'

Returning inside, I found Moses in the studio.

In his grieving state he had not ventured there as often as before but when I slid open the door of the studio that afternoon he was busy at work. The benches and tables were covered with various items: photographs, albums, notebooks, scissors, marking tape, pens and plastic trays, along with some old books arranged in size order and pamphlets. He was poring over a set of old family photographs of Adele with their daughter Agnes. He looked surprised to see me. I was inclined to leave him to his memories, understanding the pleasure to be gained from squeezing oneself back in time and space. But he beckoned me to stay.

I sat down heavily on a stool by the table and opened one of the leather-bound albums. An assortment of photographs of his immediate family – Adele, their only child Agnes – filled the pages: the yard, the well-stocked kitchen, grouped around Cotton Tree in the centre of Freetown, on holiday in Bonthe along the coast, at Lumley beach, snaps from Ghana. Their lives played themselves out in silence.

Then a purple-coloured album resting on a trestle table caught my attention. It was marked: 'England'. I laid the others aside and began turning its heavy pages for pictures of my childhood. I saw a couple that brought back those times: me pushing a bicycle up our road and playing under our neighbour's fruit trees. Not many people in my life now had known me then. I searched through the entire album and discovered only four snapshots of myself. Instead there was an abundance of images of our home: of the red living-room carpet littered with toys and picture books, a childhood bedroom with its matching cotton bedspreads. More: the contents of the kitchen cupboard, packets of Kellogg's cornflakes, Corona lemonade, assorted tins and packets, silver-plated salt and pepper cruets, burgundy-rimmed dining plates and assorted teapots; the old-fashioned washing machine with mangle. Pictures taken when we were out. Taken naked. My mother would not have liked that and I'm not sure I liked it either.

Perhaps it did not matter. I had imagined there would be more. My mother and I had assumed Uncle Moses would have some. Well, we had been wrong to entrust the recording of our family history to him when he clearly had not ever regarded it as a priority. But whatever happened to the pictures of us at Christmas time? Or the day we saw the field of buttercups? Wanting to ask not to accuse, I approached him.

'Julia, let me show you these nineteenth-century prints.'

I dragged my stool across the plain wooden floor, placed it by him and smiled.

'Decker really started something: a chain reaction here in Freetown with his photography. He was documenting for the British as far back as eighteen-seventy. Look at this one.'

'It's amazing.' Here was the port of Freetown in 1870 with its wooden buildings and port workers standing around waiting to be snapped. I stared at the image, which contained a mystery for me: where was the photographer? It seemed as though he had taken the picture from the sky – an aerial shot in 1870?

'He was famous for that,' answered Moses, 'so many unusual vantage points in his work.'

He insisted on staying by my side, asking questions, engaging me in conversation and showing me more of his studio prints. The pictures of African ladies in bustles, leaning against Grecian urns, intrigued me. I'd never seen so many prosperous turn-of-the-century costumes, so many brass buttons or stiff white sleeves in an African setting. These images were a world away from the chaotic Freetown of today. So many people have died here, but in those prints there was no sign of despair, death, war and mutilation, not a gesture to our utter degradation.

'You know, there is a story I once heard,' I told him. 'A West African artist arrives in Venice and is asked to comment on their art and culture. He looks around the city and says: "I don't understand what has happened here. The architectural monuments are extraordinary, the paintings too. But I don't find any link between the past and what I see today. Are you sure these are the same people?"'

Moses smiled. Years and years had passed, but something stood still.

'Na we, my dear, na we,' he said.

*

Two days later.

'Ooo, ooo, ooo, ooo,' like a cuckoo calling, Anita arrived, interrupting our session in the studio. 'Come look.' She was pulling my arm so hard I felt it would be yanked from the socket. I ran behind her on to the veranda, from which she pointed back to her yard.

'What?' I asked, puzzled.

'Look there!'

Citizen and Sara, in shorts and barefoot, were on their hands and knees planting some shoots in the earth she had dug up that morning and rearranged elsewhere. From our spying position it was obvious that this was a cooperative venture: the four hands were clearing holes, putting in the shoots, and patting down the earth.

'Thank God,' said Anita.

'Amen,' I replied.

Citizen had responded to Sara's new gardening with an enthusiasm that took us all by surprise. The earth was dry and the handprints in the soil where the children patted down the earth in their garden were clearly visible. Anita and I decided that this plot should be reserved for them, a site for neighbourly endeavours. 'Mek we see,' she said.

Sara, Miss Green Fingers, made no mention of her conquest of Citizen and I began to think she saw it as perfectly normal, so I said nothing either. But two days later, when she was looking especially pretty in a European-styled blue dress with a bow, she let slip after breakfast, 'He listens to me, Auntie, I give him my latest ideas.' And I knew girl-power was speaking fresh and cool as coconut milk.

Sara was the proud owner now of all my writing paper, all the pens and crayons that both households could muster, and a humble gardening assistant, Citizen-Mellors. He followed her about, waited for her bulletins of local genius and, without the slightest hint of annoyance or mimicry, obeyed her orders in the yard. As observers only, Anita and I joined them aboard their newly launched romantic ship. For me, it was a lesson in leadership, for Anita, a joke. Sara, not happy with the placing of their plants in a higgledy-piggledy order, had to have them dug up again and replanted on the other side of the patch in rows. Citizen obliged. He redug the earth, using two sharp sticks and his bare hands. We looked on. He wore an old T-shirt that was marked with mud thrown up from digging. There was mud all over his feet, on his hands and in his hair.

When the re-sowing was over Anita called out, 'Una cam wash.' She scrubbed Sara clean and shampooed and conditioned her hair with my creams, then it was Citizen's turn. He entered the bathroom naked, having dispensed with his muddy shorts and T-shirt on the stairs, and stood by the door, watching us. I ran the water and, crouching down, stirred in some aromatic oils. The air filled with the pungent smell of cypress and lavender. Citizen was still at the door.

'Come on then, time to get clean.'

He immediately came forward and stepped into the tub. He reached for my pink nailbrush, which was in the shape of a hippopotamus, and sniffed it. As he bent down I saw that his upper back was covered in marks: his mocha skin, which would otherwise have been breathtakingly smooth, had been cut by beatings and wounded with a knife. In my quivering palms I cupped the oily water, splashing it over his back. As the liquid ran gently down his skin I saw the number 439K cut into his back. Citizen, unaware, was paddling in the water with the exuberance of a duckling. Filled with misery, I urged him: 'Splash, splash the water with your hands.'

He began to play with the hippo brush and the surface of the water shimmered. As he played I applied some of the ointment Anita had used at Doria camp and rubbed it into 439K. Citizen stopped moving and sniffed the air. He sighed, fondled the miniature hippo with his left hand and stood up, allowing me to wrap him in a long green bath towel. For a moment he was in my arms, bunched together.

I watched him make for the bedroom where Anita had put him a few nights before and I followed quietly behind. I tidied up his things, relishing having him entirely to myself for a few more minutes at the end of that peopled day. Citizen lay in bed, staring straight ahead. He seemed calm and sleepy. Not much light penetrated the shutters and the smell of cypress and lavender hung in the air.

'Sweet dreams,' I said when he finally fell asleep, clutching the hippo brush. As his grasp opened, the pink animal appeared to be peeping out at the night. I too stared, mesmerized by my eight-year-old cousin. Anita and Sara had shown me the way to reach him. A few sheets of writing paper bound into a book, a well-earned token of affection from Sara, rested at his feet. I was proud he had something of mine too and that our first close exchange had been a success.

As soon as Uncle Moses saw me coming towards him, he could tell that I was pleased.

'It's the first time he has allowed someone to put him to bed,' he encouraged.

'Not really; Anita did the other night.'

'But in the middle of the night.'

He poured us both a shot of whisky and twisted round to check if I approved.

'It would be nice to have a nightcap,' I confirmed.

He wanted to bring back some semblance of normal family life by talking away the late evening.

'It would have been so different,' he said, 'if she hadn't gone to the farm.'

'You weren't often apart, were you?'

'No, only when she wanted to visit Agnes. You know their farm was so far away.'

'And before that?'

'Yes, well, you know. Once or twice. When I went back to England, she didn't want to come. Anyway we didn't have that kind of money. And she didn't like to travel too far. "Moses, you go and come," she would say.'

Outside it was pitch dark. Somewhere in the far distance we heard the squeak of a night bird and then a car. During the long silences the house spoke also. The water pipes chugged, the electricity hummed. It seemed as if the house was putting itself to rest, but Uncle Moses was still talking:

'She said, "Moses, don't limit yourself to ordinary studio work. Other people can do that." I told her, "It's our bread and butter." She said, "Look beyond what people ask you to do. Go with your own vision. You talk about the old photographs but I don't see you working on them."'

I closed my eyes and saw blackness poised to spread to eternity. It devoured everything.

'I must get to bed, Uncle. Goodnight.'

'Goodnight,' he said, 'thanks for listening.'

Rain poured, turning the night into the coolest yet. I had left my bedroom window open and a small gust of wind blew it to and fro until it woke me, or was I dreaming? A few specks of rain had spattered the bedclothes when I pulled myself up to close it. I had been lying there for some time, trying to calculate the exact physical effort required. The mosquito net was torn in parts but had so far protected me from the worst assaults. There were only two fresh bites on my ankles. I sat on the chair to massage some antihistamine cream into the bites. It was then that I noticed the light from the room opposite. Citizen must have left the bedside lamp on or perhaps he had fallen asleep while drawing. I put down the cream and went to investigate.

Gently pushing open his bedroom door, I was alarmed to

see the room on fire. I rushed to his bedside. Citizen was deeply asleep with his head still on the pillow and his face pointed straight at the ceiling, his breath audible and clear. With my fingertips, I touched his brow. He was warm but not especially hot, although flames continued to lick the walls and swirl around the old dresser. But there was no crackle of burning wood, no sign of ash, no hissing of fire. The fire made no impact on the room. Outside, rain was pouring more heavily and the night grew fiercer, but inside the house we were safe, dry and comfortable. A stray thought floated into my mind: *A child's bedroom is adapted to his life, his imaginings, his dreams.*

'Oh, God, give him peace.'

But even his smallest facial muscles spoke of pain as they twisted and relaxed.

Oh, God, give him peace! I clung to my mantra.

His breathing broke, he was choking and struggling for breath but I could not keep my eyes on his contorted expression. Anita had told me about child soldiers who set fire to villages, terrifying people, killing them in their homes, in their beds. Was that it? Citizen turned his face towards mine and his muscles continued to twist above his eyes and around his mouth.

'Oh, God, forgive him and bring him peace.' Thinking of him as a small terrified boy, not as one who terrifies, I watched the flames subside. I stood inches away from his face, checking that his breathing was normal, watching his chest rise and fall in gentle ripples. A light sheen appeared on his brow, moistening the black curls of his head. I opened the window to cool the air. A small gust entered the room and the flames vanished. Relieved that it was over, I slipped back to my own bed.

'Sleep tight,' I offered the night.

*

Anita made the tea far too strong the following morning. She remained outside, preparing snacks: in her palms she rolled small balls of nutty *gari* with chunks of onion and chilli pepper, miracles of spiciness that she tossed into a plastic bowl. 'Sara and Citizen were helping me, but you know pickin, they'd had enough after two or three,' was her early-morning report.

'Yes, I know what kids are like. I'm feeling hungry and tired.' I sat beside her.

'Never be hungry and angry and lonely and tired.'

'Some hope, hey? Just hungry and tired for now. And maybe a bit frustrated.'

I tried one more dispatch to the wise woman in my company. 'I'm thinking of going into town to talk to the people who found Citizen. I need to know more about what he was up to, his life before he was taken to Doria camp, you know.'

'You want to know everything. You can't accept just what you see. That's all. Deal with what involves you and leave the rest.' She popped the remainder of the dried *gari* into her mouth.

'But that's the point, it does involve me. I need to take it in properly and learn more; only then can I see what I can do to make a difference.' I threw some of the hard grain into my mouth. It nearly made my choke. 'Help me to see, Anita.'

Eddy appeared and put his hand out for a snack. Anita filled his palm with the nutty grain: 'Is all you getting.' The minute she looked away, he put his hand out again. She went on: 'Sit here, your hair needs doing. Who plaits it so small-small like this?'

What a cheek, to change the subject and criticize my hairdo at one go! She was waiting for an answer and I let her wait, until I realized how childish that was.

'Susan. Susan does my hair. She's done it for years.'

'And who is Susan to you?'

'She's a Jamaican girl, woman. And a friend.'

'Come.' Anita put my head between her two strong knees, clasping it tight like a hazelnut in nutcrackers. The scent of her body merged with the heavy aroma of pomade on my hair. She removed the clips, undid the tightly woven braids and gently turned my head, the better to reach each side. I surrendered my head to her, neck and muscles softening like dough at her touch. With a mixture of pleasure and pain as her hands loosened the tiny, scalp-hugging plaits, I sagged into her command, my hair all loose, pointing into the air and hanging down to my shoulders.

Gripping my shoulders firmly, she advised me: 'I'm going to fold it big for you now and you'll see things better.'

While she started to work the hair, twisting it into fulsome cornrows, fit for a market woman, I attempted to control my mind. I was observing scenes I had never witnessed before. Her big plaits were a trap, a device for opening up spaces in my head that hadn't been tampered with since I was a girl. She was using this hairdressing ritual to push African 'bush' images in those spaces. I fought back, gathering memories of London – me sampling couchillo olives in a Battersea delicatessen, me catching Eurostar at Waterloo station – but I was losing. That central parting of my head became a valley lying between high green mountains. Downstream, circles organizing themselves around my ears transformed into a ravine rushing over yellowed rocks. My head was a map of Sierra Leone, its farmland, diamond mines, mountains, ridges, people, soldiers, fighters, leaders. Up the smooth dark skin of my neck marched a band of boy and girl soldiers, young, scabby creatures in all shapes and sizes. They looked weary and might have been refugees from another era, but the modern vehicle, a mud-splattered truck at their rear, told me otherwise. A girl riding at the front of the truck, a baby at her breast, looked up at me. She paused in the middle of her feeding and stared into my eyes.

'I see much better now,' I called out to Anita. 'It's a whole cast of characters, Anita.'

'Uh . . . mm,' she said, giving my head a little push as she massaged the last of the oil into the scalp. I could sense her moving off, leaving me to work out these dramatic scenarios.

All I could see next were traces of their passage; the tracks left behind on the road and the two boys who came after the truck walking backwards, their guns pointed up into the air: the lookout for spies, seeing everything, spotting the enemy.

I closed my eyes again. I was sitting firmly on the stool, the stool in Anita's yard. Dizzily I got to my feet and waited for a further sign.

I didn't have to wait long to hear soldiers' voices; the sound of their crying filled the camp. After a seven-day forced march into the bush, rough and harsh terrain, they were made to sit on the ground and listen to a lecture on why they must fight for their rights and better times. Shocked and confused, they were asking what were rights? And then they started to cry, 'Why me, why me? What about me?'

Almost twelve years old, Abu was already as tall as a man, but the softness of his skin betrayed his true age. He felt himself losing balance as Lieutenant Ibrahim yanked him to his feet and, wielding a six-foot birch, beat his thin black legs, which shook like leaves in a breeze. Urine soaked his black cotton shorts. He held his head and felt ashamed. At this sight the smallest soldiers scattered more tears on the ground. So this was it, the day childhood finished. Without warning and for the third consecutive day, Lieutenant Ibrahim was beating Abu. In Citizen's heart, in all their hearts, the beating reverberated like a drum. When would the drum break?

As Abu fell to the ground, Lieutenant Ibrahim was shouting: 'Why? Why? Why do you cry every day? Why, why?'

Abu looked up, a last blow catching him on his head. He was both conscious and alive, what did he have to lose in answering truthfully? The lieutenant's features were dark and blurred by sun as if the light from his eyes had been siphoned off.

Abu faced him and bravely replied: 'I miss my mother.'

Lieutenant Ibrahim flinched. He had heard this one before and it was not to be tolerated: 'Well, we've been here many months without our mothers. If you cry again, we will kill you.'

Abu took himself off to where the other children sat, first blubbering as they watched him approach, then in silence. The worst thing in the world had happened but no one was crying.

Rallentando. I could feel my heartbeat slow down. Ibrahim was twenty years old. He owned a blue bandanna, a ten-year-old radio, a pocket knife and his uniform, a sleeveless jacket. He was in the habit of telling people that his uncle had given him the knife as a present when he was fourteen. This was not true. He had stolen it from a corpse on joining the army five years previously. He loved that knife, kept it by him at all times and made a point of using it every single day. It had served him well, helped him win promotion to lieutenant after two years' service. He loved his rank, second in command of his unit; he had earned it, like everything he had had in his life. Every day he was with them, his unit, number-one-burning-houses unit. They were his troops and they listened to his every word. They had to. Their lives depended on it. There was nothing he had not seen: people defecating like wild beasts in terror, parents burnt alive in front of their children, every ugly death; multiple rapes, single rape, gang rape, rape of pregnant women, daily rape, rape over a fortnight.

53

One lonely night five years ago, the man Ibrahim used to call 'uncle' appeared from the viscid darkness carrying a white candle: Ibrahim exterminated them all – killed the man, killed the darkness, killed the light.

Citizen sat by Abu. Their legs were stretched out on the ground. They did not speak, but were they to call out, however loudly, who could come? A girl approached them with tasks to be done: fetching water or going to look for food. They volunteered to fetch water and they took off together. Abu was telling Citizen about his older brother, Masu, and of how their grandfather had been attacked and burnt in the family home. Without their elderly guardian Masu and Abu were living in the forest, looking after themselves as best as they could, when the soldiers had found them. Citizen was listening. He held the stories in his head.

In a minute, in a split second, I lean forward to hear the sound of Abu's voice once more. He opens his mouth to speak, but in the background a dog is barking loud and fierce. I long to hear the boy again and reach forward. Is it too late?

The girl whom Ibrahim had taken as his 'wife', the girl who was riding in the truck, beckons to me to follow her. I point towards my chest:

'Me?'

She nods. She has observed me as one ready to slide into their lives. She leads me from the stool where I have been sitting, the stool in Anita's yard. She leads my slippery self through a door to another world. She leads. I follow.

Three

I was down on my belly in a marshy spot, struggling to breathe and pushing the dark tangles of bush and shrub out of the way, the better to spy on Citizen and his new friend, Abu. In the unremitting heat, guns cracked in the air and splinters flew. The two boys were running about a village, darting into homes and then re-emerging, sometimes empty-handed, sometimes with a fruit or a plantain or two. They stopped to skin three ripe bananas, dropping the waste on the ground. They gobbled the fruit and clutched their other finds: oranges, plantain and some onions.

Then a woman's voice shouted in Krio, 'Feed those chickens, Alex!' Yellow dust rose from the ground as Alex, wearing nothing but blue shorts, ran to obey his mother. Fluid and familiar, the life of the village went on. Two young women were hanging out washing, twisting the sheets like ropes to wring out excess water. An old man was pushing a rickety barrow full of wood back into his yard, where three small girls were throwing a ball to each other.

Citizen and Abu had retreated to a quiet spot, on a hill overlooking the centre of the village. From there they followed the action. Away from the fated scene. Citizen raised a hand to signal to the unit. En masse, a group of six boy soldiers descended on the village. The tallest had long black hair, streaking like a mane behind him. In front came Lieutenant Ibrahim, head of the unit, dressed in olive-green trousers and string vest, shouting to the others to follow. With a torch, he set the first house alight. Within seconds the fire was fierce. It demolished the house. A terrible smell came through the air. The villagers began to scream, running in all directions like insects being sprayed. In a few minutes three houses were gone. A local preacher found himself surrounded by a circle of fire and tried to manoeuvre to safety. Animals began to screech and moan as the fire smacked their lungs. Thatch flew into the skies.

'Shoot!' someone shouted from within a wooden building. 'Shoot! Shoot!'

Gunfire cracked out. Random shots: someone trying to save someone's life. Flames ripped through wooden-framed houses like scarlet-haired brigands. One of the three girls who had been playing ball ran to find her mother. She tripped on an old wire and collapsed in front of them. The father – or grandfather? – came out, clutching in sweaty hands various small things: family heirlooms, a frying pan, a toy. He dropped these and ran back inside, holding his crotch. In the middle of the village people were already gathering; one or two had managed to retrieve their makeshift beds, an occasional basket stuffed with precious items for a fiancée. A woman stood there with the cotton dress she had been mending, not realizing the clothes she was wearing had caught fire. The village school such as it was had gone, visited in seconds, consumed in minutes; the books and stools lay charred as the peculiar brightness wended its way through the village, breathless. An intense and devilish voltage, seeing off life. Finished, nothing; finished, done.

Citizen and Abu began to run back to the unit, having accomplished their part in the mission. On the way back they dived into another kitchen and snatched as much food as they could carry. Then something shifted in the bush. It was an old woman, a short granny who was vomiting on the ground. The boys stopped and stared. Abu dropped one of his oranges in front of her. She spat on it. Citizen grabbed Abu's arm and pulled him away. As they plunged into the gloom of the forest, they saw that they were lost. Which way back to camp? Citizen staggered around looking for traces on the ground: a bullet or torch from one of the others. Then he became stuck, his shorts caught on a piece of barbed wire. In the darkness he unpicked himself but all the while they heard a rustling sound and could not tell whether it was a rat or a man. He pulled at the fabric and the barbed wire ripped it, so now the shorts were split at the front, exposing him.

'Where to?' Abu asked in a new voice. 'You know this place?' he asked again, of an unresponsive Citizen.

'Listen, you hear water?' Citizen was holding back, cocking his ear.

'No, no water.' The sky had turned a dark-khaki green. All around the bush was silent, but far off in the distance they could see the lights of a camp. They began to file down, turning left towards the lights, chattering in soft voices. They were not completely alone. From time to time a peace-keeper's plane flew overhead, searching for lost boys trapped in the dark, war-torn forest.

By the time they arrived back at the camp, Citizen and Abu looked feverish and weak. 'I'm so cold,' said Citizen, collapsing in exhaustion. He pulled himself up and went in search of a blanket. He found two old woollen rugs, one of which he threw over his shoulders. The other he passed to Abu. But then something seemed to happen to Abu; as though seized by a terrible fit he began to shudder.

'It is so cold,' he told Citizen, but though he rubbed his arms and held the blanket close, the shudders continued for several minutes. Citizen tried to warm his friend, standing by him. He went off in search of another blanket and came back empty-handed.

'Blankets finish.'

The bitter cold air was relentless, just as the sun always left them weary on their day searches for food. Abu tried to get up but he could not. He rolled about in an attempt to ease pain brought on by his eating too much fruit on an empty stomach.

'I'm very cold,' Abu kept mumbling.

After hunger, no proper food. After fighting, no rest. For a while the two boys lay there, neglecting to check what the others in the unit were doing. Later, they were called to eat. There was fresh water that night. The unit settled in the darkness. Little by little, talk stopped and most of the child soldiers in the unit fell asleep. The two on night watch were smoking to stay awake. They dared not sleep. Darkness closed around the camp. In the distance the dying fires of the torched village smouldered. Their day's work was done. Citizen was trying to keep warm and to comfort Abu, who occasionally coughed and moaned.

'I want to sleep.' Citizen looked up at the darkening sky with a gaze that seemed too sad to believe that a rescue plane would come and lighten it.

'Sleep now,' said Abu. Citizen rolled on to his side and looked away from the sky. By midnight, he was asleep.

'We are number-one-burn-house unit!' Ibrahim shouted over the camp at dawn, still high on the previous night's fix. 'Listen, number-one-burn-house unit! Get up!' He leapt into the air like a frog. He seemed to come alive with the memory of his latest conquest. He was more alert, more vocal than he had seemed before. Then he called Abu and Citizen: 'Where the rations?'

They laid before him the paltry supplies they had filched. He took the oranges, though not without rebuking them for bringing back so little. Abu was feeling slightly better and the convulsions had subsided. He took the needle that was passed to him and injected into his arm. Then he passed it on to Citizen, who copied the procedure. 'Whoa!' Citizen cried out. That would keep him awake all day. He swayed about in circles as though trying to stir a liquid in his belly. 'Whoa!' he cried out again, shocked at his own condition. This was meant to protect them or make them feel strong. But instead Citizen looked like a wild creature whose limbs had been rearranged, foot for hand, upper arm for calf. He sniffed. 'Let's go,' he told Abu. Far away, guns were being fired but Citizen took no interest in the explosions.

'The mission will begin soon,' announced one of the girls, signalling that the horror of rushing into crowded villages with fire in their hands, wreaking devastation on homes, land, people, breathing the burning hair was imminent. Citizen looked unperturbed. He rubbed his stomach. Fear had deserted him. The drug had seen to that.

'Those little insects running around before us,' laughed one of the boys.

'People run, shoo, shoo, shoo, like little insects.' The speaker drank a brown liquid from a jug, spilling some on the ground.

'Don't waste it,' Abu reprimanded. Annoyed he took the jug and poured the liquid down his throat.

It would not be long before they would be at it again. Suddenly Citizen had a look in his eyes that even Abu had not seen before, an expression of despair.

'My shorts.' Remembering he had torn his only pair, he looked totally sad.

Abu shook his head and patted him on the back. 'Come on.' There was no time for feeling glum about shorts; the unit was marching off, preparing to attack.

Up ahead, about ten minutes before the unit, Abu and Citizen were on special lookout. Abu had his own gun to carry. Citizen had taken a big stick, since his ability to carry and fire was in doubt. The sun streamed down and by mid-morning it was over ninety degrees. Sweat poured down Citizen's face and soaked the roots of his hair. His hands hurt from carrying and his feet, stained a reddish brown from walking barefoot on the long march, were sore. When the insects became too troublesome, he shooed them away. There was a long silence, then voices – not human voices, but strange utterances, like the screeching of birds.

As they came up close to the next village, they realized that fighting had already broken out. 'Help!' 'Mama!' 'Help!' 'Shoot!' 'Fire!'

Thugs mingled with soldiers, village people merged with strangers. The violence was like a set piece, they had seen it all before. A man cornered by a mob was beaten with sticks and bottles until blood spilt from his head. His girlfriend, in panic, ripped her own dress. Fighting went on for hours before they were called to retreat. But they were caught in a trap.

One of the village boys, Sesay, holding a mortar for pounding yam, was beating Abu. Abu fought back, trying to reach a stone to bash Sesay's head. Citizen ran to help his friend and began punching Sesay in the ribs and in the balls, hitting out with his fists and the bundle in his hands. He did not stop, though Sesay's bloodied lips were mouthing the word 'No.' Where had he found such strength? Abu could not tell. The tearing sound of a gun being repeatedly fired into the air – *crack, crack* – assaulted their ears. Then a rumbling sound close by, louder than thunder. A great bang and pieces of metal shattered, clods of earth and debris fell on to their heads. Both were shaking. Flattening themselves against the earth, they covered their ears against the deafening sounds and stayed as still as they could. Sesay, no older than them, was also on the ground. Blood was flowing from his face, but he was alive. They were all alive.

When all was silent, Citizen wriggled forward through a tight space to where the others in his unit were lying. Abu followed though, being bigger, he found it difficult to manoeuvre. Next they heard a wailing sound, a soft whimpering cutting through the bush. Abu knew it was a person though he could see nobody. Then he spotted some tracks on the ground and followed them to where Bobo lay. It had to be Bobo. He was always forgetting to get down. 'When you hear the fire *crack, crack*, you must get down,' Abu had told him. Bobo always forgot. When he heard the fire, *crack, crack*, just as they warned, he grew excited, jumping to look.

He had a bullet in his leg and was writhing in agony on the ground. 'Help me!' In pain, Bobo bit his own lip. Abu and Citizen took his arms and set him by the truck. Abu put his hands over Bobo's hot forehead while Citizen fetched water for him to sip. Their senior commander found them all and took Sesay along. He was screaming that he wanted to find his people but shut up when the gun was pointed to his head. Gunshots, not aimed at them but still cracking the air, exploded above. Hurtling back to their unit, they collided with bushes and one another, sometimes screaming out each other's names:

'Citizen! Citizen!'

'Abu! Abu!'

New boys joined that night, not only Sesay whose mortar for pounding yam was a solitary link with home. Abu began to explain: 'We are the number-one-burn-houses unit.'

'Eh?' Sesay wanted to cry.

'We burn houses,' Citizen repeated. 'The unit burns houses.'

Sesay skidded as he tried to rush away and his ankle twisted in the attempt. He looked hurt. 'No.' He refused their comforting, but Abu was persistent. He turned from Citizen and looked deliberately towards Sesay, who was spouting tears on the ground. It must have been pity that made him keep his eyes pinned on the new recruit, whose oval-shaped face was beautiful.

'The first night is always the worst,' Abu consoled. It was the worst. Sesay had regained his balance and looked about the camp, at the weapons, at the two young women with shiny red lips and tired eyes. He looked down at his own clothes and realized that although he had killed no one they were covered in mud and blood. As he struggled to centre himself, his chest heaved. Lying on the ground but beyond his reach was an unusually shaped weapon, which he was staring at when suddenly Abu shouted, 'Don't touch those!'

'Those are bombs with stick, they hurl it like so.' Citizen continued the lesson by demonstrating the pitch. There were guns of different kinds scattered on the ground but Citizen reassured Sesay that they did not know how to fire all the weapons either. 'You stay with us on lookout. We go before, we see where the enemy is, the weapons store, and we report back. They give us groundnut or cigarette to go and sell, then we report back.'

'We go before. See if the enemy is there.'

'Who is the enemy?'

'People.'

'People who want to kill us,' added Abu.

'Yes,' confirmed Citizen.

The boys explained that orders had to be obeyed exactly. Always do what they say – 'exact', not 'more or less'. Although they did not know where they were or how well they were doing, it was best to follow orders. 'Do what they say or they will kill you.'

They wanted to be sure Sesay had understood. Some boys were very strong, good fighters. Not all. 'I failed,' Citizen said, 'I couldn't do it.' The previous week Citizen was told to flog to death another boy who had failed to fire his gun. The commander gave him a birch, shouting: 'Beat him! Beat him to death! If you don't beat him to death, I will kill you.'

'Beat him, beat him!'

Citizen had raised it high, higher, as high as he could, to bring it down on the boy's head, once, twice, but he could not raise it a third time. Again the commander shouted: 'Beat him! Beat him!' Citizen raised it high, higher, but it fell haphazardly from his hands. He had drooped, sharing the disgrace with the birch. There was worse to come. For failing to execute the boy, he himself was punished with a beating of fifty lashes.

I closed my eyes.

'I kill *beaucoup*! *Beaucoup*!' shouted a teenager, just back from the front. Citizen, Abu and Sesay were paying him no attention and looked annoyed at the trigger-happy Thomas: 'I killed ten – no, eleven people!' He was only twelve years old but his bragging and numerical precision was already well known.

'Ten or eleven?' asked Sesay.

'Eleven. I kill *beaucoup*.'

The voices of other child soldiers came over the air. They knew the fighting was not over, that what had been left undone would be revisited the next day. And the next. They stood by a single kerosene lamp, their knives, cutlass and guns by their sides waiting for instructions. Then Abu and Citizen came back. They had found Masu, Abu's elder brother. He was weak and starving and sick, but lucky to be alive. The two boys had decided to hunt for food. They stole some ripe mangoes from a market woman and ate one of them, relishing the eruption of sweet pulp in their warm saliva and they returned to the unit with the yield of fruit.

Abu was trying to feed his brother, but Masu could not hold the fruit in his mouth and coughed it out on the ground. Telling him to 'buck up himself' Abu looked over to the lieutenant to assure him that all was well. Masu feigned disinterest but knew from the dryness of his mouth that malaria had set in. Bad air. Bitter sickness. He scratched his face, his neck, his head. The sickness that had invaded his body was worse than any fever he had known. The world tipped one way, then the other. He took in what he could. Before he passed out he saw syringes lying on the ground, the back of his brother's hand and the hard yellow-blushed skin of the mango.

Towards midnight Lieutenant Ibrahim, dressed in khaki trousers, purple T-shirt and soft shoes, came to instruct them that it was time to move on. In his right hand was a bottle of whisky, which he passed to his 'wife' to share. She took one sip and handed it to the boy on her left. Ibrahim suddenly reached forward and snatched it back, pressed it to his lips, drinking hard. He glanced around shiftily, looking for a smoke, refusing to relinquish the bottle again. Clinging to it, he hesitated, then secured it under his arm, while furiously searching his trouser pockets. The bottle slipped from its cover and fell to the ground. This unleashed his rage:

'You fucking useless bastards, you good-for-nothing fools!'

His 'wife' raised the now almost empty bottle and returned it to him. He turned and hit her hard across the head so she fell to the ground where her chin hit the bottle. Holding her jaw, she struggled to her feet and stood behind him.

Out of sight a vehicle roared past. The unit made ready to move on. Abu, seeing that his older brother, though conscious, was very weak, went to his aid. 'Let me help you, Masu,' he whispered. Masu looked into his eyes and was silent. The lieutenant glimpsed this brotherly love, picked up his gun and shot Masu in the head: 'That's the first good-for-nothing bastard!'

Abu held his own flesh and blood and laid him to rest. He called the others to come round him and the congregation stood together on the blood-soiled earth warm from the day's sun and witnessed, with Abu, the passing of another life. They talked to one another and held one another. They talked to Abu and held him. Abu was crying.

'Dance,' shouted Lieutenant Ibrahim, 'I say dance!'

He scratched his face, fingered his gun and pulled his khaki trousers out at the knees. He looked as though he would shoot another one of them. His 'wife' scurried away and put on some thudding music, a dull *boom*, *boom* spiked with the clinking sounds of percussion.

The child soldiers began to move, bodies mimicking those of people in delicious ecstasy of free movement. They danced as if with this performance of contentment they might at last banish the spectre of loss and grief from their lives. This is what had been commanded: to dance like gallant soldiers. Evening approached and the sun's insistent burn was waning, but the child soldiers hurt. In a line, along with the others, Citizen and Abu danced after a fashion. Citizen tapped his feet, cautiously deferring his sorrow for later, when he would lie alone at night.

Lieutenant Ibrahim climbed on to the gnarled trunk of a tree, from which he shouted, 'Enough, that's enough.' Not one muscle in his face moved but he emitted a long sigh with the final, 'Stop, enough.'

An ominous calm descended on the child soldiers as though the imponderable weight of his regime was a force they could not withstand. The lieutenant touched his 'wife' on the buttocks and kissed her on the neck, indicating that it was time to move on. In eerie silence the child soldiers began to move about looking for their things. Citizen gathered his belongings and put Abu's together also. The forest was buzzing with insects, but he ignored them and moved about inspecting the ground for some stray item of their confined lives: a shoe, an odd blade, a missing cup. Finally the entire unit was ready to leave. Loading their possessions on to the truck one by one, they formed a line and turned away.

I stealthily sat up and gazed out at the dark towards those frail shapes marching to their next station. I listened hard for shouting, gun shots or planes flying overhead, but only a haunting melody came to my ears. The sound of children's voices, lingering on the still air, strained to mark boundary in time:

> 'When shall I see my home again?
> Oh, my home,
> Oh, my home,
> I shall never forget my home.'

Four

The journey back to Moses' house was maddening. My thoughts vacillated between disbelief at those bizarre, distressing images of Citizen's war and the desperate conviction that I could assist him now. I imagined the two of us returning to that forest in peacetime, drowsing in the shade of sky-scraping banana trees or sipping fresh pineapple juice at dawn. Away those scenes of risk and death with people screaming in terror. But wait, they were not trigger-happy snipers but half-naked kids, shrieking with fear because there was nowhere called 'home', no comfort blanket. No question, those pictures were shouting for big headlines or some magnificent bird with gigantic downy wings to stoop down and say, 'Jump here, little Citizen, let me carry you to safety.'

For hours, I lost my way. I attempted to turn right but the road twisted the other way, and judged me a novice. I stood on the correct path and beseeched it in the cold midnight to let me move forward without falling down a cliff or hurting my already weary feet. I was shepherded back. Only once did I tumble down a hill but that led me straight to Uncle Moses' house.

By the time I walked into the yard the light was becoming murky, and though the studio was in near darkness he was still at work, reading a yellowing copy of the *Sierra Leone Weekly News* from the 1970s.

'Hello. Have you had some dinner?'

'Not yet, but Anita cooked and left some soup for us. It's on the stove. Are you hungry?'

'Not very.'

'I was sorting these files out – it's something to do. Look how much rubbish I've accumulated over the years, so much *bota-bata*.'

'Easily done. I love chucking things out. I used to keep all my old magazines, bits of advice on make-up and boyfriends and what to wear, as if it was going to be useful for years on end. Then you realize they write the same stuff every month anyway. Only it took me years to work that out.'

'I'm not keeping other people's work, only my own. And my predecessors. When I went to London in seventy-six it was because of them. People had seen their pictures and they wanted more.'

'You came to us for a couple of days. Do you remember?'

'Of course I remember.'

'Do you remember the pigeons?'

He laughed.

'Oh, yes, I remember it well,' I sang in a mocking voice, attempting to imitate Maurice Chevalier, the French singer.

He unearthed a letter from the Commonwealth Institute asking about those old photographs: 'Adele and I could not believe it. We spread it out on the bedspread and read it aloud to make sure it was real. Look how the handwriting is small and scrawny. When I met the person I could not believe it. Big broad man. Big pass me.'

I took the letter and skim read:

Lewis Cole, who is one of our board members, gave me your name and suggested that I write to you about our forthcoming exhibition, 'Photos of One People', planned for spring 1977. As you may be aware we are very interested in the history of African arts and are trying to make contact with leading African photographers such as yourself who might be willing to contribute works to our exhibition.

The central aim of the exhibition will be to go beyond the ubiquitous photograph album to demonstrate the richness and variety of photography in a number of countries within the Commonwealth.

We are, unfortunately, handicapped by financial constraints in commissioning work, so we are only able to offer a small disbursement for your photographs, but you can be assured that full credits will be given in our catalogues and all other publicity.

We look forward to an early response.

Yours truly.

That spring I had changed school. Our house was as it always had been but nowadays there was a hysteria of jasmine shooting over the doorway. Those feisty sprays of yellow cut through all impressions of arthritic cold and beckoned passers-by to look up and see who was living there. We were no longer different to the point of legend; Asian families, from India, Pakistan and East Africa had moved into the area and multiculturalism was swaying in a hammock over all our heads.

I was making banana-and-walnut bread, the nearest recipe to African rice bread that I knew, when my mother told me that Uncle Moses had written to say he was coming. I would move out of my room and in with my sister for the duration, she told me. I did not mind. I anticipated him liking my teenage bedroom, the honey yellows of the walls, curtains and nylon bedcovers, the citrus boudoir to which I awoke each morning whether my adolescent mood matched its brightness or not. According to my mother, on most days it did not. She said I was 'difficult' and 'forgetting myself and trying to be like the English girls'. But I wasn't. I simply wanted some of the things that I knew they had.

Uncle Moses arrived in England at the end of January, but it was the middle of February before he came to stay with us. 'Yes, he will be here by eight o'clock,' my mother confirmed on the day after Valentine's. I rushed home from school, cleared my room and waited. At 7.30 he called from London to inform us he had been delayed and would be coming a day later. We did not take the news well. It was an evening of long silences in which we paced. After a dinner of leftovers – fish fried so deep the eyes turned stone white, topped with lukewarm gravy with onions and pepper – came the televisual feast, *Bouquet of Barbed Wire.* We liked the barbed wire best.

'I was so thrilled to see you. You said, "I can't believe she's doing O-levels already."'

After the adults had greeted one another, he pulled me to his chest, holding me so close I could hardly breathe. It was good to hear his voice again. It was deep, purely African and resonant, while my mother's was flatter and Anglicized, posher, though the African accent was still there. And I sounded as if I had come from nowhere in particular. There was a lot to talk about: Freetown and politics; they became heated over South Africa and cooled over family that evening. The talk was between Uncle Moses and my mother. I can't remember much of what was said. However, there was something about sitting together at the table, eating minced rice and cabbage, followed by Del Monte's tinned peaches with Carnation milk, that seemed to put them in nostalgic mood. They discussed someone from the past and how he drank too much at a party or some comical thing about his wife. Then they would jog each other's memory and discover more and more funny things about the person.

One particular exchange took place to which I gave more attention than the rest of their stories. Uncle Moses had pushed aside his dinner plate and said, 'I have some bad news to tell you. Pa Collins died two weeks ago.'

'Oh, no!' My mother put her hands to her face. 'That must have been a terrible blow to his wife and children.'

'Not just to them, but to us all, to us all,' said Moses. 'I think there are many who could have helped our country to develop but they just left it to the few to struggle on and do what they can. Perhaps they are too cowardly to face up to the responsibilities.'

'Cowardly . . . that's going too far. Anyway things don't improve just because a few people make a big show of themselves.'

'So who said anybody is making a big show? People have to have a chance to enjoy what they have put in.'

'Yes, what they have put in. Time and time again is people enjoying what they have not put in. So much Mercedes Benz! People just drinking and congratulating themselves, and for what? For what, eh?'

'You talk as if these men – good, solid people like Pa Collins – have led the country astray. But they haven't; they've shown what can be done. They've led the way. I for one will want to be there and show my respects. And you should too.'

'Me? No, I don't think so. I'm not saying I'm glad the man is dead. No, not that kind of wickedness. But what has he really done to improve things? Any little something and you want to clap the man on the back, like he's some saint. Are you so stupid you can't see the mistakes they're making?'

'Who are you calling stupid? Me, me?' He had stood up.
'You, you, you –' He could not finish his sentence and left it
hanging in the air, then blurted once more:

'You have any idea what life is for us now? You think you
can just sit up here in England and know better than every
damned stupid African man, don't you?'

Perhaps they found a better ending than this. It is quite
possible. At a distance of so many years, how can I truly
recall exactly what was said? Besides, I had had a long day at
school. Certainly Uncle Moses was too mild-mannered to get
this angry so easily. Now I think of it, I am sure they soon
moved on to talk of other things and everything was all right
again. When I went to bed that night I was quite happy, but
not as happy as I wished to be, given that Uncle Moses had
come to stay. The next day was better.

When I came home from school around 4.30, he was in the
living room watching the children's television programme
Blue Peter with the sound down. I sat beside him for this
after-school hour, changed the channel and turned up the
volume. Another programme was ending and then came the
Penguin biscuits advert:

When you feel a little p-peckish, pick up a, pick up a Penguin . . .

'Do you remember you started nodding like this then?'
and off we went, singing along to the chorus we remembered.

On that afternoon he had pulled me from my chair, feet
tapping, backs straight, bottoms out. We flapped round and
round the room, steered around the table and the abandoned
fruit: 'When you feel p-p-p-p-peckish, pick up a pick up a
penguin . . .'

My skinny arms flapping by my side, I had watched his
taller frame move ahead of me, mimicked every moment,
every twitch of his body, echoed everything I could make
my own. It was not so much a dance; it was a rite of passage,
a moment to cut through barriers and beat off the past with

our flippers. This was the way to slice through glaciers, to rediscover hope under the African sun. Holding no resentments, we were gliding past the internal strife that had robbed us of so many of our treasures. We ventured down to Neptune's bowers where the whitened bones of babies dead too soon floated on mossy green. The rhythm was never broken. Moses called his people and they came, unadorned, tripped into the waters where syllables of a-part-heid dispersed like froth on showers.

That night I imagined that we could do it again: land thrumming with pleasure at Freetown's shore, stand on the beach and look across the darkened city on which so much devastation had fallen during the last ten years. This place had once been a bunker for the Falkland boys, looking out on the African night and listening to water slapping against the jetties, big water rats scuttling home.

'Uncle Moses, let's call it a day,' I suggested.

'Good idea.'

'Tomorrow I'll help you sift through this stuff, and woe betide you if you hoard old magazine cuttings like me.'

'I'm not.'

'Sure?'

'Almost.'

He switched off the light and we ascended to our different rooms, different dreams. I lay awake until the sound of him pottering about in his bedroom ceased. Sitting up in bed I reached for my diary and made one short entry: 'He too remembered the penguins!'

It would have made sense to invite Anita and the girls to stay in that half-empty house with us and perhaps help to dispel the ghosts. I shivered at the thought of sleeping in that bed, in that room, which had once belonged to my cousin Agnes when she was a girl. That chair, those school books and that copy of *Kossoh Town Boy* must have belonged to her. At the end of the corridor was her parents' room. As a child would she have heard them? Would they have tried to be quiet? There, on that calm blue sea, he had loved her. There where the wooden floorboards bore witness: a few shudders of ecstasy, an impromptu dance as he hums the music of Marley's 'Kaya' into her ear, unclothing her breasts. His flesh between her teeth, biting him gently, teasing the spirals of black hair on his chest. His memory combing the curves of her body, retreating to the softness of her bottom. An aphrodisiac age. The smell of his wife: a black orchid.

I fell asleep.

'I want my mum,' a voice said. 'I want my mum!' it wailed. It was at this point that someone in my dream told me to sit bolt upright in the bed and look across the yard outside the house, where the dream was going to be finished. Down by the gate Eddy the monkey was addressing a teenage soldier who was pointing a gun at his hairy head.

'Put that down now!' shouted Eddy. 'Down, down!'

The soldier placed the gun on the ground but with a flash of speed pulled a sharp knife from his belt and brandished his newly unsheathed weapon in front of Eddy's face:

'I must cut off your hands!' repeated the soldier.

'What!' shrieked Eddy. 'You want me to give you one good slap?'

The soldier repeated: 'I must cut off your hands: no hand, no vote.'

'Stop there, you stop there! What makes you think I want to vote in your election, eh? You think I believe in your elections?' The soldier made ready to reply but Eddy was having none of it; stretching up on Aunt Adele's chair until he was as tall as a giraffe, he lunged at his assailant.

'Stop this nonsense now and go home!' he screeched, emitting an ear-splittingly intense sound that caused the soldier's once stern face to crumble. On the point of tears as he backed away, the soldier threw the useless blade to the ground and called out:

'I want my mum! I want my mum!'

'Well, go home then,' said Eddy, 'just go home.'

I woke up and realized that the sounds of the war had stormed my dreams. I was in Freetown, where monkeys do not dismiss soldiers, where fires destroy wood and the time is exactly 8 a.m. Whatever the purview of my dreams, whatever the wildness of my imaginings, a trickle of blood ran down my leg; my period arrived predictably on the twenty-eighth day.

'*Kong, kong, kong! Kong, kong, kong!*'

It was not the sound of someone knocking on my bedroom door but the voice of someone imitating a knocking sound.

'Come in.'

Elizabeth poked her head round. 'I'm going to market, you want me to buy you anything, Auntie?'

I pulled down the mosquito net and reached for my watch. It was 8.45. I flapped around for my bag. 'I thought I'd cook everyone a meal tonight. I could do my groundnut stew,' I said. 'See what you can get me.'

She thanked me for the contribution and closed the bedroom door, leaving me to rest. Little did I expect to see her still in the yard when I came down half an hour later.

'You see why marketing takes so long,' said Anita, pointing to her eldest child with her young man. 'They have been dating for a few weeks now.'

I could see that Elizabeth and her lover knew how to laugh: everything was amusing. He was haggling for more kisses and she was playing with him, moving her head about but also throwing him periodic negligée glances.

75

Anita clapped her hands: 'Go now, the market will be finished before you two reach.'

The young man picked up the empty basket and waved goodbye to Sara, who was on her bike. Elizabeth tucked the money into the top of her clothes and fixed her head-tie. She took out a lipstick and expertly readorned her full lips without the aid of a mirror.

Anita shook her head. She clapped her hands again: 'Now.'

The young man moved towards the road, Elizabeth followed him.

'Do you know what I miss most in life?' asked Anita, once they were gone.

'I don't know. What?'

'Starting little love affairs,' she said. We laughed.

'I know what you mean.'

'Elizabeth was "starting" with another young man when she found Citizen. I can't remember his name and anyway it is not important. His job is nursing. He was working at one of the centres in town, providing basic health care to the ex-child soldiers and others – reinforced milk, I think they called it, because some of them could not eat at all. Elizabeth went by one night when he was on late duty and thought she recognized Citizen among a group of boys who had been deposited there the previous day. She told her man that the boy's family had been searching for him and desperately wanted him back. He told her they should come in the morning and all arrangements would be made. She agreed.'

They passed the evening comfortably together, cooped up in a small room adjoining the hall.

La la

La la

Kiss

Their heads grew closer. A herd of small boys wandered into the office and saw them.

La la

La la

Kiss

They did not pay attention to the stragglers, who watched intently as they separated. It was a nice night, with a mild temperature. The young man shepherded the boys to bed. He did not see the extra one, lurking like a low mist. Goodnight till tomorrow.

La la

La la

Kiss

Elizabeth turned to take her leave. In the dark the fingers of a life-sized doll touched her bare arm.

La la

La la

Steal a kiss, child.

She did not hesitate in taking him home immediately. Bypassing the usual rehabilitation roadblocks, she accelerated through the lightless city streets, hope running through her veins with her neighbour's grandson in her arms. Peacekeeping troops, apprentices to such freewheeling devotion, watched her go. The impression was of light chiselling unholy ground. It was an hour's walk back. The boy was heavy in her arms but not a burden.

'Here it is,' Elizabeth told him as she turned down their road. She knew the number of paces to the front and in the gloom the weary pair breathed in the scent of 'bougainvillea in mauve passion'. She slipped into their yard, hands still shaking with excitement. It was a clear night with a moon. On the right were her sleeping sister and mother, beyond the fence Moses alone in his catacomb.

Elizabeth put Citizen on the bed and, still fully clothed, he slept. In the morning, a little after seven o'clock, she went to see Uncle Moses. He had slept fitfully the night before he said. He had had a premonition of the boy's return and was simply waiting for the clock to catch up. Elizabeth had gone alone, leaving the boy in their yard. She knew, as everyone knew, that many families resisted taking the child soldiers back. People talked about how devious and cruel they were. How they killed without thought, without pity for human life. People said child soldiers were the most destructive elements in the society and yet now they were getting everything, far beyond what the victims of war were getting. People said better throw these devils into a crypt where skeletons go to live. But Uncle Moses said:

'Let him come, let me see his face.'

When Moses set eyes on his grandson, he could barely conceal the quaking within.

Over the next few days Moses practised putting the clocks back to when the boy was just his grandson: the antebellum Citizen. Once he suggested 'hide and seek' and they tried, both of them equally. Moses hid first in his studio, throwing an old net curtain over his head, then by the door of his bedroom. Next, it was Citizen's turn. Citizen hid again in the studio. But on being found the child let out a scream so soultearing that it cut through the house and, they say, threw down the servants' quarters at the rear.

It was Elizabeth alone who responded to that scream. She ran over to Moses' house and moved through to the studio where they were. She lifted Citizen at the waist, pressing his small frame up close to Moses, so the old man could feel the boy's breath:

'Mister Moses, look into the child's face.'

'Mister Moses, you no see him mama?'

'Mister Moses, you no see him grandma?'

Moses looked at Citizen's features and recognized in him his daughter Agnes and his wife Adele. His grandson stood, not uttering a word. But, unconfined, the voices of his mother and his maternal grandmother echoed, distinctly calling their own son:

'*Na we, oh, na we!*'

So Elizabeth kept an eye as best she could, adjusting a little here and a little there until grandfather and grandson could live together most of the time unchaperoned. Moses tried to conceal his difficulties, but word slipped out. He invited people over for company and, to some degree, to help his grandson. One group of visitors approached using torchlight to guide them to the house. They were not to know that Citizen would dive for cover when he saw their beam flash over the window. No one was able to coax him from under the table. The boy looked at everyone and everything with suspicion; so almost everyone avoided looking at him. He had changed. Could he be Moses' grandson? Who would have thought an eight-year-old's eyes would bear such shadows?

Visitors continued to come. Mrs Richards, a headteacher and old school friend of Adele's, called round. She had been humbled into carrying a comfort blanket since a teenager had pointed a gun at her head, but she came nonetheless on hearing about Citizen. 'What do we do now? What do we do?'

She positioned her chair at a safe distance from Citizen and tried talking with him, but he stood dumb and staring. Others came and asked questions. Many left bewildered and distressed; Moses could not bear the look in their eyes, so he left the house to Citizen and took to his studio. With the house empty, the kitchen cold and his mattress unfamiliar, the boy wandered the bare boards, nibbled at food and ran away again. What Adele had left behind – the perfectly ironed sheets, the cleaned footwear, some faded skirts and blouses, all empty and unused –

indicated how separate the remaining family members were. Only dark space blowing between them like a barrier made their living together bearable. Torn by distance, communicating with signals and gestures as cold as serial numbers, they had passed the days until Uncle Moses called for me.

There were smiles now between Anita and me as we walked into the road, where she cut some flowers to put into a vase. She talked about what news had come from a girl-friend in Guinea who got out before '97, and then turned again to our families. She was a mother with two daughters doing what she could.

'Elizabeth had done four years of secondary school before she had to leave. We just couldn't find the money again. FSSG. Do you remember it? Her uniform is still in there.'

I did remember the school; other people I knew had gone there.

'It was mine too,' she said. 'A good school, we learned how to handle ourselves.'

'You must have been there when I first came here, you know, more than twenty years ago. How about that!'

'Yes, look how time flies.'

We were back in the kitchen and she stood on a bench to reach a vase into which she thrust the purple blooms: 'Looks lovely.'

'Is it too late now for Elizabeth to catch up with school?'

'I think so, don't you? Her mind has gone on to other things.'

'Yes, I see that.'

'But not for Sara,' she said. She peered into the vase, check-ing its possibilities. The breeze from the window carried the flowers' perfume into the room.

'I could try to help you and Sara. I would like to, you know.'

She looked at me as though something miraculous had come out of the vase. 'Don't worry,' she said, 'you have enough to be doing.'

It was long past breakfast time but I had not eaten anything all morning and was beginning to feel light-headed. I took a couple of crackers from a packet and, excusing myself, returned to my room to rest. My mind was on Anita's girls: Elizabeth with her 'mind on other things', who by now should be returning with the shopping; and nine-year-old Sara, who would be at home drawing up a new map of her world on those few sheets of paper.

And Citizen? No one's child now. 'I don't know,' Anita had told me when I asked about Citizen's parents. 'I don't know the details. The village was attacked on market day.' The entire village had been wiped out. Every couple, every farming family had been up early, preparing to sell their produce. I could see – watching her face as she told me – that she was actually visualizing their village being destroyed, like one traipsing through a landscape of catastrophe and slow death. I had tried to follow, to become more of an expert in grasping the invisible deaths, endings that left their imprint like DNA. I had watched her grab a tea towel and twist it into a knot, telling me in Krio to accept that Citizen didn't have parents any more. And her words drifted away as if the images of that village being torched were also receding.

Elizabeth came back that afternoon without the boyfriend and left her shopping in our kitchen. 'Tell me, was there plenty left?'

Her eyes were bright with pleasure. 'Plenty, plenty,' she said.

She was kind to me, taking on the adult things. The groceries were more than adequate – a chicken, big peppers, onions and a grain that looked like millet or couscous. 'Is your sister out there – will she come and help me?'

She shook her head. 'She's with a friend, not at home.'

81

Left alone, I sat down at the table and began to cut the chicken into large pieces, needing this flesh in order to ground me at home. I began the chicken groundnut stew, employing the recipe that my mother had shown me. I heated the oil in a large skillet and fried the seasoned chicken until it was crisp on all sides. I put them to one side before chopping the onions and peppers into small pieces and frying them. I loosened the knot on a bag of peanuts and poured them into a bowl, rubbed off the paper husks and left the white nuts ready. The splattering of oil from the pan was the only sound.

I had just begun pulverizing the nuts when Anita showed up, humming. 'You will have dinner with us, won't you?' I asked.

'What are you making?' She sat at the table, pretending to hold a knife and fork at the ready.

'Chicken groundnut.'

'Like that?'

'Of course like that. That's how my mother made it. And that's how Auntie Sally showed her how to make it.'

'We don't bother with all that pounding any more,' she said, 'it's so old-fashion.' She stood up and walked over to the cupboard, a cupboard that I had barely noticed before. From it she took a jar which was put down in front of me: peanut butter. 'That's what we do now.'

I continued, adapting my recipe by adding the peanut butter. The sauce bubbled up like dark mud, splattering pellets of peanut all around. Dinner was a success: the children ate hearty portions, laughter surrounded me. The adults thanked me for the trouble and there was an avuncular embrace because the groundnut stew was 'just as big Auntie Sally always made it'.

Love and peace. The love is in the taste of the food. The peace I took to bed. I undressed and laid my body on the white sheet. *Here I am again, black on white, ready to dream tonight. I will love the whole of my body and gently the waves will break and blackness will surround my eyes and music will fill my ears and I'll be jammin until dawn . . .*

Jammin . . .
Jammin . . .

Five

Sweet, wonderful sleep. It was a relief to abandon the orderliness of a Freetown day for a night without rationality elsewhere. Asleep and at the mercy of the heavy reggae incessantly playing in my head, I drifted into a landscape of black, browns and lush greens, dense foliage that looked as though it had been frequently soaked by rains. It was a long journey. The sounds were a mélange of African rhythms; above the syncopated roar of a fast-moving river crashing over rocks was the small rustle of leaves being trodden underfoot, in the distance a drumbeat, birds singing 'ka, ka, ka' from high up branches. These were rainforest sounds. Stately trees framed the rough track for miles into the heart of the forest and a pungent odour of burning wood suffused the night air. Which way to go next? I stumbled on a winding dirt track, believing it was the route to take me even deeper, towards where the child soldiers would be. Above my head a wild beast swung like a talented trapeze artist and, flying ever higher, scoffed at my confusion. Undaunted, I kept going, thinking it best to remove my sandals and proceed barefoot, in the style of one who squints on others in the night. Not for long did I have to bank on the soles of my feet to guide me. A simple road sign proclaiming PANDEBU, LAST VILLAGE showed me the way, intrepid explorer that I was.

The sun was high in the sky as I reached Pandebu. The first and surprising sign of human habitation was a lean-to mud outbuilding with a large oven; it turned out this was the village bakery where a Fula migrant supplied his rural clientele's sophisticated taste for fresh baguette. There was a strong aroma of newly baked bread, though the baker was not there. In his place was the girl who had been 'wife' to Lieutenant Ibrahim. This time she was without her baby but carried a bundle of firewood under her arm as though about to stoke the oven. She eyed me, seeming to compare me unfavourably to herself. I put on my sandals and followed her in that widening morning light to a clearing but the moment we arrived, she disappeared.

Barring my way was an old man in a half-crouched position who looked as thin as a Kenyan long-distance runner and was wearing a *coboslot* of pure white around his hips.

'Who are you?' he asked.

'I'm a visitor. Are you from around here?' I replied.

'I'm from here. Part of the senior Gola community, you know – rice, kola. Some members are interested in ivory, gold; others in land management. The women plant groundnuts.' He threw some groundnuts into the air and caught them in his mouth as they rained upon him. Then he smiled, showing off white teeth.

'And you? You here to see someone?'

'Yes, I was looking for some child soldiers.'

'Who?'

'Child soldiers, a group of about fifteen.'

'Who are they? Are they slaves?'

'Oh, no . . . sort of – yes, yes and no.'

'They've gone. All gone.'

'Who?'

'The slaves. All gone now. Listen.' He raised his arm into the cool moist air and splayed his fingers: the movement released the sound of men's feet trudging, diffuse voices and sibilant sea spray. The forest threw in a faint smell of salt, freshly spilled blood, coarse sweat. This stale odour from the past filled my nostrils and caused me to retch.

'No, they're not slaves in that sense; they are mainly soldiers, small ones . . .' I indicated the height by putting my palm on an imaginary head at about Citizen's height.

'Child soldiers! Those small boys who've been burning and ruining the villages, killing people and all?'

'Yes, those small boys.'

'I want to see them too,' he said. 'I've wanted to put an end to their terrible ways for a long time.'

The inky eyes softened. 'I will have to prepare a special call for them. Wait for me just there.' He indicated a large silk-cotton tree with sprawling thick roots about twenty yards away. Then, for no apparent reason, he tugged a chunk of wild bark from a nearby tree and disappeared into the thick of the forest. Privacy and concentration must be required for this exercise. The very words of this Mende cuckoo were beyond my comprehension. In his self-styled creolization, I caught an occasional English word surfing in the wind:

'. . . child . . . skipping-rope . . . chair . . . shoe size . . . paint . . . fingers . . . riddle . . .'

I imagined forest creatures emerging, nervously curious, to witness who might come forward. He reappeared at my side and led me back to the clearing where the girl had casually deposited me some moments before. She was standing patting her baby on the back. Her breasts were still exposed. Before they had seemed full and heavy but now brown paper cups, flapping. I was puzzled by her undersized body, her vacant eyes.

What kind of young girl are you, that you bring me to this faery clearing, dump me before this showy soothsayer, then disappear? I thought, but did not utter a word.

The old man shrugged. She was not who he was expecting clearly. He detached himself from our company and her gaze and went to sit about fifty yards away on a smooth and long black rock that looked like a bench carved of granite, roomy enough for four or five people.

I was conscious of the young woman staring at me so I broke the silence:

'What's your name?'

'Miriam.'

'And the baby's name?'

'She doesn't have a name yet. Just Baby.'

'Hello, Miriam and Baby.'

I stretched out my hand. Baby put her tiny hand in mine, belched and winked at me, indicating that she at least was feeling better. A murmur of children's voices suggested the others were on their way – the old man had succeeded. I joined him on the black rock where he sat swinging his legs.

'Thank you for calling them, Mr . . .?'

'Bemba, call me Bemba G.'

'*Tenki, tenki*, Bemba G,' I replied, inserting my small Krio vocabulary into the conversation.

Half a dozen child soldiers walked sluggishly into the clearing, looking up as they spotted us. In the lead was a youth of about sixteen with a black scarf round his head; he was smoking a cigarette and carried a black-and-silver ghetto blaster. Some of the boys had AK47s strapped to their sides, blankets slung over their shoulders or makeshift weapons constructed entirely from discarded bits of wood and metal. One member of the group was a girl aged about six who, drawn by the aura of our host, came to sit at his feet, leaning her back against his legs. She was as black as syrup and, though her clothes were filthy and torn around the neckline, she maintained a bearing of gaunt assurance.

'Come in, everyone, come in and sit down by halfway silk-cotton tree,' said Bemba G. Obediently they came and sat. After the first few, a group of four boys including Citizen and

Abu turned up. None of them paid much attention to me, though Citizen gave a slight nod of recognition in my direction. I could remember nothing between leaving Uncle Moses' house and arriving in the Gola Forest with Bemba G, as if I had been miraculously translated into the war zone with no effort on my part. Citizen must have decided to abandon his grandfather's house too, leaving his playmate and the beloved crayons.

'Is you who called us?' asked one boy.

'I asked this old man, Bemba G, to call you here,' I owned up.

'That's good,' said the young man. 'My name is Peter. I've been fighting now two or three times a week for three years and I am tired of the war.'

'Do you know what you are fighting for?' I asked Peter. About to reply, he was cut short.

'Listen, boys, I have to tell you this is not the way to carry on,' said Bemba G. 'You don't do anything worthwhile, no, no. Show me, what do you know?' Peter opened his weapon, took out the bullets and refilled the barrel. He lifted the gun to his shoulder, twisted it around his head three or four times and pointed it at the old man's head by way of introduction.

There was no talk: he did not say he would kill old Bemba G, but his actions were enough to suggest this. Peter moved adeptly like a cowboy shooting his way out of a saloon, and his stony expression, the cool glint in his black eyes suggested he was as tough. He stared straight ahead, his eyes enlarged, ready to take on another opponent.

'Stop that now,' called out one of his mates, who sauntered over and offered Peter a cigarette. Bemba G did not stir; his hands did not tremble, nor did his lips move. Peter put down the gun and lit up. As he smoked he rolled another spliff in a tobacco leaf, ready for later, and put it in his trouser pocket. He was in khaki, nothing boyish but a soldier wearing soldiering clothes, close as pelt. On the ground, next to Peter's gun, the other boy dropped his possessions, which were wrapped loosely in a grey rag. Introducing himself as Hinga, he sprang forward to shake hands. He had large brown eyes and long lashes. He opened the bundle – everything he owned was there: a brown bottle of pills, a wooden box, a pair of worn-out trainers and a black T-shirt. Not much for a young boy. I thought Bemba G might recoil from his guests but he did not. His eyes glimmered with curiosity and he asked:

'How old are you, Hinga?'

'Twelve years old, sir.'

Hinga bent down and opened his wooden box. It was empty. He shrugged. To my eyes, he looked too small for a twelve-year-old – I would have guessed eight – though his manner suggested a young adult.

'Let me ask you something, Mr Twelve-year-old,' said Bemba G. 'What is five and seven?'

'Twelve,' everyone shouted, including Hinga and Peter.

'What is twelve times twelve?' persisted Bemba G.

'One hundred and forty-four,' a few voices shouted back.

'What's the square root of twelve?'

The clearing was silent and filled with airy breezes. From the middle rows came muttering, something to the effect of 'not fair' and 'we never heard about square root'. Then silence again while all eyes turned to see what more Bemba G had to say about number twelve.

'You see,' Bemba G was saying, 'you need an education.' He went up to the towering silk-cotton tree and pulled from the centre of it a board on which were scribbled numbers, equations and signs. His fingers approached the board and extracted the square root sign: it glistened before our eyes; everyone gasped. It was hard to tell whether they were gasping because of the board that lived in a tree or at the glittering square root sign, but still they gasped.

'The square root of one hundred and forty-four is twelve.'
Everyone nodded.

Hinga licked his lips. 'That's something new,' he said honestly. 'That's something I never heard before.' For a few minutes he relished this novel dimension of his age. Meanwhile, the boy with the ghetto blaster, who had been nursing his machine in his arms, let it hit the ground like a dead weight as he repeated to himself: 'The square root of one hundred and forty-four is twelve.'

This old man was clearly an expert in mind control or teaching. He gave each child soldier something mathematical to do and before long they were immersed in their own projects. Miriam, carrying Baby on her back and holding the little girl's hand, was measuring spaces. Peter and Hinga, set to calculating further square roots, wrote on the board, producing strong dashes and curves to represent the newly introduced symbols. Bemba G was with Abu and Citizen, explaining about probabilities in agriculture. The compound heaved with activity and the energizing effect of so much adventure. Bemba G had even dragooned two of the older recruits into tackling more complicated mathematical calculations of forest clearance. Then, on leaving this lanky pair, the small dark girl appeared as if from nowhere to announce that the number of paces between the black rock and the silk-cotton tree was fifty-two and one half.

As the late afternoon gave way to evening, devouring the light, I witnessed the children's reawakened interest in a delightfully modest world of sums. They provided more data than expected: there were fifteen logs in the corner, six calabashes, two brooms; pee can fly more than six feet. Rubbing his hands over his bald head, Bemba G called the group back together.

'It is important to know about numbers,' he said, 'the numbers that shape your life.'

He then told a story that showed his interest in numbers was not impersonal. One day, when he was nine, during a family massage session he had overheard his mother talking to other female relatives about land changes. Amid the cries of 'Mmm, that feels good,' and 'Rub my back,' young Bemba G had learned that the forest was to be divided in a straight line thirteen degrees west of Paris. The two officials – one French, one English – in charge of the division were strangers to the family and their neighbours. Bemba G's father, a powerful hunter and storyteller, had trained his son well: at the eve of his teenage years and newly versed in how the forest was run, he had resolved not to lose the advantage. Bemba G had sat beneath the gigantic silk-cotton tree and, unaware of the dangerous fabrications called 'geography', arrived at a scientific plan:

Method:
Find the straight line 13 degrees west of Paris.
Check to see if my home and silk-cotton tree is in the middle or not.
Make plans accordingly.

Result: (after much searching)
Failed to discover the straight line.

Conclusion: (after much reflection)
Decided to live at a slight angle from this universe i.e. hunting, storytelling and netting other orbs.
Decided to rename silk-cotton tree 'halfway silk-cotton tree'.

'That is what I did,' he nodded and scribbled this version of his story on the board for all to see how the scientific experiment was carried out. The child soldiers tracked every movement.

'Go now,' he ended. 'Go one by one so I can see each of you. Let me watch you file out.'

I tried to thank him for his time but he waved his hand. 'Come again soon. Visit me again soon. Come any time. I'm tired now. I need to rest. I haven't done so much talking in . . .'

He drifted off before finishing his sentence and we were left regarding the top of his bald head. I turned to go. Then Abu asked, 'How much rest is he going to need?'

'Old men need two days to rest,' offered Peter, 'that's what my grandfather told me.'

'In that time,' continued Abu, 'we could bring some stories of our own. That way, when he's finished his, it will be our turn.'

'OK, everybody: two days to find some stories of your own and we meet back here.'

'Back here again?' asked Abu, pointing dramatically to the ground.

'Yes, in two days.'

Mathematics roots you to the ground; mathematics, the place where magic is infinitesimal and mayhem self-induced. I watched the child soldiers disappear and the old man's head droop tiredly, his cleverness folding away its bright wings. Miriam, the girl soldier who had beckoned me, was clearly delighted with the way things had turned out: she bounced Baby on her lap and thanked me. It had been a good afternoon sitting with the child soldiers and finding out how mathematics had come to the rainforest. Until the light began to change in the forest, until the canopy grew in and lizards returned to their rocks for rest, the child soldiers had watched as figures, signs and symbols were proffered to their incredulous eyes.

Six

In all these journeys there were certain similarities. Energy. Night. Solitude. The split from Uncle Moses' Freetown house to the Gola forest, which no one in their right minds would step into alone at night. The war was over and they said the region was still not safe, but I had to look – to press my Afro-Brit nose into Gola Forest business and discover whether other multidimensional events might occur there. What does a London-Freetown-Gola Forest adventure look like?

Perhaps something of the war spirit had entered me, a belligerent vitality I did not own in London, which impelled me to ask a hundred questions, seek out children who knew about death and fingered guns like bonbons, children such as my young cousin Citizen. Like all forests, the Gola has an intoxicating magical order: scrupulously structured and tinged with babble, unreliable clocks and tracks. Mooching along here Gola-style requires little planning and is wholly instructive. In quite a different way, life with Uncle Moses was also teaching me things.

In the morning Moses was supposed to make an early start filing away materials and fixing up the studio, but he was still lying in bed at nine o'clock. Much later when we met in the studio he laid out papers and documents in neat piles on the desk, on the floor and on a small table. He worked slowly and thoughtfully, compiling a list of things he wanted to keep and occasionally passing me an item to look over. The first interesting one was a photo album that he propped in front of me, like an invitation into his private life.

'This is what this studio looked like when we first moved in. Can you imagine?'

It was hard to. I was interested in seeing what the house had looked like before his time, for in my mind his life had been unchanging and secure. What I loved most about that house was the sense of permanence: Moses had lived here for thirty years and had never thrown anything away. In England we had frowned upon the idea of keeping still; we moved twice in five years, once into draughty rented rooms and then again to a small private house. Our possessions went in and out of newspaper wrapping, like fish and chips, and accidents happened with my radio-record player and my mother's porcelain.

But here there was such stability: the bone china and upright piano dated back to his parents' time; the record player was, like me, pushing forty; even the crayon drawings we had made back in the 1970s were still upstairs.

In the album there were pictures of the studio, some of Uncle Moses at work, but none quite captured the sense of pride he felt in his achievements.

'Everybody wanted to have their picture taken. School children came from FSSG and Grammar School, choirs, even one brass band, the Mothers' Union from Rodean Street Methodist Church, group sittings where everybody put in one or two leone. One sitting, many prints – everyone was happy. Maria came to help me on Saturdays.'

He pointed to a slim teenager in grey pinafore and slingbacks, posing for a single shot. 'She was a good girl.' Pretty too.

'I told Adele. I said, "Adele, this is what I want to do. Help the ordinary people to see themselves the way they want to."' He took a sip from his cup of water. 'And she would say, "Well, just do it then, Moses." Then I said, "Well, if it doesn't work, what will we do?"

'And she said, "We'll manage."' He cast a quick look for approval and acknowledgement in my direction. 'So I did it, and we managed. We always managed ourselves.'

'It's a family trait,' I said, 'we always manage ourselves. Somehow.' I was thinking of Citizen battling away.

'Even manage to get some love?'

'Oh, yes, somehow or other. You know how it is.' Was I ready to share with him my tales of coupling? I hesitated too long and he let me off the hook.

'I remember one girl, one English girl, telling me to get a move on,' Moses said. 'I felt so stupid fumbling about with rubbers.'

I tried to read the look that played around his eyes and mouth; we were both recalling naked pleasures, intimacies we had never ventured to talk about.

'For a long time it was touch and go for us. Adele and me.'

'How so?'

'We didn't know if we could have a child. Adele gave up on me. Not three years after we married. So much fuss about those English girls. She found some pictures. There.' He indicated a small drawer.

'I told her. It was before. B-E-F-O-R-E.' He spelt it out for me as he had done for her.

'That must have been hard.'

'You don't know our women, Julia. They can be so . . .'

'Well, it's difficult.'

He seemed torn between the love of his life and the memory of what he called 'those salad days'. 'I always said to Adele, "It's salad days." Salad days love.'

'But she forgave you?'

'Eventually. Yes.'

'And you had Agnes?'

'Eventually. Yes.'

'And then a grandson too.'

The sun was high in the sky, the day too warm for serious work. We took refuge in the yard and sucked on huge yellow mangoes, the string hanging from our teeth with delicious abandon.

'Our women,' he began, 'like rules, discipline.'

'Too much discipline, you mean?'

'Yes, too much. All too strict. Take Aunt Sally.'

I remembered hearing about her. She had terrified everyone. She was long dead now but it was odd how a memory almost thirty years old could be so vivid. She would sit on a cushioned straight-back chair on the veranda at her colonial-style house in Murray Town, cleaning her big teeth with a knobby chaw stick and spitting out the wooden bits. Aunt Sally alarmed the house girls who worked for her with her Bible talk, her frowning and legendary economy. She had put in years with the civil service and they were to be up at dawn, obeying her orders:

'Come and cut the onions and peppers, small small!'

'Trim the okra, properly!'

'Make the akara beans fine!'

Even my own rather strict mother could do a modest imitation of Big Aunt Sally.

'So what is it?' I asked Uncle Moses. 'Why are we, they, so strict?'

I was down to the mango seed, holding half of it in my mouth at one go.

'God alone knows. Maybe it *is* God. Our religion.'

'Christianity?'

'Yes, and our history. Were we ever really free?'

'I think so. Don't you?'

'Free to be ourselves? No.'

'And here we are in Freetown,' I mumbled.

The sun was dipping, withdrawing its graces from the sky, and reminding us that there was work to be done back in the studio. Uncle Moses peeked at me to check if I was ready.

'This is what you people must do, not be held back by as many rules as we were. Be free!'

I understood what he meant, yet what had we achieved with our freedom? War. He was reading my thoughts.

'It has been a terrible time,' he said, 'a terrible time.'

The rest of the afternoon was peacefully spent looking over the photographs. There was Aunt Sally. We laughed together. 'She knew how to give you bad eye.' There was Uncle Moses, sitting on her veranda in a wicker chair, legs splayed out, feasting on the akara that some small girl had prepared. He showed me pictures of the centuries-old Freetown, buildings that had now lost their glamour: FSSG, Central Law Courts; busy street scenes with cars bumper to bumper, office workers in crisp white shirtsleeves, African women in gowns. I could imagine the hooting and shouts of people desperate to get away from hot tarmac at the end of the working day.

Then Uncle Moses arrived at the family photos. There were pictures of them as a young couple: in one of these he was wearing nothing but white shorts. He had his arm around Adele's waist and was nibbling her ear.

'After the reconciliation?' I asked.

'Yes, peacetime. Oh my Adele,' he said, 'my one and only Adele.'

He told me how that very evening she had cooked some snapper fish stew the way he liked it but not the way she preferred to cook it and he had offered all the reassurances he could. He told her again about the day they had met and reminisced about how the English autumn sun striped the lawn at his lodgings. When, later that night she had decided to take a warm bath, he had filled the tub for her, scattering in blue salts before she climbed in. He had watched from the bathroom door as she had unpicked her plaited hair, a small tug and the cornrow gave in to her hand. One row at a time, she had ploughed up and down until an unfurled field patterned her scalp. She had placed some oil in the palm of her hand and massaged it in. Deep into the roots, she had kneaded and rubbed. Her hair had bounced back in response. Then, removing her robe, she had sank into the blue water, her head protruding above. He had remained by the bathroom door, mesmerized.

I turned again to the family album and saw pictures of Citizen as a baby and at every stage of his young life. A wave of sorrow came over me. I saw the small rounded nose of his baby face; him lying on his back, on a white coverlet of antique lace, his eyes closed tight; being carried in Agnes's arms, a baby with a strong back and softly curved shoulders that glistened with oil. These images of Agnes with her boy shook me to the core.

Uncle Moses guided my viewing: 'On Sundays, his mother pressed his shirt for school and folded his socks into pairs – the ones for sport and playing outside and the ones for best. She grew lemons, made lemonade from scratch and bottled it, to sell. There she is rolling them to soften, and rinsing, squeezing out the juices, putting in sugar, water and herbs. She'd call to Citizen: "Come and taste." He left his truck and appeared at her side. He tasted, pulled a face, so they added more sugar and more again until it was sweet enough. It was one of their rituals.'

Uncle Moses remembered Agnes telling him that this was the ritual Citizen loved best. He called it 'cooking lemonade'. Agnes was not born a country girl, but she had soaked up all the knowledge she could about farming. By leasing land, life in the country might be hard but it was affordable and she had made extra money by selling produce to the Guinea markets. There she could also pick up unusual lappa outfits not available in Sierra Leone. In one photograph, Citizen, dressed in an African suit in burnt sienna, stood between his parents, looking up to his father, Kole. His features, in every way down to the tiniest detail, were the image of his father. It was little wonder that, looking at the two men in her life, Agnes had a broad smile on her face.

'That was his first day at school.'

'That's when they first had the farm. It was rainy season. Adele went up there as often as she could to help out.' It looked like a smallholding rather than a farm as such. Attractive, though: anyone would fall in love with the place.

'They look alike, don't they? Everyone said she resembled her mother.' I paused over the print of Agnes with Auntie Adele, both in green-patterned dresses, doing a mother–daughter pose.

'It was a good Christmas, that one. We made it to Lumley beach eventually.' Three generations, two hampers, one family outing.

'You did have a lot of food, just for the five of you.'

'There were plates, cutlery, bottles of ginger beer and clothes in one. In truth, that was modest; some families took generators.'

Creole people like big celebrations, the public consumption of huge quantities of food. Agnes and Adele were like the rest.

As Uncle Moses and I reminisced, our words sounded cool but our memories were crackling with fire.

'Half the people there probably had even more.'

'Joloff? Christmas cake, rice bread, other breads, potato leaf, ginger beer!'

'More!'

'Perfect.' I closed the album.

Elizabeth came in with a cup of tea.

'Mister Moses, no need to worry, but I found the place

where Citizen was sleeping outside. Over there!' She pointed vaguely towards the road.

'Found the place?'

'There was a cardboard box of his small things. Some rags, a knife, a small towel. Nothing much.'

'Have you thrown them all out?'

'The box, yes, Julia, and the dirty things. The towel I wash and put away.'

'Thanks.'

'Why did she tell me that?' he asked behind her back.

'Maybe keeping the record straight, I guess. So we know.'

He avoided my gaze, returned the family album to the shelf and continued: 'I knew a child would come and disrupt my life. I did not know how.'

'That's a strange thing to say.'

'I'll tell you later. It is not his fault. I'll tell you later.'

We agreed to call it a day. Tidying piles of personal papers, letters, cards, bills, the detritus of life is tedious at the best of times. I offered encouragement: 'We are doing OK.'

He casually reread a letter and went to turn off the light.

'You have changed. When you were a girl I always saw you as such a dreamer, not at all practical or thinking about the future.'

'I did think about it. Well, I worried about it. But now it's different.'

'How is it different?'

'Because, with the war and everything, the future's so close.'

Did he understand what I was saying? That we had to do better now as uncle and niece and there was no more time to waste on empty kernels, the scant communication of these last twenty years, with their resentments. Life was too short, so much death had taught us that.

Back in my bedroom I reflected wistfully on his criticisms of women: was he now a liberal? The last time I had looked to him for support, when I had longed for him to open wide his arms and affirm me, I had been badly let down. A reluctance to rupture our new-found harmony had stopped me from reminding him. After years with scarcely a word exchanged, I would not damage what we had now. *But it was death that had made him call you back*, I said to myself, *death and loss and loneliness.*

Unlike dear Elizabeth next door, I wasn't home with Mother at twenty and yet I could not roam. Unlike young Elizabeth, I had finished school with good results but I did not feel ready for the unpredictable territory of adult life. One October evening, back at my mother's house in the wall-to-wall carpeted living room, with display cabinets in attendance, we entered the ring for the inevitable showdown. In the left corner, Mother, hot on fault-finding with sharp tongue; in the right corner, Miss Jobless, impeccable tap dancer with wooden shield and visor.

'Mummy, I've been thinking. I might go abroad at the end of this year.'

'Oh.'

'Yes, a friend of mine – Jenny – suggested Paris and we could share a flat.'

'Who exactly is this Jenny? What kind of people are they?'

'Well, you don't know her really, but she's very nice and her mother's a teacher too.'

'And what sort of work will you do?'

My heart sank; I realized I had no idea. I blurted: 'There's a chance of a job with her father.'

'So both her parents are in Paris then?'

'Not exactly. Her father's there, her mother's still in Scotland.'

She paused, sniffing the divorce. Gathering speed and confidence, she charged: 'Don't you mean you'll be sharing with her father?'

'No, not really . . . well, maybe at first till we find a place of our own.'

'I'm not sure I like the idea of you going off all over Europe sleeping in the house of some man we don't know. We're not that kind of people. I've told you a thousand times, I didn't come to this country to join in their nonsense! What kind of work does this man do?'

'He owns an agency involved in . . . design.'

'Don't they have agencies involved in design right here? Why do you have to go so far away from *me*? You are so keen on these English ways and this wild life.'

'You know that's not it at all.'

'Well, what is it then? What is it?'

'It's just that I need to move on. I can't stay here.'

'You two use this place as a hotel. Your uncle has always said this is a good family home, not just a place to drop in from time to time. If you go to Paris, when will you come home?'

'Honestly, I don't know. I might come back in three months, say, or even less. I just need to go for a while and see.'

'A while?' The clock ticked. 'When I think how I kept close to my mother . . .'

'Don't say that, I *am* close to you. You could always come and visit. You'd be very welcome.'

'Have you told this Jenny's father that you're coming?'

'Oh, no, I said I had to talk it over with my family first.'

'Well, tell him your family needs you here.'

We sailed for France. The white gulls hovering above the cliffs of Dover, littered with carrion feathers, looked ennobled that morning. Our pockets were light with a couple of 100-franc notes each. I did not know how we would live, but as we stood on deck munching our Rich Tea biscuits, bought half-price in Tesco, we were happy.

We stayed with Jenny's father in his Port St Cloud apartment, where he lived with his lover, Carole, a Parisian of about thirty, who spent evenings draped on the lime-green chaise, her eyes covered with cucumber slices. We looked for jobs but schoolgirl French and giggles hampered our prospects. Jenny's father offered us hours doing errands at the agency where he worked. I wrote to Uncle Moses that I had a job in the design business and that, like him, I wanted to make my way in the creative world. With more caution gnawing my ballpoint for an afternoon, I wrote to my mother about the job, the apartment, life; and waited. Jenny and I talked over our wishes and dreams, sharing plans while skirting the subject of returning home, which panicked us both.

Finally, one morning, as I was leaving for work, a postcard arrived from Uncle Moses:

My dear Julia,

I am glad to know you are enjoying this new line of work. Thank you for asking after everybody in the family. We are all well. Nevertheless the recovery from the attack of malaria fever has had a telling effect on my system, but I am thankful to God that it never laid me low for long.

I continued at the agency until the winter set in. At last the sky let go of the snow and one morning Paris was dusted white. Christmas came. Only when Jenny and I went into other people's homes, saw their cards or windows decked in lights did the season really register. By then we were sharing a studio apartment with a sloping ceiling, up four flights of narrow stairs on the Left Bank, but it was home and the place from which we sent appropriate greetings to our parents. Mid-January a tissue-thin air letter floated across the Atlantic:

My dear Julia,

A happy New Year to you and may it be full of happy pleasant surprises. (I flatter myself to wish that this may be one.) I have had it in mind to write you for some time. I hope it was not like a stepping stone, like the way to that place – always full of good intentions!

I told your mother I was going to write and broach a subject that has been on my mind for some time. Straight to it: have you thought about coming home and teaching here? You could get a post at FSSG or, if that does not suit, one of the smaller schools.

I confess ignorance of the scale of salaries but above all that you will have the satisfaction of contributing to the development of your home.

If you do not like the idea of teaching you could do something else. Do you know that your cousin is now working for the Civil Service? You may even think of Unesco, etc. Reflect on the possibilities.

Think how your ancestors would feel in their resting place . . .

All said and done, think what it would mean for your mother? It is not my wish to convince you in one letter but please think of it and weigh everything carefully.

. . . Please reply, even if it is No. No chance.

Take care and God bless.

A sharp slap from across the ocean. I felt so disappointed, I could not imagine feeling any other emotion again. Why could he not understand me and support me? Why did he not see that I was trying to find my way here? I gripped my Paris dream hard. I kept the thin blue letter at the bottom of my underwear drawer, the place for secret things, the safest hiding place.

*

At eight o'clock I rose to the sound of Elizabeth singing in the yard next door. It was a song that was popular here some years back; every bar and every radio programme had it. Sara knew it too and joined in, singing it to Citizen. She could give him this, a morning song for a little boy.

'Another late night?' asked Anita, as Elizabeth did nothing to conceal her merriment from the night before.

'We were just walking down on the beach and talking till late,' she threw us in answer to our questioning glances. Anita wanted some more information about this recent young man and continued to inquire about his family. I did not wait to learn how Elizabeth's romance was taking shape, but left with my teacup for Uncle's studio.

The moment I entered he began to talk as though only drawing breath between phrases.

'You said the archive. Let's get straight to it.'

I offered to take notes and do any odd jobs required while he organized materials.

'Good, thank you. I've been thinking,' Uncle Moses said, 'that Alphonso Lisk-Carew deserves more of my attention. J. P. Decker was always my man because I liked his approach and his family gave me that camera.'

There were several cameras around the room but I realized he meant one of those heavy metallic items with two bulky lenses that had to be screwed on and off and had different scales for calculating focus.

'Now, Lisk-Carew had his studio down Westmoreland Street.' Uncle Moses pushed some more prints in front of me. None of these were from a studio but showed Mende people up-country, miles away. 'Made his name by taking pictures of all the top men in the colonial administration and the Duke and Duchess of Cornwall.' I could visualize this nineteenth-century African in their arboured grounds, making small talk, giving thanks for their patronage, witty, erudite, conscious. The work on display told another story, photographs of village women pounding yam with long poles, thick as birches, an African family of five fishing with a wide big circular net, their feet deep in the river, behind which a railway bridge looms.

'Look at this one. Why did we never go up country on the train?' A look of intense puzzlement flashed across his face.

'Because there's no railway there now. That was the nineteen-tens.'

When Alphonso was alive he was able to make a train trip up country to record everyday life and no doubt he thought nothing of it. I imagined him sitting bolt upright in the sunny train carriage gazing out at the scenery as the train pulled away from Freetown, with its bustling stores and pavements, to the outlying factories, timber-yards, and finally to the open fields up-country. People must have been pleased to welcome him and surprised that such a distinguished-looking and well-educated gentleman was coming to visit them.

Uncle Moses was pouting and showing me a map. 'That's where some of the worst of the fighting was.' His long finger wandered over Pandebu and other villages in the northern province.

'I'd like to know who was taking pictures then. Would you know?'

'Certainly. There were rumours about a young chap filming in Super-eight and sending stuff abroad.' He said this with a deliberate display of confidence.

I nodded, raising my brows in an attempt encourage him. 'People were lined up against a wall with bags over their heads. Men and women. There –' he was pointing again '– and there.'

Alphonso would never have dreamt such things might happen in this place. What had we allowed to happen there up-country, where life was supposed to be sweet? Dancing. Singing. Cutting the bush. Planting. All that fighting, war and mutilation.

From where he was standing Uncle Moses could not see my face, but he tapped the table for a return to work: 'Alphonso Lisk-Carew died in sixty-nine, two years after we came back.' I added the date to the card. Then he left me, saying, 'Add: "Most famous for –" er . . . just put there: "Patronized by the Duke and Duchess of Connaught".'

Alphonso, a pioneer photographer whose portraits, land-scapes and cityscapes were respected across the West African region, though not technically inventive, was one of Uncle Moses' favourites. While I completed his notes, Uncle Moses took the unusual step of standing close by my side and put-ting his arms around my shoulders.

'Good. Put that he worked with his brother Arthur. Put it under family connections. That'll do on Alphonso for now. We can always come back to him. Let's get to my man J. P. Decker. He's the one whose camera changed my for-tunes.'

Anita came across from her home in the darkness and into Uncle Moses' studio. He had gone upstairs to change his clothes, having splashed some tomato sauce on his white shirt at dinner. (Tonight Sara and Citizen, dressed in match-ing shorts, had assisted Elizabeth in making the meal; it was a case of too many cooks. Citizen had cut up the vegetables, onions and peppers in ungainly chunks; Sara had made the salad, which was fine, and the sauce, which was too salty. Both youngsters had been thanked for their endeavours and both were now in bed.)

Anita was holding a can of 7-Up. She tugged open the ring before settling on a stool beside me. 'A good day?'

'We've been through these archives and some family

photos. There's so much here, but I've sorted some and labelled most.'

'It's looking good. Much better.'

'Do you think so?'

She looked more closely at the pile of photographs, ordered and labelled on the table, then she went on: 'Yes, but this is only a part of it.'

'There are many more?'

'No, not photos. You need balance.'

'What are you saying?'

'You need to look forward, say what will come next – not always back.' She jumped off the stool and stood up, leaning her head back against the wall and taking a further slug. 'And it is not always this or that. It could be both.'

'Oh, really.' She was not helping.

'I think you should let him know if you've decided anything.'

'I'd like to talk to him some more and spend more time. Time together, you know – Moses, Citizen and me . . . well, all of us really. Do you understand?'

'Yes, up to a point. But it doesn't matter if you spend time together, all three of you. It is just for you to decide about Citizen.'

'I will. I will as soon as I can.'

I thought that would be the end of it for now. For a moment, she stood gazing around the studio in silence. 'Yes,' she said eventually and gave a nod, 'as soon as you can. I suppose you want to weigh it for yourself. In England, you don't take family just like that?'

I wanted to believe she was trying to be fair, just frankly speaking her mind, but suddenly I felt myself accused of being mean-spirited.

'What happened after you and Elizabeth found him? Did you learn any more?'

'He had been sick. They said malnutrition. And confused.'
She put down her can on a tray by her side and seated herself
again. It was one of those simple statements that falls like
rain, directly into place. Malnutrition. Confused.

I looked at her to continue. 'We were not supposed to take
him like that. But we had to. He said he had done it, but not
with his hands.'

This time it was my turn to nod in silence.

Anita said, 'The only chance to help him was to take him
home.'

'And now?'

'Now? Yes, the same is true.'

'But he is home, Anita. This is where he belongs.'

'It's too much for Mr Moses and you are his family.'

'Perhaps too much for him.'

Uncle Moses reappeared wearing a loose blue-and-white
shirt with embroidery around the neck. We retired to the
lounge for a drink. He poured a glass of water for himself.

There was a small flickering light from outside the lounge,
someone walking with a torch. I stood up and pulled off my
sandals, better to tiptoe upstairs to bed, but something made
me sit again. Tired as I was, I sensed that Uncle Moses
wanted to talk. This was the cheeriest I had seen him. Anita
and Elizabeth had both settled on the sofa. Anita looked
tired. She had surely been up more than eighteen hours but
she would never suggest we rested, not at this moment. And
Elizabeth, her long legs tucked up, her upper body with the
cleavage exposed, was toppling in the direction of her
mother's lap. Every one of us should have retired to bed, but
we stayed, knowing instinctively how important it was that
Uncle Moses be allowed to recount this story. He presented
us with every detail of those times, every conversation, with
photographic precision.

*

On a fine summer's evening, in the early 1970s, Moses had been taking pictures of the cast during the premiere of *Juliohs Siza*, which Thomas Decker had translated from Shakespeare into Krio. In the wings, Adele was watching, relishing the cheering and curtain calls, when she spotted the playwright standing opposite. Adele pointed out her husband to Thomas Decker and, as Moses was putting his cameras away, she tapped him on the shoulder:

'Moses, this is Decker. I've invited him back.'

Decker followed in his car and parked behind Moses. Once in the house, he waited alone in Moses' studio for drinks to be brought. Adele came back in, with husband in tow, carrying a wooden tray with a white linen cloth, two glasses, a jug of water, whisky and some eats. She apologized for not joining them but settled for a ten-minute chat about that night's performance.

Decker stayed and they spoke about making art: Moses' photography, Decker's plays and sketches. They poured another round of whisky. Decker, getting into his stride, pulled out an article he had been reading on language: 'Listen, listen, how will they like this? . . . "There are three distinct Creeo dialects. The first is peculiar to the numerically insignificant group of Creeo 'Intellectuals and Aristocrats and Professionals who belong to the top-most stratum of black society' . . ."' So pleased with himself he winked at Moses and read on: '"English words are pronounced almost exactly as an Englishman would pronounce them."'

Moses was concentrating. 'Go on, yes.'

'"The second is peculiar to about sixty per cent . . . and is the most widely spoken of the dialects and" – this is the point – "will become standard and written Creeo . . ."'

'Then we can all spell!' announced Moses. 'Power is p-a-w-a and tower is t-a-w-a.'

'And hour is h-a-w-a,' Decker butted in, knowing it to be wrong.

'A-w-a,' said Moses, laughing too. He began to feel rather maudlin; caution said to keep himself to himself, but he wanted to talk. Apart from conversations with Adele, he hardly ever took time to discuss ideas like this. He began tentatively. Decker was so confident of his own ideas and sure that history would prove him right, yet he seemed a sympathetic listener. Moses told him frankly how hard it was to make ends meet and watch 'those young boys who were behind me at school move into government service'. He did not like the sound of his own complaining voice but the more he talked, the more easily the words flowed.

Decker listened for a while, then joined in again. 'Yes, sir, and when you've worked and worked, some people still have the cheek to complain about the final product and say they could have done better.'

'That's right,' added Moses.

'And for less money.'

Moses agreed. They had another round of drinks. By the time they were saying goodnight, Decker had promised to introduce Moses to a contact of his called Harris, who would put some civil service work his way. He also said he had an old camera that he wanted to pass on, 'a gift for a master'.

One oppressively hot morning, Decker came by with the camera. He and Moses went off for a long walk, taking a flask with them. Their destination was not fixed but they found themselves in a restaurant whose lunch menu included pepper soup and some imported desserts. Later, settled on a black leather sofa at a bar, they consumed the third beer of the afternoon. Although they had only walked for less than half an hour the sweat was getting on their nerves and they wished one of them had insisted on driving. 'This heat,' said Moses.

'It's too much,' agreed Decker. 'The office ventilation has broken down. The insects are taking over.'

'The insects still have work even when you boys don't,' said Moses.

'Even the papers I need I can't have: machine's broken down,' continued Decker.

'My work goes on. I have things to do. And I want to see if that old camera can produce something for me.'

'It can, and I've fixed for Harris to come and see you from Government House. He'll see you all right. He took over from Pa Collins – good man.'

'Fine. Very good.'

They stopped the banter to admire some schoolgirls who were passing in white cotton dresses. 'One day soon, that will be my Agnes,' said Moses.

The afternoon heat was intense. They decided to start back and to take a taxi halfway to save time. On the way back they discussed Decker's sketches:

'Of course they are full of politics, but you want me to tell them that?'

'If they asked, what would you say?'

'It's our local custom.' As they turned into Westmoreland Street, he tripped on the paving.

'Be careful how you go,' said Moses.

'I am careful. You can't be too careful here.'

At that moment Agnes's teacher Miss Wright had stuck her head out of her car window and shouted out: 'I'm going your way.'

'What a good woman!' exclaimed Moses as they headed in her direction.

Decker was as good as his word. Harris, early thirties and ambitious, had called to commission Moses to take some government photos. On the morning that Harris was to call to collect his package, Moses sat up at the edge of the bed, rubbed his eyelids and stretched his jawline. He pushed aside the mosquito netting and glanced at Adele, who was sleeping peacefully in the middle of the bed. With his feet he began feeling under the bed for the brown leather slippers that would take him back down to the studio. At his bedside, there was a lamp, a small clock reading 4.50 and a glass of water fetched up the night before after a heavy meal. He found the slippers, dressed by pulling up a pair of cotton shorts and slipped out of the bedroom.

'The set of prints must be ready for Harris by nine o'clock,' he said aloud to himself on the way down. This announcement constituted the agenda for the morning and was all he needed to stay on track. Back in the studio – in disorder after a long and hard day during which, unusually, his Saturday assistant Maria had come to lend a hand with the rush order – Moses felt the roughness of his beard. He decided to ignore it until later and felt instead a surge of enthusiasm about his project.

Outside in the kitchen, Adele's footsteps were now audible. She swept the floor, picked up three empty beer bottles from the kitchen counter, removed a dead mosquito from the pail she had left outside and began to make breakfast. Eddy came and sat on her chair by the kitchen door. He looked worn out and droopy, so she dropped two well-ripe bananas in his lap and left him to eat. The food ready, 'Come and eat something,' she called to her husband.

The soft alto voice did not penetrate the first time. The blue lappa that hung between them was separating Moses from his morning feed. He put the set of prints in a folder, wrote out the invoice and marked the package for 'JOSEPH HARRIS ESQ.'. He took the long broom that had been standing in the corner and swept the studio clean. He sorted some papers into a pile and placed them in a drawer for later. He checked again in his diary to confirm the time Harris was due to call. Only then did he realize that he was hungry. He left the studio and went into the kitchen. Pilchards, slices of fresh tomato and bread lay on the white platter.

'I passed by Annie's yesterday, but they said she was not in town.'

'No,' confirmed Moses, 'I hear she went to England.'

Sitting motionless on his stool by the door, Moses traced in his mind his own movements from Freetown to London many years before; it was a journey to remember. He became aware of a dish being handed to him. He smiled. 'Annie is sending her eldest to school there, boarding school. Must be plenty money.'

Adele followed his thinking. It was as traceable as a tear. 'That will be one more England lady coming back,' she said.

Moses finished his breakfast without tasting the food and turned to go back to work.

'What are you thinking about now?' asked Adele.

'I'm thinking we could make a little more money,' he said, 'a bit more.'

At nine the civil service work was ready.

'Show me,' said Harris. He reached into his pocket and pulled out a pack of cigarettes. He lit a cigarette and smoked while Moses unpacked the photographs to present to his client. Harris lit another cigarette with the butt, mused for a long time by the table on which discarded prints of a local secondary school group lay, before coming across to look at his own set.

'What do you think of them?' Moses asked, fingering the edge of the cloth where the work he had just finished was lying.

Harris answered, 'Yes, this is what we needed.' He hesitated a moment before going on: 'Those school children, you took them and their teachers?'

At first Moses did not want to answer, for these were teachers agitating for their back pay. 'It was me,' he said finally.

Harris did not blink but, eyeing Moses, said, 'Those teachers need us back in power.'

He threw down the cigarette butt and crossed the room. When he reached the door he said: 'We need to make our country a success. You can help.'

Some shouting from the street interrupted their exchange. Moses rushed out to see what was happening. A fierce-looking dog was attacking a small boy; the mother was trying to comfort him. He saw the boy's distraught face, the mother's shocked expression and the dog baring its teeth. Then the woman started shouting at the dog, 'Come out of here, come out!' while the boy, who was no more than five years old, began to shriek. Moses led them away back to the house. Harris wanted to know if they were acquainted and whether he had seen her before. Moses said no, and continued to give his whole attention to the couple in distress.

'We will talk again,' said Harris, turning to go. 'We will talk.'

As soon as the boy and his mother were calmer, they left. Moses returned to his studio. It was still too early to leave for the day's assignment, so he went back through the prints he had made over the previous three days, ordering them according to region – Bo, Kenema, Freetown – and, as far as possible, stacking them in date order for easy reference. After that he went for a short walk, during which he saw the same dog from the morning's attack. This time the dog was lying on the ground, haunches spread out like a drunk on siesta, drying out.

A month later, Harris called to say that the photographs were good. He even apologized for having been so reticent on their first meeting, and said with a laugh: 'Our department chief says the photographs are very good.' They needed more and would let him know of what and when and how.

Moses left his house a little after seven o'clock that evening to meet Harris at a bar within sight of Lumley beach. The drive took him longer than he had imagined it would. The past five days in Freetown had been difficult. More often than not, electricity was cut. In the darkness, occasional private generators threw their cones of light on to the stony pot-holed roads and people walking about the city gleamed in the headlights of passing cars. It was a nocturnal tableau of tired people illuminated in a haze of dust and fumes.

'You've got no reason to worry,' Harris said, as he lit his third cigarette of the evening, 'we know you are with us.'

Moses said: 'I'm not really a politics man. I take pictures. People come from far away asking me to take their pictures. They like to be photographed by me for their albums. They know my photographs can make them look good, and they like that. In fact my photographs can help people. You see what I am saying? The photograph can help them see the truth of who they are. That's what I do. I am not a politics man.'

'No reason to worry about that,' said Harris. He rolled up his shirtsleeves. Reaching for the whisky bottle that sat on the table between them, he poured a small amount into the cut-glass tumbler. 'With one month to the election, we need photographs now to publish when we win. And your photographs are the best ones we can have.'

There would be money up front. There would be benefits. All pros, no cons. Harris poured another small whisky and downed it in one. And another small one. There would be money up front, he was saying for the third time, all pros, no cons. How could Moses refuse?

As Moses turned his car to head home, he had the impression of returning to a different reality. He had seen Adele that morning as she left for market in her flared floral dress made of cloth bought long ago and pale yellow open-back shoes she had been wearing since England. She seemed disposed to remain in that garb for many years to come. But now that image scattered like a flock of birds frightened by a stranger and he saw her anew with clothes he had not imagined before. As he passed through the town near the wharf, the stench of rotten fish hung in the air. He covered his nose with a handkerchief and blew. Home in fifteen minutes.

The next morning he woke up at his regular time, 5.50 a.m., ready for the new project. He would talk to schoolteachers, government officers, bank officials, press people, doctors and other hospital staff – the ordinary people who made life tick. It was a chance to get out and document their lives, to show what progress was being made and to capture it all in photography. And the deal was good. He would have access to all the colour facilities paid for by the government, the pictures would be used far and wide. He would make a name for himself.

Harris called by to see how it was going. He smoked two cigarettes while reminding Moses of the benefits of this work: all pros, no cons. His manner was completely normal but his breath suffered from the drinking sessions of past nights and his face from the wear and tear of manoeuvring. 'We will buy everything we can use,' he said on leaving.

Over the next fortnight, Moses made several attempts to generate photographs that would show how well the government was doing. He listened to people's stories without making any comment and with an apparently neutral attitude, but really looking to conclude that their successes were government-induced and their problems self-induced. One day he was on his way to town when he bumped into Agnes's teacher, Miss Wright.

'How are your subjects doing?' Moses asked with a smile.

'Mine are doing well. Reading and learning and blooming. What about yours?'

Moses bit his lip and looked squarely in her face: 'What do you mean?'

'I don't know. I hear tell you're doing some government project.'

Moses had hesitated in a way that should have made Miss Wright suspicious. 'I've just come from the hospital down Westmoreland Street. Our doctors need more resources. They are not doing so well.'

'And neither are we,' Miss Wright reminded him in a more serious tone. 'Pay day comes and goes without the pay coming.' They said goodbye and Moses went on his way.

Harris called him to view the prints at Government House. Before they entered the room, Harris said they were to scrub their hands up to the elbows. Moses followed him into the men's room and copied his scrupulous washing. Then Harris led him into an ante-room where the prints were laid out on the table. 'We have to avoid more contamination.' He pointed to the set of prints and apparently explained why surgical washing was required before viewing.

Moses recognized the work as his own: shots of the president on tour, with officials in a motorcade, up-country, in Freetown making speeches, shaking hands, admiring babies, engaging with teachers and nurses, patting a small boy on the head, laughing heartily at a cultural evening.

'There's no one left in the building,' Harris had interrupted the viewing, 'no one to overhear anything you might want to tell me.'

Moses realized that the moment belonged completely to him; the noise of the office workers had subsided. Harris leant against the door. He took out a cigarette then, thinking better of it, returned it to the packet. He was keeping his hands clean.

'Now that the work is finished,' Moses began with an embarrassed smile, nodding towards the prints, 'what more is to be done?'

Harris pressed his thin hips against the door and folded his arms. The office building was shrouded in silence. Moses stepped closer to the prints and picked up a couple of them. Then he saw a faintly sketched figure hovering over the head of the president. It was the figure of a small boy holding a gun. In each print the figure appeared – distinct but soft like a breath.

What shocked Moses was that he felt neither horror nor surprise. Yet, knowing Harris's eyes were upon him, he uttered a low 'Oho.'

Moses pursed his lips and let his eyelids shut as though prayers were about to be said. He felt excited. He thought they were both the most fantastic and the most winning images he had ever taken. The truth appeared as a shadow on the print. Then a surge of fear swept through him, a fear that they would hold him accountable for the shadow. This seemed a moment when all the things he had struggled for – money, security, a good reputation – were in doubt. He looked again at the shadow; a small child barely recognizable, rising as a bruise must in response to a blow, scar tissue to a wound.

'A drink?' asked Harris, pulling a cigarette out as he opened the door. Moses followed him down the empty corridor and out of the building to a bar, where a teenage waitress put two cool beers in front of them without waiting for an order. Harris was leaning forward over the small table placed between them. 'Any ideas?' he was asking.

Moses shook his head. He had no answers to satisfy Harris, the civil service or the government. Jumbled images crowded his mind. Nothing that would help him came within his grasp. Not the long dark nights of working on the project, the days of trailing the president. He thought of the various characters they had met on the campaign trail – chiefs and officers, shake-hands men with their neat bribes, drinks sellers and talkers. He remembered the talking, the promises, the noise of the political cavalcade. 'I have no idea what happened,' he assured Harris.

'Some kind of crazy thing, isn't it?' laughed Harris as they finished their drinks and made ready to leave.

'It could be dust on the lens,' Moses lied, attempting to close the gap between himself and Harris. 'Yes, some kind of crazy thing.'

Something was stirring uncomfortably in the pit of his stomach, a longing to address the boy in the photo, when reality raked him back to Harris.

'Did I tell you we have brought in another photographer?'

'No.'

'Well, you left us no choice.'

'No.'

'So, must be going now.' Harris took a final swig of his drink and lit up. He left one photograph with Moses. In his tired state Moses peered at the print but in the evening light he failed to see the shadow there; it was as though the boy was refusing to come out again. Nevertheless he took the one print, the only evidence he had of his work for the government's election campaign, and shuffled towards his car. Such noise, it was always worse in town.

With relief Moses turned his car into their road, noticed the friendly bougainvillea outside his house. The evening was touching night, an attendant moon bringing serene light. He went into his studio and placed the offending photograph in a brown paper envelope, sealing it with thick tape. He put it in a drawer without labelling the package, confident that he would never forget.

He was tired but not ready for bed. He drank some water

and that revived him. He walked idly into the yard and leaned against the plane tree, with the camera in his hands. It was so old, it could hardly be expected to serve again. He felt as if he had walked into a trap. *Foolish me.* The night was so still that even the leaves of the tree did not waver as he stood there. The camera weighed heavy, its double lens faced the moonlit sky, silent and unrepentant. The inner workings of the camera were now so completely exhausted that only imagination could conjure up what they once had been. The flapping wings of a bird beat the air; afterwards there was silence again. The silence penetrated to the place where bones hurt.

Moses stood in the moonlit silence as if waiting for God to direct him and give the word, but nothing came. All that was there was what he had always known and feared. It was something fixed that seemed to increase and grow more rocklike over time. He wanted to heave his entire weight against this obstacle called Fate, but what was the point? *Just go on, go on.* He let his shoulders relax and fall. 'That is how it is.'

A bird overhead offered a little sympathy.

Suddenly the lights in the house went out. Adele, weary of waiting, had gone to bed. Moses returned the camera to the studio. Before, he had thought about hurling it into the rubbish to corrode. Now, he took his handkerchief and wiped the double lens. He did this so carefully that no contamination or fault could attach itself to future prints. He did this so lovingly that the future tears of the boy soldier were gradually wiped away.

Seven

The silent, blackish water of a little stream running through marshy land gave me no clue of my whereabouts in the night's journey. I skimmed the top of the water with my fingers and pulled up a handful of tiny glittering leaves, which shone in the dark like guiding angels on my labyrinthine wanderings. When I was a girl, I had gathered acorns and russet-coloured leaves but never did they glow in the dark. Once the terrain was illuminated, I noticed I had a large feline companion: a stealthy leopard, its pelt gleaming yellow with rosetted spots, was strolling along a thickly forested ridge above me. Usually when people around these parts say 'the leopard has come to town' (*lepet don kam na ton*), they mean that problems from the rainforest have entered the city. My sense of direction is poor, but I was certain that the leopard I spotted was walking into town. The only possible reason she stopped, flicked her tail and contemplated me was sympathy. Foolish maybe, but I was carrying my increasing knowledge of town life back into the forest.

In the morning, the clarity of light was divine. Although I was walking on a rocky footpath with a margin of weeds and nettles, my spirits were high. I was looking forward to buying a baguette from the Fula bakery frequented by the diamond diggers when I spotted Miriam's black-and-red patterned shawl.

'Hello, Miriam, no Baby today?'

'No, Baby is sitting with Hinga.'

'I thought we'd go to the bakery and pick up some baguette – can you lead the way?'

'The bakery isn't near here.'

'No?'

'It's far, right on the border with Liberia. I'm not going back there with you. When you enter the forest you are coming like a person who is asleep and I have to do so much to put you right, but when we reach you are all right.'

When we arrived at Bemba G's compound, he was roasting coffee beans. He pounded them to a coarse powder and brewed me a strong and pungent beverage. I regretted not having baguette to go with it, but relished the taste of the morning brew and his hospitality after such a long journey.

After coffee, he gave me a tour of the land around his home. He realized that I was a novice to his regional ways, for local people all knew about crop rotation, which plants and shrubs to use for medicinal or recreational purposes and why land was left fallow for up to ten years, while I was agog as he taught me. This seemed to him so amusing that he exclaimed with delight:

'No forests in your parts?'

'Sorry? No – definitely urban stock. My closest is called the New Forest.'

'New? Never mind –' with laughter '– you can learn.'

His dark eyes fixed on my face as he marinated me in forest lore, the details of rice cultivation, the value of elephant-dung rice, a local speciality, shape-shifter stories about men and elephants that made me laugh for the first time since landing again in Africa. On our way back to our original meeting point, we strolled along a riverbank and up a slope covered with dark glistening rubble towards his wooden hut.

'Are all your stories true or do you make them up?'

'When it's history, I show the sign for "true story".' He raised an old green gin bottle broken at the neck above his head.

'And when the story is not true?'

'Who needs to know?'

'Tell me a story then,' I pleaded. 'Tell me a true story about the rainforest.'

'All right. This is the story of salt.' He raised the old gin bottle above his head and began: 'You know salt, yes?'

I nodded. 'Yes, for putting on food.'

He nodded. 'Yes, that is salt.' He then explained how the taste for salt among his people had brought trade and trouble.

'Trouble?'

'Too much trouble. And it all began with the hunters who came looking for elephants.'

'Elephants?'

'Yes, elephants.' He told a story about Keba and Babu; the former, using his magic powers, turned himself into a bird to spot elephants, spotted a woman making dinner and observed that she had no salt, so he gave her some. The resulting weakness for salt led to one of the most over-generous transactions of goods he had ever heard of in which his people handed over sixty strong young men, skins of zebra, duiker and pangolin and much more besides.

'Too much salt is bad for you,' I countered.

'I never liked too much salt either,' he said.

'But was that the only trouble?'

'No. The hunters took the young men as far as the coast and sold them.'

'Oh, no.'

'Oh, yes.'

He had grown pale with the telling and mopped his brow. I asked whether he had seen the bird-man who was hunting elephants in the forest.

'I once met a man,' he said, 'who could turn himself into a bird.'

'Oh!' I blinked hard. 'Where did you meet him?'

'Up in that tree.'

Hunters had brought animal skins like zebra, duiker, pangolin and other items I had never heard of.

'This is fantastic!'

He smiled at me.

'Thank you. Life is made of story. Take names. Like the village Mathora. Thora is "put down". A traveller was passing a group of huts and he asked the name of the village. "Come to think of it, we don't have a name for it, but since I'm about to put down these bags of salt, let us call it Thora." Put down. See?'

I did. In the early evening light, sitting on fine woven mats in red and purples, I spotted a calabash of fruits from which I was invited to help myself. Birds burbled over our heads, their sounds falling like sunbeams in our midst. Flies and midges did not trouble me; like a contented vessel at low tide, I drifted for a while. An age passed. Then there were shouts, a series of loud noises, and I realized I must have dozed off. In front of me was a group of children, hissing.

'Are you the same children who left me here only two days ago?'

'Na we, oh, na we!' they cried.

'But what happened to you?'

The child soldiers stood before us, torrid red with shame and anger, their faces looking wizened like raisins.

'What happened to you?'

Peter answered first: 'I met Killer on the road. He made me go back and fight; if I didn't fight he would kill me. Then the fear gripped me. He said I must follow him. When I followed he took me to some place. He gave me some rice and meat. For so many months now I did not eat rice and meat.

So I eat till my belly full. Killer give me something to drink. I drink all. He said if I turn my back or try to run he would kill me. I did not turn my back. I didn't run. When he was sleeping I cut his foot so he could not follow me.'

'Who is Killer? Did you know him before?'

'He was fighting with me. Seo Cut and Killer and me – we were in the one unit.'

'What were you doing with him?'

'Where could I go? What could I do?' asked Peter. 'And it is your fault. You called us here and then you left us. Where would we go? All of us, where would we go, eh?'

'Were you all together?'

'No, I was with Abu and Hakim,' said one older boy.

'I was with Baby and I took this one along,' said Miriam, indicating the little girl of six, who piped up: 'My name is Isata.'

'Yes,' confirmed Miriam, 'I was with Isata and Baby.'

'And we were together after I cut Killer's foot,' added Peter, pointing to Hinga and another teenage boy.

Then there were cries of: 'I was alone!'

'Me too,' shouted someone else.

'And me too.'

I looked at these solitary travellers. 'What's your name?' I asked each in turn.

'Thomas.'

'Victor.'

'K.T.'

Victor said: 'I killed many people this time. The first time I was afraid but then I was just shooting all over the place. I didn't know what to do. Then the drink finished in me. I felt bad. I know I am bad. I killed people.'

'If you don't kill people, they will kill you,' someone chimed in logically.

All eyes were fixed upon me.

'I had fallen to the bottom of a ditch,' said K.T., 'when the soldiers came and took me, they said I must have run away, so they would beat me. They beat me till I was blue, then I was bleeding – the blood soak all my clothes.' Bloody red liquid spurted from his skin and a festering wound on his leg from a rat bite that would not heal was exposed to full view.

Bemba G bowed his head in silence, his eyes troubled, his face creased with anguish. He seemed even more distraught than me but I spoke first. 'I'm sorry, I'm really sorry.'

My insistent curiosity about seeing child soldiers had led to this disastrous outcome. They were right to be bewildered and angry. Who was I to ask for a peepshow of their experiences? I kept saying, 'I'm sorry, I'm very sorry.' It did not seem that anyone was accepting my apology even though I repeated it several times.

Citizen did not approach me. He stopped short, taken aback, and gave me a puzzled look while I clambered off Black Rock to sit on the ground. The children stood shoulder to shoulder, their faces reddened with crusted blood, their lips chalky dry and whispers of melancholy grey streaking their hair. The gang looked me over with suspicion. They were beginning to perceive the elaborate web of chaos I had created by my search for child soldiers.

The first one to move was Isata. She came up to me and almost threw her body into my lap, a bundle of girlhood unaware that her skin had turned rough and hard like an old lemon. She sighed, laying her head against my bosom, then she shivered and fell asleep.

The others, however, prised open their dry mouths and spewed out rage, shouting about being abducted, forced to fight and kill:

'I was a street child. I didn't have anybody.'

'They forced me to join.'

'They killed my small brother and forced me to join.'

'They gave me a gun and made me shoot.'

'My head is blowing, my head is blowing up!'

I felt myself sag.

'Don't blame her,' said Bemba G. 'It is not her fault.' He had begun to move about now, stopping in front of each child as he spoke, examining each face for signs of contrition. Eventually, he flopped down on Black Rock and addressed the group as if they were local elders:

'We said to come back in two days and you cannot reach Black Rock before the time you say. It is strict on time. It is not her fault. Let's be honest; we have a problem. That's why you are old, old before your time. But I have things I want to tell you.'

I raised my palm: 'Now they are here, the children need to rest and to have some food before we go any further.'

He nodded and was gone.

Although they hardly budged from their positions, the child soldiers relaxed, knowing that dinner was on its way. Bemba G laid before them steaming mounds of cassava, black-eyed beans in palm oil served hot from big metal pots, a bowl of greens flavoured with herbs and topped with nuts. The sheer abundance of his supplies made them grow quiet. Still uncertain and no doubt afraid, Miriam took the girl Isata by the hand and, in a contorted but linked position, they fed each other. On seeing the high platters, the stout youth Peter began to cry, at which point Citizen and Abu came and patted him on the back. Famished, eating with their fingers, the children bunched the solid fufu into balls and dipped it into the hot sauces; with relish, they pushed lumps of meat and fish into their mouths until nothing remained.

Imagine, I used to think that 'sandwich' was lunch! Well, full-belly gourmands, the world began to look different to me. These child soldiers, among the most sharp-witted young people I had ever met, threw their dishes up in the air and caught them, as a sign of appreciation for good food freely given. The place erupted into a scene of juggling dishes. The old man Bemba G was grateful and decided to serenade them. He brought out a woodwind instrument reminiscent of a medieval pipe and played for them, a melodious tune that I named 'Ode to Pepper Soup'. When the music stopped, the child soldiers were quiet. The girls stretched their legs out on the ground while the boys, in the fashion of Romans at the baths, propped up on their elbows, reclined in pairs chatting about the day's events. The mood was changing. Who would have thought that an hour or so earlier they had been like belligerent thugs, dragging Bemba G and me back into their miserable tales? I looked over at my young cousin, Citizen. He was in his child-soldier dress of ragged-cut jeans and holed top, but he too looked calm and free of vengeance. Eventually the entire group grew tired and, one by one, they fell asleep.

Bemba G's large hut was surrounded by tall trees, while the adjoining compound was spacious and clear except for his beloved halfway silk-cotton tree in the centre and Black Rock a few yards before the hut. If the child soldiers were to stay here, they would need shelter, for which I located good logs, thick branches, straw mats and hammocks.

I took a walk down to the stream. There was silence. Nothing moved. Strange blue birds looked from their perches and the fish kept their heads down, but the atmosphere was perfect. Here by the stream the air was soft; here, children could become themselves again, soft-limbed, soft-voiced and free. I returned to the compound where, as in a school dormitory, their physical closeness belied the private reality of sleep. Bemba G asked me to keep an eye on them, explaining that he had some work to do. He disappeared between the trees, the white of his cotton *coboslot* visible for only seconds before he was gone. I wanted to nap too. I longed to let this dense canopy of trees – safe home to elephant, lizard, monkey or rat – welcome me too. In the late afternoon heat, with the sun beating down on the wooden building, I became tranquil. But I refrained from sleep. Flies came to inspect my sleeping charges and were dismissed with the flick of a wrist. To all the forest creatures the heat, the sounds and scents were familiar, but it was a struggle for me not to surrender to the heat and allow it to befriend the grooves of my body.

When the child soldiers finally woke, they each seemed slightly restored, no longer a grotesque sight of youngsters with grey-white hair, dry, twisted skins and terrible yellowing eyes. Isata gazed at everyone, like a child who had just heard a bizarre fairy story about her parents, and, relieved to see all was back to normal, proceeded to pat everyone on the head. Bemba G returned rubbing his palms over his balding head as though smoothing back hair.

'It is done – three-hundred-and-fifty paces each way from halfway silk-cotton tree is safe ground,' he announced to me alone.

'Will they know when they've reached the boundary? Is there some marker?'

'They will know.'

'Good, very good.' I smiled at him. So Gola forest was neither keening nor bent on our destruction, but our den.

Around nine in the evening, we sat down. Bemba was impatient to get on. 'Here with me they will have good stories and good food,' he said.

'Can you do that – give them good stories and good food?' I checked.

'That's what I said. Let me talk to them now.'

'Yes.' I sighed. 'Any time you're ready.'

'They will be all right in time,' he said.

Trusting him more, I gave a little laugh. 'Thank you. You

can talk to them, but let me go first. I have something to say too.' I cleared my throat and began.

'Children, you have no idea how relieved I feel that you have come back to us. We have been worried all day about you. In fact, your return to being yourselves is the best thing that could happen. I feel reassured.' It was good to see how relaxed and beautiful they seemed, with their original colouring, curling black hair and lively eyes. Citizen, too, was like a child being rescued and given wings . . .

As I spoke, I became aware of distant gunfire behind me in the bushes. Bemba G acknowledged my anxious glance with a smile to go on and the children showed no sign of unease at all.

'You see, what we've done today – at last – is to make you truly welcome here in the rainforest. We should have prepared for you before, really prepared the space before asking you to come. It was an oversight; we made a mistake. But we've resolved that now – it's a safe place. I've gathered some materials to build huts. Please make them now and be comfortable here.'

Another distant boom provoked a few worried glances. Citizen jumped to his feet, pulling his T-shirt up over his ears.

'Don't worry about that. Don't even think about it. The space here, our safe space, extends more than three-hundred-and-fifty paces from halfway silk-cotton tree. This is like a walled garden. Enjoy the hush of Gola forest, children, you need not be afraid. Now listen to our host Bemba G.'

I watched them intently to see whether my words had made any sense to them. Against my cheek I felt a warm breeze. I savoured its tenderness. Above us, a dark blue sky, and in our midst insects frolicked but the other forest creatures were not heard. The forest had fallen into silence.

Miriam plunged through the bush, walking confidently and with huge strides. I had to charge along in spurts to keep up with her athletic pace while Isata trotted dutifully by my side. Sometimes, I feared Miriam was trying to shake us off but she always waited for us and even before we glimpsed Bemba G's familiar hut I was offering prayerful thanks for her guidance. I wanted to sit and drink some cool water after the morning's walk, but as soon as we saw Bemba G approaching, fingers to his lips bidding silence, it became clear something untoward had occurred. All the child soldiers were huddled on the ground, still fast asleep, having failed to make their huts as I had suggested.

'What's happened?'

'We will drink our coffee and wait for them,' began Bemba G. 'Last night after you left they were very restless and fighting broke out.'

'Why? Who were they fighting?'

'Each other. They wanted to tell stories.'

'Yes, it's true; they said that the very first day we all met.'

'I said they could tell them one by one.'

'And that made them fight?'

'No, not exactly.' He scratched his bald head. 'Help me. Do you know John Rambo?'

I told him I did not know him personally, though I could picture him shooting his way out of the some American back-woods.

'They all know him.' Bemba G stretched his arm in the direction of the sleeping child soldiers and recalled some of the American's lines from the night before.

'Did that make them fight?'

'They will probably say it wasn't him, but I think it was.' Bemba G paused to look at me, then added, 'Hinga said he was in charge of the force to capture John Rambo and he gave instructions for the weapons and ammunition that they needed. Peter disagreed.'

'And then the fight? Who really started it?'

'Hinga and Peter started it. You see how Peter likes to be in charge, so he was the commander. He told Hinga to order his men to send two B-52s and F-15Es and to join him at command base. Then Hinga said, no, he was not sending them, all he had left in the hangar was two F-16s and two B-1s. That's how it started. Peter said he knew what they had, since he was in charge, let him send them or else. Hinga was shaking with anger. He said Peter reminded him of the commander of his unit: "I know you – you mad, you mad with power," he tossed taunts like that into the air. Peter could not ignore these accusations and started punching. The others took sides, cheering either Peter or Hinga; they wanted to fight it out, all except Miriam. She said every time you ask child soldiers to tell stories, it leads to trouble. She rescued Baby and Isata from the mêlée and warned them: "No more stories." . . .'

Bemba G's voice was faint. He paced up and down, hands on hips, muttered, stopped, began again. 'I thought I was doing the right thing letting them tell stories, but I was wrong. Where do they find these strange tales?'

I scrutinized his kind old face. 'Maybe they were showing off. I have a plan. You tell them stories, set a good example and show how it's done. Make it clear we're not prepared to hear theirs until they behave. And they must build those shelters, not sleep out rough like beggars.'

I fixed him with a stare. Bemba G's inky-black eyes revealed nothing. He said in a relaxed way, 'There's no hurry on my part. My work is to tell them stories and when they are ready . . .'

'. . . they will tell their own.' I finished his sentence for him. He nodded, breathed in deeply of the morning air and went off to make more coffee. I heard him busying himself grinding the beans and shuffling through possessions. Then suddenly he came out: 'Ah, ha! Mm, yes.' He had located what he wanted.

An hour later, after too much coffee, the child soldiers began to stir, most of them in good humour and all of them hungry. He gave them breakfast and told them what we had decided. He flexed his hands, cracked each bone and called out: 'A new direction.'

The sun came out stronger, blinding, warning of change. In the warm yellow light Bemba G had them sit to listen to his stories. Some of them were recited solo but many had choruses. He told of trees that talked in the night, men who became spiders; he told forest stories that amused the eager listeners and reminded them not to fight over narrative lines. He explained the difference between 'true' and 'made-up' stories and those that change direction. His eyes locked upon their faces, assessing whether they were learning. Sometimes he paced between the trees, calling on the lushness of the forest to assist him. All afternoon the sun kept us alert, passing under our clothes like a rude and sexy hand. Once he was satisfied they had learned enough, he sent them to build their shelters, which they did willingly.

'What happens now?' asked Hinga.

'Now we play my games.' A light laugh came from Bemba G. 'Everyone run around as fast as you can, then when I say "Stop!" the person at Black Rock can have a go.'

Movement began. Black dots dashed, circling their globe, cries criss-crossed the air.

'Stop!' It was never loud enough for everyone to hear first time; one or two looked across at Black Rock too late. Citizen won first time. Everyone went again.

'Stop!' Then it was Isata. A third time it was K.T. They kept to their individual paths, heading for Black Rock as often as they could but each time only one was there at the right moment, like high voltage accurately wired. It was a popular game and everyone joined in, creating their own passages, puzzling each other with their speed. Bemba G watched them intently and before boredom had begun to set in he called out:

'Next game is "HA". The second I say, "HA," you say, "HA!"'

They tried. They got it. They missed it. They fell about laughing. Everyone was in a good mood now, shouting out and jumping into the air.

'HA!'

'HA!'

'HA!'

'HA!'

'HA!'

How light and full of fun they were, trying to say 'HA!' in each other's faces while watching Bemba G. It looked easy, but it was hard to stay together. I left them to their games and took a stroll as far as the river bank. A cool breeze wafted over the water, the sun dipped slightly over the tops of the trees. Wonderful land, rich fertile soil. Once the ground had been prepared it was good for planting groundnuts, cassava, rice, corn and kola. *Wouldn't you relish this for ever?* I turned back and heard the medley of voices long before I saw them again. Country voices, Krio accents, Mende and Temne tones rippling through the forest. Evidently whatever Bemba G was up to was not over yet. I came back past the hut and saw them in a large circle.

He had them shouting bizarre sounds into the air, one after the other in rapid succession. A tongue twister: 'Stop that tick-tock, clock!' Then, with accompanying arm and leg actions: 'Zap, bam, puff, zizz!' 'Zap, bam, puff, zizz!' over and over. Sometimes he shouted out 'again' or 'good' before going on to the next one. Occasionally, I recognized a Greek word – 'EUREKAAAAAAAAA' came hurtling out of fifteen mouths on to the forest floor and then up into the skies.

'Whisper it,' he called out. Into the quiet of the afternoon floated a subtle silvery 'Eurekaaaaaaaaaaaaaaaaaaaaaaaaaa,' from all fifteen.

Could it be softer still? 'Eurekaaaaaaaaaaaaaaaaaaaa.'

'Softer, yes?'

'Eurekaaaaaaaaaaaaaaaaaaaaaaa . . .'

'Proceed once more!'

'Eurekaaaaaaaaaaaaaaa,' they answered, savouring the Greek. There were many eyes turned towards the sunlight, heads flung back, lips wide open: laughing children. A silver banner that ran for yards from the middle of halfway silk-cotton tree was pulled out, Citizen holding one end and Peter the other. Standing on Black Rock, Bemba G shouted, 'Give me audience, children, these lines are good for you!' There proceeded ten or more disconnected lines, in English, Krio or Mende, which everyone repeated without any sign of irritation.

'Try this for size: "Some nice boonoonoonous lady!"' It was a bouncy female New World sound that bumped into me like a Jamaican higgler woman.

'Some nice boonoonoonous lady!' they repeated, pouting over the 'boonoonoonous'.

Several times they repeated it: loudly; in whispers.

'Is all this going somewhere? Do you have a plan?' I wondered. He was changing the games but we seemed to be in the same place. Besides, the children were becoming loud and Black Rock looked threateningly curvaceous, like a huge mouth.

Bemba G disappeared into his hut and re-emerged with a book.

'They can do it! I will feed them this!'

The book was not passed to me with the solemnity of the Bible. It was not shoved at me with the casualness of a circular. It was thrown into the air, veering towards Black Rock only after it had looped with splendid equipoise over my head. The book that landed in my lap had a grey cover, a frontispiece reading in exceptionally fine markings in black ink: 'Ex libris Bemba G'.

I stared at the titles centred on the same page:

Julius Caesar by William Shakespeare
and
Juliohs Siza by Thomas Decker from c.1599 to c.1995
or longer

I leafed through the tome; its thin pages were like rice paper and covered with scribbles. Each line by William Shakespeare was tracked by another by Thomas Decker.

'What, you will teach them this?'

My question remained in the air. Black Rock was firm beneath me. In front of me the boy child soldiers were climbing trees calling out to one another:

'Citizen, Citizen.'

'Peter, Peter.'

'Abu, Abu.'

Miriam was sitting on a mat, fixing Isata's hair into braids.

'Why am I *here*?' I imagined a different scene, an afternoon at a haberdashery store like the one I used to traipse through with my mother, staring at the walls lined with wide bolts of good cloth, the counters displaying cotton threads of many colours. 'What would madam like today?'

And another voice: *'Three small but useful items, please: scissors to trim this heavy title in half, gingham ribbons to tie up Isata's plaits, straight pins to perforate this playground sorcerer!'*

Eight

Repetition is the ground for the new and the same. These were the words that flashed in my mind as I lay under the night sky. It did not matter which way I looked from Freetown to England, from one generation of the family to another, scenes replayed with intimations of sameness. We were a family, with its own customs handed down from Aunt Sally's generation to Citizen's. Much of this familiar practice had been adhered to so tightly that two world wars, several political coups, and even civil war would not eradicate it. There were words and exchanges that signified the family bond but could still resonate of an emotional terra incognita.

'Miss Adele loved to munch fish head!'

'My mother did too.'

'Always after you with your chicken bones.'

'Mine too.'

A small pile of chicken bones lies on a table for someone to clear away.

'How hungry are you all?'

'Very hungry!'

'Better cook all then.'

A one-pound packet of long-grain rice is tipped into the hot red sauce and shushes in oil at the bottom of an iron pan. On tiptoe the children peer in, longing for the hard white grains to soften and change colour. The mother takes a long slotted spoon and dots the outstretched palms with tomato sauce. 'Ready?' she asks.

Visitors come.

'These are the little ones?'

'Oh, ya! Look whey dem don big!'

'Let me look at you.'

'This is the baby.'

'Just like the father.'

'The father's nose.'

'And his eyes.'

'That's his colouring.'

'The baby. The little baby.'

The African child does not know why his skin, his colour, his height make women snatch their handkerchiefs and weep with joy.

We travel across Europe, across the Atlantic, unaware that the welcome will be a mixture of suspicion, self-imposed curfew, waiting for news from 'home', unfamiliar sounds, the eloquent country of dreams.

'How long are you staying here?'

'A while.'

'What do you mean when you say "a while"?'

'Well, you see, I don't know at the moment.'

'Do you see how we do things here?'

'I think so.'

We travel nonetheless, perhaps unconsciously desiring a return ticket to the period when it was possible to travel over a wide area of Europe, western Asia and North Africa needing no passport, speaking one widely understood language and using one generally understood currency. These conditions greatly assisted the interchange of ideas and beliefs as well as material objects. Such was life in the Roman Empire.

The evening after Uncle Moses talked about the boy in the photograph, a distant cousin, Miss Ida, whose long, grey-streaked hair was up in a bun, came to visit. She had been curious to meet me and to discover what was happening with Moses and Citizen. We settled down to eat sweet snacks of coconut cake and akara outside in the yard and drank the three bottles of stout she had brought as a present. She was glad to see that Citizen was at home.

'But he has nothing to say about what he did?' Moses and I shook our heads. The two of them faced each other in the yard where Citizen was lying by the tree.

Uncle Moses was quick to say how pleased he was that I had come because the little boy did seem more settled. Miss Ida said that was something.

'Do you want to taste the stout, too?' She spoke to Citizen in Krio, softening her voice. He nodded and emerged eagerly from the side of the tree.

'Fetch a small glass and put some water in it.'

Citizen went into the house and returned with a tumbler half-filled with water, to which Miss Ida added about a thimbleful of stout. While he gulped this diluted drink, she looked him over, freely commenting on his condition as though he could not hear.

'He's not too bad. I've seen much, much worse.' She ran her hand gently over Citizen's head and he went inside with the empty glass. Miss Ida then spoke of some boy she had found, quite mad, sleeping under a tarpaulin, cold in the night. He had nowhere to go and could not find his people. He had spent a few nights at her house – five, six, seven, she said. But how long could it go on? The boy would not settle.

'Sometimes he says he prefers to fight.' That made her afraid.

'What can we do?' Uncle Moses shrugged. 'This is the tragedy we have all had to face.'

We also spoke about Auntie Adele. Since Uncle Moses had shared some of his more intimate thoughts with me, it had become easier to talk about her and we all did, as a kindness to him and for our own sakes. We were able to reminisce about her perfect baking, her obsession with Bronnley's Lily of the Valley soap, which we bought by the crate-load from London for her boudoir, her laugh and her life in 1960s England.

Miss Ida agreed with what Uncle Moses said: Adele had been unworldly. In the 'swinging 60s' of the Beatles, Black Power and Flower Power, Adele held to clean living, church attendance and family. Miss Ida had been the one to rescue her when she first arrived in England. Adele's first bitter mistake had come on the day of her arrival. She had been standing at the bustling Liverpool railway station, looking about her for somewhere to take tea, when she was approached by a helpful traveller with light-brown hair, sugar-pink lips, a whiff of light perfume.

'Can I help you, dear?'

A friendly face, Adele had thought. 'I wanted to take tea but I need the lavatory. Is it close by?'

'I'll show you, dear.'

The toilet pan had been bearable but Adele hesitated to stoop among the scattered cigarette ends and wet paper on the dirty floor.

'Let me take your things, dear?' the woman had offered.

Indecision resolved, Adele had passed her handbag to the bare white-braceleted arm and moved back into the cubicle, raised her skirts to pee. Just as the release came, quick as a flash, the door had banged shut.

Gone, the whiff of perfume, not even a trace left now around Liverpool station; gone, Adele's money, passport.

As she had emerged from the lavatory, Miss Ida spotted her, realized at once that she was distressed, that her clothes suggested a new arrival, and hugged Adele until she forgave herself.

Miss Ida had many such family stories. When Uncle Moses went inside, Anita, Elizabeth and Sara came over to join us and Miss Ida continued to talk.

'Adele would be shamed to see this place now. That boys' place looks nasty like that Liverpool latrine.' The makeshift house where the servants had slept had all but collapsed and all sorts of muck was heaped there. 'They say his boys went to fight. Fighting for their rights, eh? One of those girls said that to me. So,' she said, warming to her audience, 'they packed up everything and no doubt stole from your uncle –' she nodded at me '– and set off by foot.'

According to Miss Ida, 'No sooner did they reach the first Bo-Kenema checkpoint, when they were stopped and searched. Could they answer the questions? No. Did they reach their people? No. Landmine got them both, so the girl said. And what's the place she told me? Emme . . . err, near Pandebu.'

All of us nodded solemnly and Miss Ida lifted her magazine to fan her face, though the sun had long since gone in.

Elizabeth was frowning. 'They just go and die for nothing.' She put her little sister to sit on her lap and bounced her. 'Look how our people have suffered, for nothing.'

'We must make a decision about Moses, how can he manage now?' Miss Ida took back the baton. 'They say his sight is not good. He can't go on with that photography business again.' She paused.

'But Citizen is here and for now, Julia. She'll make sure he is all right. Not so, my dear?'

'His sight isn't so bad in any case.' I was earnestly explaining that I was dispensable.

'Older people need to be assured that the young care,' said Miss Ida, smiling confidently.

*

I was enjoying Freetown, enjoying the company of Sara and Elizabeth especially, and wanted to defer the call back to the rainforest for as long as I could so that I could consider how best to operate among the child soldiers given that foreign texts were flying about. But, a short time after Miss Ida left us, when darkness had surrounded the entire capital city, I rushed back into the 'bush' without even brushing my hair. The journey was easy; I had no trouble making out the paths, knew the rivers, the flying beasts and how to greet the leopard stalking the high ridges.

I was comforted when I spotted Miriam, who told me that a few more child soldiers were expected since my last disappearance, word having spread that this compound was open to them. I was in time to see them arriving. There were about thirty-five of them, mainly boys. They said they had walked miles to reach us and their ragged jeans and soiled clothes confirmed it. One had a torn smelly blanket over his head and dragged an AK47 along the ground.

'Is this military barracks?'

'No, it's a friendly camp for former child soldiers.'

'We're playing a game called Julius Caesar,' Isata explained.

'OK, I'm coming.' As he unfolded the blanket, cups and ammunition cascaded down.

'No weapons allowed here!' I warned. 'There's a store over there.'

The boys who trailed after him were speaking a variety of languages but in spite of their raggedness continued to march in line, left-right, left-right, as a matter of habit. I recognized the boy at the end both by his smile and the drum he was carrying: it was Corporal Kalashnikov bringing up the rear with Sally.

'They attacked our camp,' Sally told me, 'we walked days to reach here.'

The newcomers did not take long to settle in, thanks to our hospitality and their quick-wittedness. There was to be a formal initiation, a ritual led by Peter and encouraged by Bemba G, in which company rules would be devised and posted on a tree. When this was completed, K.T. (who I noticed had one foot longer than the other) read them aloud, stopping just long enough after each item for the company to respond: 'Agreed!'

Mornings

Make sure everyone eats plenty of fruit.

Always work on mathematics first thing after breakfast.

Games everyone can learn or join in: animal games, tag, arm-wrestling, hide-and-seek, and dancing.

Afternoons

Playtime: work with words for *Juliohs Siza*!

Child soldiers' stories.

Rest.

Share food.

Sleep (don't make noise).

They had finished their mathematics – an introduction to trigonometry – and Hinga had put on 1970s soul music for them to dance to, their most popular pastime now that they were free to relish the suppleness of their bodies. 'Put Barry White!' K.T. bellowed to Hinga, who obliged, making this the first hit of the day's session. The children joined in the singing, trying to make their teenage voices as gravelly as possible. And the moves? For Citizen, lewd and suggestive gyrating; Peter made brilliant leaps into the air; Victor, twirling palms like a chorus girl; Abu, limbo dancer *extraordinaire*. Such dazzling exuberance from the girls too. At the instant when Bemba G shouted, 'Playtime!', everyone stopped what they were doing and focused on their story work. No one missed the moment, no one complained about the hard work.

Then they were at it for several hours until early evening: learning to combine words with actions – standing tall with arms raised, 'Friends, Romans, countrymen, lend me your ears,' and bending down, palms open and outstretched, 'I come to bury Caesar, not to praise him.'

Everyone was given something to do. Even the smallest ones were enthusiastic about learning new words. They enjoyed reciting long speeches in unison and when Bemba G said this practice no longer made sense and they would have 'roles' instead, the result was not good. How careless we were not to realize they would look reproachfully at this idea of 'rank'. A rapid explanation about sharing and fun had to be posted for all to see.

Bemba G took charge of casting, calling us to assemble around Black Rock for his pronouncements:

'The big man is Julius Caesar, a great soldier,' he explained. 'He comes back from war but people plot to kill him.'

'Oh, shame,' murmured the child soldiers.

'But his ghost comes to haunt the plotters,' he went on.

'And they die?'

'Yes; they fight among themselves.'

'Good,' said Abu. 'I want to be in the plotters' group.'

'Me too.'

'And me.'

'Yes, you two. Abu, you will be Cassius. Hinga, you will be Anthony. I think I will play Brutus.'

'So it won't be just the child soldiers?' I asked.

I was unsure whether I had slipped in an awkward question, as for a moment Bemba G sat there stiffly, continuing to look at the cast of characters.

'They will have enough to do. I will play Brutus.' I knew

by his intonation that he wanted to *play* but I did not care; I was content to assist in whatever way seemed necessary.

'All right,' I agreed. Then I repeated to the group, 'Hinga is Mark Anthony. Abu is Cassius, you, Bemba G, as Brutus – that was quick and easy.'

'And I want to be the great soldier,' added Peter.

'But he gets killed.' Abu sounded concerned.

'But his death is the main event – everyone has to think again,' Bemba G assured them.

'Do they plot and fight in the bush like us?' asked Victor.

'Yes, in the bush, like you.'

'Will there be a part for me?' Miriam had left Baby with Hinga again, but Isata had followed closely behind her.

'How about the wife of Brutus?'

'Who is Brutus?'

'Me,' affirmed Bemba G.

'Oh, Mr G, you are too old for me!' She giggled behind her right hand. He took the other hand and said:

'You are my true and honourable wife

As dear to me as are the ruddy drops

That visit my sad heart.'

'That's beautiful.' Isata put her hands together to clap and off went the two girls.

'You will be soldiers and townspeople.' Bemba G waved his hand over several heads. They bobbed away leaving the two of us sitting on Black Rock.

'Those are the main parts, but I'd like Citizen to have one of the smaller roles,' I said.

'But he hasn't opened his mouth yet.'

It was my turn to negotiate for something. In all the days I'd known Bemba G, I had been cautious, patiently expecting his decisions but clearly not pushing my own. 'We might have to work with him to learn a few lines, but I'm sure he can do it.' With a look of incredulity, he put the playscript to one side, stood up and scuffled away a few feet. I shouted after him: 'He just needs time, a bit of time.'

He faltered to a stop and nodded. 'Find him something then, give him time.'

I smiled back, relieved that he understood. I searched the body of the script for a small part for Citizen; it had to be a speaking part. I longed for the moment when he dared to speak again. Then I looked around the compound for him.

Citizen was standing on top of a boulder, waving at someone approaching from the thicket. I watched the friendly glow scattered across his face, the boyish enthusiasm as his arms swung into the air when he jumped down to greet Peter. They were young boys, affectionate, true and sturdy. Off they went together, their black figures disappearing into the forest, Peter's shoulders higher than Citizen's, acting as an umbrella to the two of them. They were brothers at arms. Citizen needed a big brother maybe more than a parent, I thought. Turning back to the list of characters, I chose for his role Lucius, a servant to Brutus. With Bemba G playing Brutus, Citizen would in effect be in his care.

Before I set off to tell Citizen to prepare to take part, I had to massage a place in my head that had begun to hurt. The scalp was very dry though not damaged, not as bad as it might have been, but nevertheless in need of care. It is the only part of me that bears the scars of this journey. I massaged my head, moved my fingers over the scalp, encouraging the tired parts to relax. At last my head began to feel better. 'Better,' I said to myself, standing up from Black Rock. I waited by the forest edge but Peter and Citizen showed no sign of emerging. A lively mood had overtaken the child soldiers. The very idea of a play about soldiers had appealed to them.

Victor put his finger on it: 'Do they fight in the bush like us?'

147

'Just like you . . .'

*Our tale begins in a beautiful land, a land inhabited by free
and brave people though some have slave ancestors. To a city
sore from internal strife, where warring, shifting groups never
rest, returns a victorious general, famous both at home and
abroad. The common people swell to honour this ruler supreme,
celebrating their great good fortune. But among those in the
body politic the mood is different – they plot, they meet at
night and plan his demise.*

*They scheme to be rid of him with clever speeches and devi-
ous ways. Unnatural happenings! Uneasy alliances! Some
claim exalted motives for their actions. Others hunger for power,
long for equal glory.*

*What results is a bloody end: the general's demise. Then the
stage is set for a long civil war, defeat and the death of thousands . . .*

Miriam punctuated my pride in this synposis. Leaning
close to me and in lowered voice, she explained: 'No point in
telling them the whole story. We're doing it bit by bit. You
have no idea how quickly child soldiers forget things like
this. They will remember one part and forget the next.'

I felt suddenly sad. 'Look, they just want to play,' she
whispered. 'They want to dress up, you know, and say clever
things.'

Miriam had a way of introducing common sense into our
lives and I recognized at once the voice of a precocious daughter of a bossy mama. What a child-woman, all of fourteen
years old, taking such pains to conceal her desire to dress up
and play a part! Then she suddenly asked, 'Is all the big parts
for men and boys?' and my heart melted for her.

'What do you like doing, Miriam?'

'Well, Miss Julia, I love to be by the river with my friends.

We go there to launder, fetch water and meet our boyfriends. Especially Saturday. We make an arrangement: "Meet me by such and such." Or sometimes I go by myself in the evening to think. It is so peaceful and quiet.'

'And do you swim?'

'Oh, yes, and when people come from the city, they don't know how to swim. No city girl knows how to swim and we say, "Come over here and we will dive you."' She laughed.

'Dive you? Like knock them over in the water?'

She laughed again. 'We also play games in the water. We form a circle. There are loads of stones and sand underneath. Then you pick a dish you want to make and you remember all the ingredients – say, potato leaf dish. You go under the water and come up, saying each one. "Payemba says I should give you salt, Payemba says I should give you rice, Payemba says I should give you pepper."'

She loved this game. 'And when it's finish you come up and say, "Payemba is dead!"'

'And then?'

'You celebrate in the water. Splashing the water!'

'We must go to the river one day,' I replied.

We crossed the compound to Black Rock, which had curved itself into a semicircular bench, roomy enough for most of them. Storytelling was in progress. For this, simple guidelines had been agreed: first, true stories about soldier days; second, inventions that everyone could understand. Whenever they heard a well-told tale they applauded loudly and cheered, like children anywhere. But for unclear stories the failing storyteller was pelted with criticism. That morning I witnessed one such assault. The boy in question was Victor. He did his best, but the hurdy-gurdy of his mind blocked his attempt to tell them what he'd experienced during the war.

'Go away!'

'Go away!'

'Use the B-M-E way Bemba showed us!' K.T. reminded him.

'Yes, use B-M-E!' Isata urged also.

Victor, his eyes glazed, blurted out something. He was not making sense. Non-sequiturs, babble poured from his lips. Embarrassed by these strange dark nuggets of a meaningless tale, some moved away. Those who stayed began chanting:

'Beginning, middle and end!'

'Beginning, middle and end!'

They shook their fists at him, shooed him away, calling out: 'It's time for another tale,' and mulishly, less able to speak than before, Victor drifted away.

It was not long after the casting was done, two or three days later, that Bemba G met his first hurdle in the play-acting. They had begun to work on a fight scene. Hinga, convinced of the necessity to show a real fight, had picked up his knife and descended, bare-chested, on his opponent. As we realized what he was doing, everyone began screaming at him to put it down.

'Drop it, drop it!' shouted Bemba G. 'This is not bush fighting.'

Black Rock flashed bright lights, switching on and off, and then the compound went dark. At that everything seemed to go back to normal. Hinga, looking bemused as though struck by temporary insanity, seemed to lose balance on standing up. Then, without warning, Bemba G started to move Hinga's arms and bend his legs, changing the boy's shape. In front he placed one arm, next adjusted a leg, then the other arm up in the air. Again another position, then movement. We all watched for several minutes as this operation went on.

Two of the others tried it.

'No bush fighting. I am showing you how to stage fight,' called Bemba G.

They reassembled as he continued to work with Hinga then left him in a pose.

'Come, watch me one more time.' Taking aside Abu who was playing Cassius, K.T. and Victor, he performed before them a series of moves like t'ai chi, his arms and legs flowing in graceful rhythm like water cascading. He demonstrated. They followed.

I watched the others while they watched Abu, K.T. and Victor. They did not realize I was watching them, that they had become spectacular.

'Look.' He moved again and this time his arm seemed to cut through one of the boys who was playing a soldier:

'Yet, countrymen, O, yet hold up your heads!'

Throughout the afternoon there were further demonstrations, with Bemba G holding the children's arms and legs in new positions whenever necessary until each one, in turn, learned how to make the slow and liquid moves.

'It is like fighting with the air,' said Hinga.

'You don't see anything, you don't feel anything,' said K.T.

'But you feel powerful,' said Hinga.

> *Dear child*
> *You feel the flow of blood in your veins*
> *The beat of your heart*
> *You are powerful, indeed.*

All was in order; we were making progress. In the following days they spent much time tending to the original *Julius Caesar*, but between the acts the old general repeatedly raised his bloody head, grabbed one of the children by the neck and hauled him into chaos. Victor was the first victim Caesar unsettled. I can still see him in my mind's eye, being sucked into that intemperate violence like a woody branch into a cyclone. Between the everyday acts in the compound the bloody Caesar and his pack were always exercising their influence on the child soldiers and they, small boys and girls, were all desperate to tell their own stories.

I was whiling away one afternoon sitting on a bench and swaying my legs when Victor came and stood before me, shouting: 'My head is blowing up!'

'What?'

'My head is blowing up!'

I told him to sit on the ground in front of me rather than on the bench, so that I could examine his head. I saw meaningless letters – M Z L – sculpted on the back of the scalp. I registered two wounds still healing from when the inscription was made. Obviously he could not see these but he must have felt them, sensed them.

'Victor, give me your hand.'

I took the short black fingers and helped him retrace the letters: 'Do you remember this?'

He folded up my question and put it away. He said, 'The war entered my village in ninety-one. We had to flee to Liberia.' Sitting on the bare ground, he began twitching his toes as though a song were going through his mind. Nervously, he bounced his legs up and down, the knees rising six inches into the air. His body jigged and he threw his back roughly against the bench in some frenzied dance. But there could be no music in his head, no melody, no rhythm.

I thought, *This boy should be sitting on his parents' airy porch eating a mango.* I heard him sniffing loudly like a dog and I thought, *This boy should smell of perfumed soap, clean sheets and a leather satchel.*

I went on: 'And what happened then?'

'I was captured, separated from my people, my mother and my three sisters. My father was dead already. I had to fight on the war front.' He told me how he fought in Liberia and when he returned his village had been destroyed.

Flies hummed about his head. I shooed them away.

Victor mumbled: 'My head gives me trouble.'

Every few minutes he scratched the scalp. I tried to help by rubbing his head in my palms. I held his head still and asked him to sit on the bench beside me. We sat together, his head in my hands. It was clear from the look in his eyes that he was not sleeping well. His stomach bulged against his shirt. His lips were dry and on his face was the beginning of a rash.

Then he said, very distinctly: 'My head is blowing up.'

I asked him about his life before the war. There was no reply, so I tried a second time and a third. 'Can't you tell me what you liked before?'

He stood up and walked about, then returned, carrying a branch in his hand. He said, 'I had plenty of things I liked, but why should I tell you any?' Then he was quiet.

'Tell me something. I want to spy your life,' I said, to soften him up.

'I know,' he said and began to bring out the Victor he had been, the Victor who was lying motionless somewhere under some other sky.

Victor, long separated from his people, cast a long dark shadow when he sat with me. He made me an offering from the darkness of his memory of things he used to like – food roasted outside; milk in his own cup; milk moustache on his lips; his harmonica; his bicycle.

I looked at him for a long while before saying: 'Tell me something about your life in the war. What did you do?'

'If you want to hear it, let me tell you. I am many people, you know.' He was describing the bad ones.

'I know,' I said, waiting to face one of the demons.

He told me how every morning he would swig the blood of ex-prisoners and fresh blood of the recently killed: it was warm and filled his stomach, but it gave him a wild head and a thin voice. The more he drank, the less he remembered who he was. He was not the Victor he had once known himself to be; not a whole boy of flesh and blood, but pieces dismembered, blown into valleys and over the seas.

I looked past his head. 'It wasn't your fault, Victor . . .' My voice trailed off.

'What can I do now? What work must I do?'

'After this you will go to school perhaps or learn a trade.' It sounded obvious but in truth I had no idea what would become of him. He did not respond. He stood up and dragged the branch in the earth. He scratched his head.

'Don't you want to talk any more?' He craned his head as though listening for something. Perhaps the Victor he had known was coming. But no, here was Victor. He didn't know how to piece himself together and that was why his head was blowing up. He came and sat with me.

Rubbing the hardened skin on the soles of his feet calmed him and helped him forget. I put the soles of his feet in the prayer position. We sat together in the late afternoon, and swayed past the daily ritual of acting in the compound beyond.

Now that they had movements and roles, the child soldiers were enthusiastic. Most of them wanted to act, to say something; even if they had only a few lines, or one line to shout out, they were proud of their speeches. But there were occasional skirmishes on other matters: entering too soon or occupying too much space. Miriam and Peter took it upon themselves to sort out those minor problems, sensing, I think, that a confrontation would put paid to 'playtime'.

Several days seemed to rush together and it is difficult for me to separate one from another. Day by day the children just grew into their characters and into a company. Miriam, Peter and Isata made bold, unstinting attempts to help others learn their lines and come and go at the right moment, projecting their voices across the scene. It was up to Isata to indicate to each actor if he was going too fast or too slow by counting his strides for him: 'Four too many!' she called out at Hinga during one rehearsal. They pulled together to make it work.

Hinga had been watching me carefully, perhaps trying to assess whether I was a conventionally serious adult or a wayward visitor with nothing better to do. I caught him looking at me sideways whenever I was talking to Bemba G about the children. And the day after I had helped Victor, Hinga came to say his head was also 'blowing up'.

'How do you mean?' I asked him.

'It is open wide, can't you see, Julia? It is raining in my brain!' He laughed, throwing his head back to the sky.

'Well, shut it up or get an umbrella,' I quipped as he ran off, guffawing while I shouted at his back: 'There's no way I am massaging everyone's feet day in and day out!'

But some of the children took things very seriously. K.T. was concerned about settling back into ordinary life. He said, 'If I was a rich man, I'd pay a doctor to put my foot right, but you see I am poor for now.'

'What will you do to become rich?'

'Be a lawyer and pass laws to bring peace.'

We were sitting under halfway silk-cotton tree, and he had the play book in his lap.

'K.T., which one do you prefer, Krio or Shakespeare's language?'

The thirteen-year-old moved his head rhythmically from side to side, looking at both scripts: 'They are both sweet to talk. I like this Brutus speech, here:

'"Grant that, and then is death a benefit:
So are we Caesar's friends, that have abridged

His time of fearing death. Stoop, Romans, stoop,
And let us bathe our hands in Caesar's blood
Up to the elbows, and besmear our swords;
Then walk we forth, even to the market-place,
And waving our red weapons o'er our heads
Let's all cry, 'Peace, freedom, and liberty!'""

'Shall I try the Krio version, K.T.? Correct me if I go wrong, will you?' I read:

"*'Na so; dat min sey dai dohn du sohm gud.*
Wi na Siza fren, wey wi dohn shohtin
In tem foh freyd dai. Una butu,
Meyk wi was wi an na Siza blohd
Rich wi elbo, en rohb sohm pan wi sohd
Den wi go waka go to di makit,
Dey paspas wi red sohd oba wi eyd,
Meyk wi ohl ala: Pis, fridohm en libati.'"

'Again, Julia!'
'Yes, I need to practise.'
We laughed, and talked of the play, his future career and dreams. K.T. was an only child, with a soft-spoken manner and beautiful Krio turns of phrase that it occurred to me sounded classical. Even his simplest use of words – 'I apologize for my left hand' and 'I did not spoil the laws' – were redolent of an ancient world.

The next day the ground was damp and cold so we settled in one of the open huts to spend the afternoon working on the pivotal act of the play, Act 3, which opens with the arrival and murder of Caesar in the Capitol. The group was, as usual, solidly there and ready once Bemba G called. They put aside their games and finished conversations, the better to work: Hinga, Peter, Victor, Citizen, Miriam, all of them waiting for Bemba G to lead the next act, bring out something new.

'I'm not going to tell you how to start this part, just do it as you did yesterday,' he said, emanating calm steady focus, 'and think about the words.'

Caesar and the soothsayer began:

> 'The Ides of March are come.
> Ay, Caesar, but not gone.'

The children ran through it three times, improving in flow and movement each time. Then they began again. This was the fourth time of going for the beginning of Act 3. Peter, the only one who had not learned his lines before that rehearsal, was beginning to feel the verse. I thought I saw him shiver once or twice with recognition at:

> '"Be not fond
> To think that Caesar bears such rebel blood
> That will be thawed from the true quality
> With that which melteth fools."'

He came to the end of his speech and frowned deeply: 'Let's stop,' he called out.

'Why do you want to stop?' asked Bemba G.

'I feel it, I feel I can't trust anyone here,' answered Peter seriously. There was no pretence in his statement. Peter was never one to lie. He was implacably and precisely honest. He was becoming Caesar, sensing that his murder was about to take place, smelling treachery as it pushed to its conclusion. He stopped still. Silent. He had everyone's attention: Citizen, Victor, all of them were there in the Capitol. They had become conspirators.

'Let's go on!' shouted an impatient Hinga from the side, bringing the group back to work.

'OK, let's go on again,' agreed Peter.

Standing well back from the action, waiting in the wings, Hinga as Mark Anthony hated the duplicity of the scene. Anyone looking closely at him, as I did then, could see the fury that was starting to rise in his body. He wanted the scene to be closed and pushed aside, finished without any more breaks. He wanted to show Caesar that it was over. *This is the fucking end of it, Caesar. Mark Anthony tells you so!*

They had entered the politics of the Capitol as though they had always known this moment would come. It might have been the power of drama and the effect of the place. By early evening when the sun was no longer our companion, the atmosphere grew thick. I sat immobile on a bench, following the actions and words. This scene was becoming so familiar yet was somehow unexpected too. They seemed like politicians and fighters facing one another with hidden weapons, smuggling ammunition in their clothes.

Caesar entered the Senate for the last time, the conspirators milled around him, moving steadfastly from plot to action, from talk to rebel blood. It was as if they had slipped effortlessly into another time, reminding each other that these verses were alive and useful.

'Liberty! Freedom! Tyranny is dead!'

'Run hence, proclaim, cry it about the streets.'

By the end of the seventh run-through that day, their movements were smoother and more subtle. They had needed no instructions on movements since Bemba's earlier class on 'fighting'; they had instinctively found whatever was needed, their own gestures almost always apt. Once or twice Bemba G stopped them to practise a mime around the body of Caesar, stepped in to make them hold the positions and see the total picture.

'Go fetch all your weapons again,' he called out. They ran from their places and returned with the guns and make-believe guns they had arrived with so many days before. They reassembled with their weapons to hand. Bemba G called out: 'All stop for one minute. Freeze!'

In an instant it was done. They froze.

What happened next took only two seconds to experience but would take hours to describe adequately. In appearance nothing changed. The child soldiers held their positions, the life of the forest continued, but something else was being transmitted. Call it an ending of amnesia, if you like, or some collective unconscious that I did not know existed. But the child soldiers got it, meeting themselves in the play. They understood their place in the scheme of things. I suddenly felt that we could not be alone in this: Bemba G and thirty-five child soldiers and me. The ancestors must be looking on – the generations of men, women and children who had led us to this place, this moment. I shouted out:

'We are not alone, there are other people here watching us, listening – can't you feel them?'

The child soldiers had stopped, frozen in their positions.

A long time had passed since they first completed that scene but if I closed my eyes, I would find them in the same places, timeless human sculptures against the purplish night sky.

Between the acting of a dreadful thing
And the first motion, all the interim is
Like a phantasma or a hideous dream . . .

Nine

It was late morning when Miriam, Isata and I caught sight of some of the boys on their way to bathe in the river. In the lead were K.T. and Thomas, carrying a large, circular net Bemba G had lent them for fishing. Trailing at the rear came Peter and Citizen, who apparently had not wanted to swim that day. Usually girls bathe separately from boys so Miriam's reluctance did not surprise me, but after we talked it over she agreed to come down with Isata and me for company. Miriam sat on the banks hugging her knees close and watched as we prepared to slip into the glinting waters. I tried to persuade her to join in but she shook her head and, with a look half annoyed and half amused, remained silent.

The silky, sweet-tasting waters enveloped me as I swam rhythmically up and down, dipping my face below the surface. When tired, I stood up in the middle of the river letting the ripples tease my waist and thighs. Sharp stones dug into my feet, but it was clear nearer the top. Afloat again, I came upon water-babies, Isata and Citizen, keeping company in the depths. She screwed up her face and he grimaced back. The river shifted between them like a playful friend, massaging their slim legs pleasurably. Isata was the first to emerge. She needed help styling her hair and ran to Miriam who was still on the bank. Miriam made her crouch down, letting the moisture run on to her lap, and towelled her dry. For a long time, Miriam worked, squeezing out the moisture, brushing and parting the locks ready for the long hair to be plaited up once more.

The boys raced, swimming breaststroke down the river to where Miriam was hairdressing on the bank. 'Dive him, dive him,' they shouted whenever another boy jumped in, and those already in the water swooped upon the newcomer, attempting to knock him off-balance. K.T. liked floating on his back, kicking his legs up from time to time, and bumping into Citizen. But Citizen swam on his own. He was a strong swimmer. He pushed himself up and down the river, flipping over to wave to Isata and Miriam whenever he reached their side. Then, metamorphosis, he became a ruddy-brown butterfly boy, his arms circling the air in rapid motion.

We spent all afternoon on the reedy banks, lazing in the sunshine. Some of the boys who had been fishing found a spot under a tree, far away from us, where they could show off their catch to one another. It was dusk when K.T. and Peter came out of the water, put on their shorts and headed back. Miriam and Isata had left much earlier. Dipping my toes in for one final wash, I realized Citizen was the only child left. 'Let's go and join the others.' I glanced at him every so often to make sure all was well. He was standing by some dry bushes, his rounded back towards me. I assumed he was urinating, but ten minutes later he was still there. 'Come on, let's go.'

He was crouching down on the ground, oblivious to my gaze and ignoring my entreaties. I moved closer, sensing something was amiss. 'Hey, come on – what's happening?'

He stood still, signalling distrust by turning his eyes down and away from me. He was giving me a wide berth and wanted me to reciprocate. Had I kept my distance and refrained from intruding perhaps he would have joined me, but he was not interested. I moved right up to him and looked down to see that he was holding a knife with a short blade.

'You know weapons are not allowed.' He was silent; a sphere of distrust moved between us. 'Give it to me.'

At that moment he turned, gripping the knife more tightly and pointing the blade in my direction. It was all but dark now. A sudden fierce terror billowed inside me but my feet were rooted to the spot. Citizen held on to the knife, proving he was in charge. A boy soldier to the last, he stared at my anxious face, knowing that I wanted to run but could not. Gritting my teeth, I moved away. He was coming after me, his footsteps gathering pace. I surged ahead, angry and determined to be back with the others, but still he came, eventually running until he reached my side. I held my breath, refusing to look at him.

And then he spoke: 'Wait,' he whispered.

I spat a bilious liquid from my mouth and began to shake, my feet and ankles giving way. I found it hard to stand – to stand up to the boy soldier.

He spoke again: 'Please wait.' Taking care to protect the blade from my hand, he gave up the knife, which fell on to my quivering palm. In an instant, I felt deep gratitude towards him and rage that he had tested my trust.

Within ten minutes we were back at Bemba G's – two silent figures, so full of fear we could have blocked the light of the sun. We went our separate ways.

That was the only time the child soldiers saw me angry enough to avoid their company. Once the knife was back in the weapons store, I drank some water, washed my face and retreated to a quiet spot. One of the boys, a skinny, pimply chatterbox, came to tell me that Peter and Hinga were fighting over Sally, but I sent him away, trying to doze or at least forget. With my arms above my head, I gazed at the skies and drifted off.

When I awoke, Citizen was standing over me. He had obviously been waiting patiently for some time. He passed me a cup of cold water and waited until I was upright again.

'Citizen, is something wrong? What do you have there?' As I reached for the brown object he was holding, he bent forward trying to conceal whatever it was. 'Show me.'

He hesitated but then my outstretched arm was rewarded as he placed a block of wood in my hand. It was about twelve-inches long and four-inches wide and weighed no more than a couple of pounds. Into the grubby wood he had carved or rather dug out his number: 439K, the cold beauty of which stored the mystery of his time in the war. I ran my fingers along the razor-sharp incisions. Citizen had memorized the feel of 439K on his skin. Like a pianist committing a sonata to memory, he had learned it digit by digit so that he could play it out in the dark. For him there would be no applause, but I thought, looking at the discarded lump of dead wood, someone somewhere should be screaming. I tried returning the block of wood to him, but could not give it up. Citizen, lingering behind me, looked relieved, as though he had given up a world.

The block of wood rested on the mat before me. I could barely keep my eyes off it, so assertive was its presence. Citizen had needed to make it and I had needed to see it. He must have asked himself many questions as to 'why' he had become 439K and finding no satisfactory answer had put 439K somewhere else. With no adequate answer of my own, I began with a wish for the future: that the 439K scar would not follow him to his grave, that Citizen be free of 439K.

The child soldiers were readying themselves for bed when I made up my mind what we should do with that block. I found Citizen with Abu and asked him to follow me. Not hesitating this time, he came. I pushed into the thickest part of the forest where the trees, a dense mass of vegetation, remained undisturbed by humans, to a quiet place, yards from where the others were.

'Let's bury this,' I suggested, 'let's lay it to rest.'

He agreed.

'Is this a good place?'

He nodded.

We had found a small lush tree that was not as large as many that surrounded it but had constructed its own arch of leaves descending almost to the ground. We took sticks and began to scratch at the soil under that arch. The earth was dark brown on the surface, but as we dug it became a paler ochre and moist. The clods resisted, but on our hands and knees we dug a hole almost two-feet deep. While he was in the war Citizen had learned how to make do with bare earth as bed, comfort, shithole. He had learned how the beautiful landscape could be transformed into tunnels, caves and graves; he had tumbled into an adult awareness of the earth. As we worked together, I was humbled by his toughness. He went at it with both hands, forcing the earth to part, tearing out stones that were in his way. He worked hard and fast, producing a deep hole in the ground. Then he took the block and buried it. Its descent was quick and clean. Citizen pushed back the soil, patting it down until 439K was covered.

On the way back, walking in front, his head upright, he kept his hands cradled before him as though to protect his clothing from their mud. He stepped lightly over the forest floor and ignored me completely. Against the white snows of the Antarctic his small black frame would not have looked more distinct: when you are as lonely as that, even nature cannot touch you.

By the time we reached the compound, I could barely keep my eyes open but I saw him to his mat; as he lay down to sleep, I covered his legs with my own lappa.

I slept soundly and had no idea what time it was when I awoke and walked down to the river to bathe. On my return I was keen to see how rehearsals were progressing. Across the forest compound noises poured. One voice, another voice, a third child's voice protesting, shouting: loud – Peter's voice; anxious, painful – Miriam's voice; the high-pitched addition – Isata's voice. All were telling me the same thing, commanding my attention: 'all day long', 'just sleeping', 'won't wake up'. They were telling me that Citizen had been sleeping for a whole day.

Citizen awoke later that afternoon, looking rested. There was a warm glow on his face: no sign that he needed our attention – he was taking care of himself. He ate some fruit and nuts and, rubbing his eyes like a toddler, fell asleep again. I stood over him and looked down at his face. His eyelashes flickered through a number of scenes, Rolodex fast-forward then backwards.

What did he dream? Did he remember the face of a man who could be trusted, a grandfather who wore black trousers and a white cotton shirt, and smelt of warm cinnamon and bent down, planting a kiss on his cheek? Another scene must have come into view because he rolled over, still smiling, a child again, afloat in a world of mother's making:

'Sing the song, then,' she urges. He begins singing for her, copying the tune on the radio. He knows the chorus, has memorized it well: 'Happy birthday to you, happy birthday to you, happy birthday . . .' The music breaks. Another time, another tempo. How the colours and sounds of memory fuse and separate! How brightly the fruits ripen above his head, turning yellow then green and red. How much must he stretch to reach them? In his sleep he raises a hand, beckons an extended tree branch towards him, willing it to cascade fruits upon his head. Come down, ripe, sweet and bountiful fruits. There was his mother walking towards him from the house, her skin a burnt sienna in the sunlight. With great strides she advances; he is happy and

excited. 'Leave that tree alone.' The branch is lower now, its green leaves hanging tantalizingly above his head. He rolls over on to his stomach, switching his view to the ochre-coloured earth. It is a good year: the trees have spread their branches generously across the wall at the end of their field, from the house there is a fine view of the harvest to come. She is there now, standing by him: 'I told you to leave that tree. Come in with me now.' He follows, knowing that at any moment he will float again and be merged with her. His arms stretch back to the place that was home. He wakes.

When Citizen woke, the child soldiers were already working on the play. He looked about. There was no longer a dream to continue; he was awake, but he did not join the others immediately, he could not without betraying the boy in the dream. Instead he sat on his heels and let the brilliant sunshine lather his brown back, remembering how his mother had touched him. He looked like a freshly washed child, a much loved child.

Nothing disturbed the tranquillity of our days until the following sweltering morning when even Miriam, always at home in the rainforest heat, complained of feeling lethargic as we prepared some fruits.

'It is so hot, Julia.' She had taken to calling my attention by emphasizing my name in a way that excluded the others.

'It is very, very hot, Miriam,' I replied.

The next morning, the youngest children were slow to rise and when slices of orange and chunks of mango were offered to them at breakfast they examined the fruit with suspicion. Even Baby, given a small plug of orange by Isata, spat it out. Across the compound two boys were gesticulating, troubled by the flies buzzing about their heads as they prepared for the storytelling session.

Bemba G appeared, chomping on his morning chawstick, a fistful of roots in each hand. He called the children to gather round, chewing and spitting on the wooden stick while they assembled. 'Now this is the time I have been waiting for,' he said. 'We are going to perform the play. You will be ready.'

'When will they be ready?' I asked. The child soldiers did not follow what he was saying.

'Five days!' he answered.

He walked purposefully back to his hut, leaving me with the group. The idea of a public performance of *Julius Caesar* caused some giggles, teasing and a display of vanity. From that day onwards brushing hair, grooming skin, standing tall and 'going away to *focus*' became the style of child soldiery. In the compound the mood had changed.

Citizen's shyness did not change much but he seemed more at ease. He knew he had some lines and would be expected to speak, to open up in front of adults, and the other child soldiers knew this too. Whenever, by chance, someone left the book lying about, another child soldier would retrieve it. Citizen, no; he never went near the book. But just as he never claimed it, so Abu and Hinga almost snatched it from others' hands. These two were enchanted by the lines and engrossed by the actions.

Then it was time to take the child soldiers through their actions, remind them to look decisive when coming on and going off. Most of them listened dutifully, some chatted about going fishing or setting up a dance competition. One endless party of dancing, storytelling, eating and sleeping – no one would give it up willingly. But Bemba G was thinking about when we would be ready to leave. He had never said we could stay as long as we wanted, of that I was certain.

'Hinga says you must come and make the stage.'

Miriam sounded tired. She was leaning on a typical African broom with twigs tied together at one end, her eyes watering as she yawned. She was talking to Citizen who was lying in a hammock. No one else knew about the block. But

Miriam guessed that he was changing and seemed cross that she did not understand why.

He rolled out of the hammock on to the ground in one movement. After the earlier rain, the earth was soft though the sun blazed down as brightly as ever. On the ground some-one had left a calabash with some cashew nuts to which Citizen helped himself.

Miriam thrust the broom into his hands. 'Learn to sweep,' she said. She watched while he busied himself sweeping dust from the compound floor, occasionally stopping to admire his work. The area we had chosen for the stage was taking shape. Hinga pulled up the stubborn weeds, with a hoe, K.T. broke up clods of earth and Victor cleared away these and the small stones.

'Put them far away,' called out Hinga, not wanting Victor to misunderstand the task.

The boys laboured all afternoon in comradely silence, heads bent, torsos bare but gleaming, making their compound ready for visitors. Halfway through the afternoon, they stopped and took a rest. 'Where is Peter?' asked Hinga. He had not seen his friend all day. 'Peter said we shouldn't bother to make a stage. He says, "This is the bush," and the bush is hard and a terrible place to fight,' Victor chimed.

K.T. said Peter was right, but the bush could change. 'Shame,' he said. It was a shame. Peter had turned morose and was influencing the younger ones, who looked to him to indicate their feelings so that now some were thinking the play a waste of time. Sitting in the sunshine, under halfway silk-cotton tree, the group finished the calabash of cashews, then went to find cold water to drink. 'Put lime inside the water,' suggested K.T. to the rest.

After drinking the lime-flavoured water, they finished cleaning the stage under the clear blue afternoon sky. In the dying heat of the day, Hinga had another good idea.

'Let's make seats for them,' he said. Although they had already worked hard in the sun, and patches of sweat darkened their shorts, they agreed to construct seating with whatever materials came to hand. K.T. and Hinga pulled a huge log with a scooped-out centre and shouted loudly to one another:

'Turn this way, turn, turn! Now go back. Slow, wait, slow!'

Hinga, as the boss, revealed great physical strength and a confidence that I found impressive. K.T. stiffened when Hinga insisted he alter his position: 'Do it like me,' he was calling. In the end they managed to move it, and rolled it over to lean against the bottom of Black Rock. They sighed with satisfaction and sat on it. They had needed more seating. Black Rock looked very different – no longer a long bench for reclining; now it shot up into the sky like a tower and sent out a gentle white light, illuminating the darkening compound.

The day following Bemba G's announcement, he made a salad of mangoes for breakfast using kerosene mangoes, Guinea mangoes and sweet-sharp mangoes. Thomas, usually so thoughtful and appreciative, said he was sick of fruit, why not have a plate of rice for breakfast? He was not the only one to complain. Others moaned about the mathematics or the work, which they quit early to play the drums with Corporal Kalashnikov. Skirmishing broke out. The Corporal, disliking the interference, hurled his drum at Isata's head. She howled.

By late afternoon, I had the impression the compound was turning against us when Miriam caught a bird that had fallen out of the tree, its wings twisted. Baby crumpled into tears. Abandoning the company even before we had shared our food, Bemba G went to sit outside his hut. He brewed a little coffee and smoked some blackish tobacco.

Victor shouted: 'Why no one give me a cigarette to change up my mind?'

'Nothing to smoke here,' came a lazy reply.

'Let's dance!' called out one helpless soul.

'No, I want a cigarette,' Victor said again.

K.T. dragged his foot along the ground towards my bench, waiting to see if I could come up with something: 'You have a cigarette for Victor?'

I shook my head. He dragged his foot back to the group. What to expect but an hour or two on the hard bench, more waiting.

Later Peter appeared from nowhere, carrying a long stick across his chest, and jumped on to Black Rock. Victor, yards away, turned and sprinted towards him: 'The noble Peter is ascended. Silence.'

With practised ease, Peter imitated Bemba G's style:

'Krio boys, country boys and lovers – listen.'

Laughter broke out: Peter had pointed to Sally and Miriam when he said 'lovers'.

'You all know me and trust me. Some of you fought with me in the bush so you know me well and trust me even more. So listen when I talk to you. Bemba G is a good man but he doesn't know your needs as I do. He wants to make a performance with us. What for? So people come and look at us, laugh at us? Who wants people to come and laugh at us? Anybody here?'

'No.' Peter pushed on. 'This is what I say. If Bemba G wants us to perform for him, he must give us something. Something to make us better. Something to make us strong!'

'Money!' shouted Victor.

'Not money, something to take, some powder fix to make us strong. So if people come and laugh at us, what will we care? We will be stronger than them. They will be like so many little insects fleeing in the dust before us. Where is Bemba G? Let him come meet me. If he refuses, I will cut one lip or slice one arm for him!'

'Ten cuts!' shouted Victor, running around the back of Black Rock.

'Twenty cuts!' shouted Victor dashing to the front of Black Rock.

'Twenty thousand cuts!' Victor was shouting from the back of Black Rock again.

'What do you say, everybody? Something to take!' Peter ignored Victor's cries.

'Yes.' The assembled child soldiers punctuated the darkness with their response.

'Louder!' Peter called out to the ranks beneath him.

'Yes: something to take,' they clamoured. The child soldiers followed Peter's command like chained prisoners held captive by Bemba G and demanding release.

'Powder fix!' added Victor, climbing Black Rock and thrusting an arm around Peter's shoulder. Peter gave him one look, one push and he stumbled off.

'Powder fix!' shouted Thomas, turning round to encourage others to join in. And they did. Without any break in their breathing, without any sign of disunity, they all shouted out:

'Powder fix!'

'Powder fix!'

Without a trace of doubt, standing shoulder to shoulder, they shouted:

'Powder fix!'

'Powder fix!'

Some of the boys had grabbed sticks and began beating the ground. It was obvious that Peter was waiting for them to join him on the high wire of rebellion, from which there would be no way back.

'Please, Peter, stop this! What are you trying to do? Destroy everything?' I said. He gave me and these questions a disinterested glare, pulled himself up to his full height, swung back his shoulders, pushed out his broad chest. With his solid-looking torso and right arm raised in the air, he looked impressive:

'Give us something to take,' he insisted in a low whisper that emphasized his power, 'or we will not go before strangers.'

'Yes, what if they try to destroy us?' asked K.T. He had stopped in front of me and groaned deeply as though in pain. I moved to one side to allow this one-legged boy to pass and join Thomas to my right.

'They won't do that. They'll want to hear the story.' He could not hear me above the din.

'Powder fix!'

'Powder fix!'

All the child soldiers were looking intently at Peter, still leading the chant. Their mouths looked red and sore. I caught sight of sticks and rods. If they had been cannons and guns, it would not have been more frightening. I shut my eyes. I began to tremble.

Darkness came and made things worse. The child soldiers were physically tired: this was the hour when they would normally be winding down, holding quiet conversations and gradually getting ready to sleep. Instead, increasingly agitated, their anger was rising. Sometime later, with a resignation that chilled my heart, I went to sit by halfway silk-cotton tree. The sky was clear and the moon seemed to filter down on to the heads of the child soldiers. From halfway silk-cotton tree, I saw that Miriam had taken Isata a few feeble paces away from the boys. Citizen was still in the main group but gave several quick looks across at the girls. His eyes darted back to Peter's face. He was in a different place then: a place where obedience was life.

Peter was drilling Citizen with a stare. All Citizen had to do was to let Peter have his way and he would be a safe member of the group. It would have required no effort, yet

Citizen was so aroused he refused to look back at Peter, staring instead at the ground as if conjuring up the spirits of murderous rage. Then, without raising his head an inch, he began to rush Peter, like a bull butting his head against the bigger boy. Peter grabbed him by the neck and shoved him to the ground. Citizen pulled Peter down towards him and they wrestled, kicking and punching. Citizen grabbed an arm and bit hard into Peter's flesh, leaving teeth marks. Excited, others leapt in. Victor first, then Hinga and Thomas.

Thomas pulled Peter off Citizen, shouting: 'No, no, let him go!'

Miriam leapt to her feet and dashed up to them. She dragged Citizen out of the mêlée: 'You fool,' she said, obviously upset, 'you come back to the bush to die?'

Citizen's lip was bleeding from the punches. He could not resist the slow drooping of his head, but otherwise, he was fine.

'You did well,' whispered Miriam to him. Citizen looked pleased, an air of dignity about him. Despite my recent feelings of terror, now that Citizen was out of the fray, I felt a slight softening in my stomach.

The fighting stopped. It had cleared the air. K.T. stepped up on Black Rock. 'You should apologize, Peter, to Citizen and to us all.'

But Peter would not apologize to anyone.

Although the fight was over and the shouting had stopped, some company members were not sure if Peter was right after all. They looked puzzled. Peter's willingness to challenge Bemba G and the wisdom of facing strangers worried them. Not just the youngest, either. It was not more than five minutes later when Abu and Sally, who had been totally absorbed by Peter's speech and the battle cry, looked about to see what I, Miriam, Citizen and Isata were doing and saying. Abu tugged at Sally's arm and muttered something to her. They both moved back from the larger group, though Abu was still protesting to himself, 'Maybe we will need something to take,' albeit with diminishing vigour.

Throughout the entire episode there was no sign of our old host. I left the group and went in search of Bemba G, running into him just as he was coming to see what had been going on. He had been resting, he said, but the noise had woken him.

'I don't know how long I slept,' he said, 'but I felt there was trouble.' To my gesticulating movements and drawn expression, he responded quickly:

'It is Peter again: Caesar has gone to his head.'

Bemba G approached Black Rock and the boy. 'Get down,' he said in a low, quiet voice. It was as though he wanted a private conversation with Peter, who was so whipped up into a rage that his lips were parched dry.

'We are not going on unless you give us something to take,' insisted Peter, climbing back on top of Black Rock. With his right hand in the air he signalled for others to be silent. 'Give us a powder fix,' he repeated.

Bemba G shook his head. He paced around the back of Black Rock and again in a low voice asked Peter to come down. Peter did not budge. His determination was grim and blind. He pushed both hands further up into the air and twisted both wrists in a gesture of pure defiance. The company of child soldiers retreated a little further, favouring the centre of the compound as the safest place from which to watch the confrontation. As confidently as a god who reigns the forest, Bemba G, feet wide apart, spoke directly to Black Rock itself: 'Bring Peter down.'

Black Rock split itself down the middle, emitting a flame-coloured dust. Splinters were splattered all over the dry ground; they were completely odourless chips of charcoal.

Everyone was silent. My heart stopped, then beat really

fast. There was a noise of crunching charcoal, and Bemba G, standing before Peter, said: 'You are a rude and foolish boy, Peter.' He slowly turned away. I knew he would have to do more to put the matter to rest. He walked around the child soldiers. 'Wait here, wait for me,' he instructed them.

To me he whispered, 'Stay with them; they are afraid.'

During his absence the child soldiers were again agitated, asking whether Peter was right or not and not easily reassured by me.

'But Peter can drink blood,' Thomas insisted. 'Peter is very brave.'

Twitching and jerking, Victor thrashed about. Citizen looked calm and pleased to have broken up the revolt. He sat far away with Miriam and Isata and two others. Bemba G was taking too long and I decided to go and find him. Just as before, I bumped into him coming to rejoin us. He was carrying a jug of water into which he scattered some brownish powder.

'You are right, all of you; there will be fear, but it will be small. The fear for fighting is like this.' He opened his arms out, stretching his fingertips into the air. He told them how fear for fighting comes into the body, making it cold at night. He explained how it presses on the bowels; how they empty themselves before you know; how fear in fighting sits inside your belly so that when you find food, the belly cannot take it.

'Is that fear in fighting?' he asked.

Most of the child soldiers said he was more or less right. Six-year-old Isata said she did not know about fear. One morning she had been playing in her mother's room when she heard footsteps and hid under the bed. A man entered and took all her mother's precious things from a drawer: her golden lappa, jewellery, some china cups. When she went downstairs, her mother was lying dead in the kitchen, so Isata had gone back upstairs to play under the bed.

'What is fear?' she asked.

Thomas suddenly said he wanted to talk about his friend being killed with 'a power saw': the electric saw cut him dead in three slices. 'After that, every night I was too frightened to sleep.'

At that Isata laughed out loud and returned to Miriam's side.

The talks about fear continued late into the night. Most admitted to knowing what it was and several shared experiences of pure terror. Bemba G walked up and down, listening. Once in a while there was silence as they thought over each other's stories. It was after midnight when into the silence a small boy remarked: 'I miss my mother.' The conversation had lapsed and more silence ensued: mothers were rarely talked about. Into that long silence came a murmur and we turned in astonishment to witness Citizen's almost noiseless tears. He shivered and the tears rolled.

Shiver in remembrance of the day when suddenly there was nowhere to live.

Cry for the empty belly left without solid food for days on end, save some roots: the pain so intense it causes tears. Remember dirty water to fill the belly in the hope that it will hold the body together. Remember how dirty water breaks the body, driving through muscles and joints, pressing against bowels. Remember how dirty water is emptied in the bush and rushes back into the mud: the pain so intense it causes tears.

Every dream is shared, every longing is common. All are living without Mother and do without her image.

From early morning till night, labour in the sun or the rain: burn villages, kill people, cut limbs, clean and polish guns, gather water; steal food, cut bush, stack grain. Risk life.

If there is nothing to eat or drink, complete the tasks and fall again into sleep or into fighting. If there is nothing to eat or drink, smoke, so suddenly the time is in the middle of another time, far away from the first day.

Sleep little because what should have been the place for sleeping is no longer there. Instead there is a bush. Behind every bush is a feeling correctly named fear. Whenever some commander comes upon the fears secreted behind every bush, watch how he collects them and orders them to spread themselves all over the child soldiers.

Now every nightmare is shared and every longing is common.

The light gauze of dawn was upon us when Citizen had dried his eyes and they all agreed to make the sign for the big fear of fighting, opening their arms and stretching their fingertips into the air. The child soldiers sat down on the ground after this. Bemba G pressed his thumb close to his finger, allowing a tiny filter of light to pass through them.

'Small-small fear,' he told them, 'not at all like before.' He beckoned to me to join him and to copy the gesture, adding: 'They call it stage fright, it is very small.'

So the two of us stood before them, mirroring one another. Everybody copied us, putting thumbs and fingers close together to show how small stage fright is.

'But I will give you something.' Bemba G was being conciliatory.

'Powder!' repeated Victor.

Ignoring this, Bemba G continued, 'It is a rainforest drink, my favourite from when I was a boy no bigger than you.' He looked into their faces. I peered at the jug's contents as he poured out for each one. The dark liquid looked delicious – a tonic for the enraged ones; each of the child soldiers lined up for a cup. It was almost a mud brown, much darker than apple juice but without the ruddy glow of berries. And it seemed to guarantee satisfaction, judging by the belching that started. The child soldiers each in turn pronounced the brown drink very tasty. They drained the last drop from the jug, Victor attempting to scoop the remains with the end of his tongue.

Victor said he felt 'very strong'.

'Courageous?' I asked, trying to judge what exactly were the properties of this drink.

He nodded.

'And calm?' I persisted.

Again he nodded his head.

Anger is always in search of calm, so I was not surprised that almost immediately the atmosphere in the compound began to change. Bemba G paid special attention to Peter, rubbing some balm on his forehead.

'Peter, is the company ready to perform?' Bemba G asked, acknowledging Peter's leadership power.

'Company is ready!' answered Peter.

A sense of well-being seemed to come over them. After the forest drink, their mouths were soft and their lips pretty browns and pinks again.

'I've never felt better than this,' said K.T. He wiped his brow, removing the perspiration and memory of their recent clangour. The children who had withdrawn – Miriam, Isata, Abu and Citizen – were also back in the larger group, mixing freely with the mutineers just as on previous days. Their routine for morning socializing picked up its usual tempo: conversations and games, a song from Miriam to Isata. It was a fitting ending to a turbulent time.

Peter had put aside his cockiness about controlling the others. He sensed that since a courage-inducing powder had been served and his command asserted, total humiliation had been averted. As they made ready for sleep, everyone was quiet. I went in search of Bemba G but he was not in his hut. There by the empty jug was a packet of the brown powder he'd employed for the rainforest concoction. I resisted the temptation to sample it while still wondering if its taste was akin to anything that had amused my palate before.

That day we let them relax until supper-time, then early to rest.

The afternoon was scorching hot. The cooking pots had been cleared away and Bemba G, who had been working hard, went to his hut to nap. Hearing the children screaming and shouting, and certain they would disturb the old man, Sally thought a quiet game would be fitting. All of them wanted their usual 'playtime'. They looked to me to set something up but as I had nothing planned, I had to think quickly.

Did I mishandle the situation? Was it some secret word that Bemba G had let drop that made them so quick and articulate in responding to me? Reviewing the whole session later I was filled with frustration. How to summarize what happened? They were quick and clever, grasping the essence of the play easily; every game or exercise they achieved in a matter of minutes. There was the whole business of powerful statesmen. I asked them to divide into small groups and gave them thirty minutes to explore ideas about acquiring and maintaining power in modern states. Within minutes Miriam and Hinga were back with impeccable results from their groups. Evidently every child soldier knew about secret societies, tampering with food supplies, bearing arms, political coups and bribery at elections. 'Good, very good, excellent. Now tell me, how do people seize power?' Again, the same result; within minutes they were done. I walked around the compound checking on their progress and at one point overheard Peter and Hinga (who were working with Citizen) demonstrate how much they had learned about negotiating power.

'You are right, Peter,' said Hinga. 'We must not press Citizen to say "yes" if he wants time to think. I apologize. Let us give him time to think.'

With most children you might still be explaining the

rules, but not with this group. Not only were they diligent, but in a short space of time they had understood the entire plot of the play more fully than I had when drafting my synopsis. Leisurely and considered discussions, punctuated by sudden realizations when someone shouted out 'EUREKA!' were taking place all over the compound. This unusual assembly of boys and girls discussed life in Sierra Leone, the challenges facing small farmers and their own education. Occasionally, during the afternoon, two boys would withdraw to lie in adjoining hammocks and discuss how they might solve one of their difficulties. I listened, astounded by their talent for thinking up ideas. 'Certainly,' said K.T., 'we have so many languages here, let us lend each other books in different languages.'

As they worked on the play or discussed other matters, I noticed that language was never the problem. It turned out that child soldiers had the knack of discerning meaning in each other's languages. Now they were not afraid of foreign words, inventing words or flipping between languages. The next day, as I listened to them saying their lines, whether in Krio or English there was evidence of confident fluency. Even children who had known only a hundred English words before enjoyed the new taste of Shakespeare on their tongues. And they were patient with one another, asking for help to master their parts when need be.

But Citizen was not drawn into this group behaviour. With the performance days away, that was a worry and it was a conundrum, for he had been good at joining in games. I alone had pushed for him to be given a speaking part but the truth of it was that I had not watched him in rehearsal for days. Finding the reticent boy sitting with Abu gave me a last opportunity with him.

Isata was standing in for Caesar's Ghost. In fact she still hoped to play the Ghost. I lay flat on the ground to watch, a few yards away from them. Abu was offering stage directions to Citizen, who was playing Lucius:

'Make like you are very tired. Yawn and then make like you are sleeping.'

'Say: "The strings, my lord, are false".'

Citizen collapsed in a tired heap on the ground and mumbled the lines Abu had said. Abu persevered and they ran through the scene a few times in similar fashion until Isata grew bored and left him to read Brutus:

'Now I have taken heart, thou vanishest

Ill spirit, I would hold more talk with thee

Boy! Lucius!'

No one had explained Citizen's behaviour, but it was clear that he was more afraid than most: afraid of saying the wrong words at the wrong time, tempting blame and condemnation. The strained expression on his face when confronted with the lines was enough to persuade Bemba G to help out. He stayed with him, going over them. The following afternoon, when the others were dancing about, Bemba G suggested a song instead.

'Do you like to sing, little soldier? Do you know a song you can sing on your own?'

Citizen said he did and they agreed that if he had music to offer that would be more than enough. He sang the Malian love song:

'With you I'll share the joys that life will bring me

Happiness doesn't always protect us from pain,

Near you, I'll share your pain

Yes, young one, only death can separate us.'

The text for the most part was uncut. We were following the original structure of the play – so powerful, so enigmatic – but we had our own take on things. Bemba G had promised that singing and dancing would be included. First the singing. All the child soldiers would come on to the stage with the weapons and ammunition they had brought and throw down the whole lot in front of the audience. As the guns, cutlasses, knives, Victor's two-pistol grip and the makeshift weapons fell on to the sheet on the ground, from offstage I was to shout: 'Playtime, Playtime!' They would then form a circle and Hinga would say, 'Let's sing our song.' Then two rounds of 'If you're happy and you know it, clap your hands . . .'

Meanwhile the small boys and girls were playing their usual games, dancing if they wished. Then Bemba G came forward with: 'Are you the child soldiers?'

'*Na we, na we*!' to be shouted back as loud as ever.

'Well, you don't have time for child's play. Let me show you a story about people in the forest who have been plotting to bring down our rulers.'

'True story or made-up story?' asked Isata.

'True story,' from Bemba G.

At that point Isata was to raise the old gin bottle – the symbol of true stories from former times – above her head. She and the small boys were to leave their games (and stop dancing) and join the audience, who by then should be set-tling on the planks and benches set in a circle around our stage. The rest put on their costumes. Then Caesar entered, calling for Calpurnia.

Peter was very good there; calm and measured for his entrance.

'Calpurnia!'

Out came Sally.

Sally was fidgeting with her long plaited hair, impatient to be on stage for the first full rehearsal. The conspirators were going over their scene with Brutus and Miriam, who was playing his wife Portia. Abu, Sally and I sat to one side.

'Do you know how boring it is to have to watch this scene played over and over again in one day?' moaned Sally.

'I don't care what you think about it, Sally,' teased Abu, 'you're just one man's wife; just sit and listen.'

'I am not just any wife,' returned Sally, pushing her long plaited hair up in a bun style, 'I told him not to go out today and he didn't listen. It's fate talking when you don't listen to your wife.'

They were at the end of their scene. Break was called before another act. The child soldiers packed around the tree and Hinga put on the ghetto blaster, choosing a striking love song for the company; across the Gola Forest Celine Dion sang with Luciano Pavarotti:

'I'd like to run away from you,
But if I were to leave you, I would die . . .'

Peter rushed over from the spot where he had been lying and came up to his Calpurnia, teenage Sally. He took her in his arms and they started to dance close in a revealing skin-to-skin moment. Her plaits rested on her neck, her lips were tightly pressed together. Around the edge, the child soldiers watched enviously as the couple twirled to the romantic duet. Their singing voices and the soft light began to affect Peter. He moved steadily. The more he danced, the more mesmerized he became. His mood was lifting. His years of soldiering were passing. Still he kept on seeing the bloody knife at his side, but he was dancing. He was holding a woman in his arms and twirling with her to music. He put his cheek against her cheek. The knife was still there, staring back at him. But there was music.

Other child soldiers began pairing up to dance. Some of the boys smiled cunningly at Peter as they danced past the first couple. Peter responded with a happy expression of his own. Jealously, he held his girl. Sally held him more tightly in her arms as she moved with the music. He smiled back at her and sang along:

> 'Impossible to live with you
> But I could never live
> Without you . . .'

The crowded dance floor, with boys and girls slipping over the earth, occasionally colliding into one another, rang out with singing. They moved freely. When the excitement took over, they shook their bodies or threw their arms into the air. Couples danced politely, gracefully. They touched the rhythm of joyful abandon. They danced into new relationships.

Only one stayed outside the rhythm: Hinga. He was pacing up and down, talking to himself, apparently oblivious to the dancers swaying to the beat. The music changed and he returned to the group, pushing some small boys out of his way to reach Sally, and she caught him in her arms as he lurched forward.

'Let me dance with her now,' Hinga told Peter.

Peter hedged, having taken a real interest in Sally, but then he gave way to Hinga: 'You two dance.' Sally laughed at their possessiveness. She was tired but continued to dance because Hinga, she realized, was feeling left out and needed to taste the new good mood.

Bemba G had done the group proud: the food that night, more bountiful than the day before, was festive and delicious. Wooden platters packed high with fried plantains, calabash of greens, hot pepper sauce, fried fish and akara beans and rice. Isata came to rest beside me.

'I like it when there is a lot of food,' she said. 'When I grow up I want to wash pans and clean plates.'

'That's nice, let's hope you have a big family then, with lots of pans and plates to wash and clean.'

Hinga was sitting next to Sally when Peter came over to join them, breaking up the impromptu private partnership.

'Come and eat now,' I said. All three helped themselves to generous portions of food.

Peter began to talk about the play. 'I die but I come back as a ghost,' he said.

'After you die, you come back and people can see you good-good fashion,' Sally consoled him.

'Mmm, dead people like to come back.'

'If you cook big food, fufu and plasas with bologi, and then drop some on the ground it is people who have gone who see the food and snatch it,' said Peter.

'Yes, and my gran'ma always said to them, "If you wanted to eat fufu and plasas and bologi you should not have gone,"' added Hinga.

'Yes, and when we open spirit to drink, then we put for them first.'

'I want to be the ghost,' said Isata, 'then I can take your food.'

'No, silly, you too small to be the ghost.'

'The ghost comes and goes in one minute and there's no food,' I told Isata.

'He is a hungry empty ghost?' questioned Miriam.

'In a way, yes; hungry for revenge.'

There was something we did not touch: those other dead, our victims. An invisible thread runs between the hungry empty ghosts and our earthly selves. As time passes, the veil between our worlds thins. I can feel these souls deeply. They are the same as us but without the blood. Adele, are you not there among them, hungry for revenge?

*

The last rehearsal days were for just this: attending to personal needs, mending the slips, gathering their forces. Citizen's musical achievement did not go unnoticed. Hinga and Peter stood by him. Hinga told me that Citizen was brave to break his silence even if it meant only a song. Peter said he knew that survival depended upon knowing exactly what to say and when to say it, knowing who could be trusted with speech and who not. We were sitting by the Black Rock twin speakers that final evening, eating kerosene mangoes; half playful, half serious, Hinga patted Citizen on the back:

'Can talk now, eh, Citizen, no worries.'

That penultimate evening I sat beside him as he fell asleep. The wind stirred the tops of the trees. A bird cawed deep in the forest. Night closed in.

The sky was clear the next morning and we all went for a long walk down to the stream, swam and played at the water's edge.

It was impossible to guess that the day would change so drastically. Menacing colours suddenly appeared overhead in the afternoon. The sky turned dark green. Rain threatened. Bemba G, the children and I ducked under the thick tresses of forest and waited. Everyone was quiet. The only sounds beckoning were the shuffling lizards caught and confined to Peter's empty wooden box by Abu and Victor. These forest pets were protesting their lifestyle until Victor, who was holding the box tight, opened the lid, exposing their courgette-green heads. The sky turned black and pitiless. A crash of thunder came screeching through the air. Citizen let out a thin cry. Victor dropped his box and the lizards leapt to freedom to laze again on the rocks.

The rain beat down on the forest, though our patch remained a dry protected belt. After a short spell, the sun shone more brightly than before and we stepped out into the blue haze and strolled back. Along the way Miriam observed rivulets of oil gleaming on the wet road. 'Let's be sure to stay close together tonight,' she urged.

Darkness had fallen. She planned to keep a solitary vigil if necessary to watch over Isata, Sally and me. 'Only we four have to worry,' she explained.

'Because they're boys?'

'The oil on the road, didn't you see?' she answered. 'It means vehicles have passed here, soldiers passed this way.'

She was right. The military must have passed nearby – who else would have come here? She looked utterly terrified and was rushing ahead, back to the hut, slowing only when I caught up with her and muttered a few sympathetic words.

Her agitated mood softened slightly as she repeated her request: 'Who will keep watch?'

'I will.' I nodded to double the power of my reassurance.

'Soldiers pin you down,' she said. For the first time I saw that she was ready to talk to me about what had happened.

That night in the rainforest the air was cold. I snuggled up to Isata and Miriam and watched over them dutifully as they slept. During the night Miriam woke several times and once she spoke to me for a while, telling me how she used to keep watch at night for the commanders so that they could sleep. I fought off the tiredness but as dawn approached I too fell into a deep slumber and had a dream. We three were on a small island floating on a cobalt sea. Dressed in brightly coloured silks we were singing rounds when I saw some men dressed in dapper pinstriped suits with collar and tie, walking towards us. 'Which way to the gangplank?' one of them asked. I pointed it out and they went in that direction.

The next morning I awoke with the elation of revenge. To Miriam, I said, 'You see we are quite safe.'

Tears were welling in her eyes: 'If we stay together we are safe.'

I took her hand as a token of female affection: we are safe.

'They attacked our home. They took me from my mother's house and beat my mother. They forced me to go with them and to carry a load on my head: their clothes, pots and sometimes the guns. We started to travel every night from seven o'clock until six in the morning.'

'Why at night?'

'Because of the jets. Every night we travelled and they raped me. Two of them.'

'Who?'

'One was the captain. The other I did not know his name but he was older than me.'

'Oh, God.'

'They only stopped when they fell asleep.' That was the only time she could breathe freely, she said; but she had bled for days. 'I fell pregnant for one of them. I went to a herbalist to give me medicine to drink but it would not come out. I tried again but it would not come out.'

'It' was 'Baby'.

'When was Baby born?'

'June fifth.'

'And when you look at her do you think of them, Miriam?'

'There is no reason to think of them. She is a beautiful Baby.'

The night Miriam gave birth she squatted on the ground pressing her fingers against her belly to help push the baby out. There were no women from her village to assist her and no one to walk with her to the amber-coloured river where she bathed Baby's head for the first time. She was just relieved it was all over. Repeatedly raped, her clothes spattered with their semen and her blood, Miriam had sensed in herself a potential for butchery and, although she had no protection or support, she entered a state of grace. At first she had thought the men would kill her. But then realizing she was alive and well, she did not know how to cope with life until she hit on the idea of guiding those who wandered through the rainforest. So many people seemed to need her guidance, her chosen mission absorbed her completely and she did not rest until she had led the day's wandering souls to their safe destination.

'And how did you see me?'

'I felt you wanting to come.'

She thought for a moment and then added: 'Running from tears.'

'That's not good,' I put in defensively.

'His tears,' she said.

Back into the heart of the compound, back with the Bemba G who, just as I'd guessed, was on a storytelling marathon, propping up the tree, recounting true tales and made-up yarns. On tonight's menu was a round-the-world fest, the already familiar treat for child soldiers: an Englishman who looked like an elephant, an Indian guru who translated for animals, an inmate of Robben Island who skated around his cell at night. My mind darted between Miriam and the group's anxieties about the next day's performance. But the child soldiers were enjoying it, stuffing themselves with the forest stories; like fire-eaters they swallowed the lot – hot, hot, hot.

Miriam and I needed time to talk but the perfect moment did not present itself. The moon was up, shining luxuriantly over the compound, before I had a chance to speak with her again. It seemed that we must be prepared to leave the forest, filled though it is with wondrous plant and animal life, and be able to travel and explore. This had to be true for Miriam and later for Baby. And the first step in any lifetime? Be named, be somebody, not an enigma.

'Baby should have her own name.'

'What name will you give her then?' asked Miriam, quite reasonably.

'Adele,' I told her without a moment's hesitation.

'Baby will be Adele now,' she said, closing the matter.

I glanced around. Isata was standing nearby, just behind Black Rock, holding the infant in her arms. Citizen was playing with Baby's toes and did not see us. Isata's nursery-school brown eyes flitted over to me. In turn, I looked hard at her, thinking: *Be careful, you are holding little Adele.* To have created such a namesake for Adele was not something I had ever sought or desired. Nevertheless I wanted to ask Auntie Adele, who though not blood was family, to accept as descendants these three embattled children – Citizen, Isata and Baby Adele.

Rain falls overnight, making imperfect curves on the soil. The trees along the back wall of the farm bend their trunks, hurling leafy branches into an embracing vault over Adele's head. Her body settles into the soft dark ground: it has waited for this wandering sister and accepts her.

She cannot see the top of the mountains looking over Sierra Leone. She had never seen them in her lifetime. But her eyes in spirit recognize the trees whose fruits are edible and her nostrils in remembrance know the smell of fresh oranges, the acid of the dark room, the passion of purple bougainvillea.

Adele passes under the waters of the River Rokel and hears it singing:

> *'I am the River Rokel*
> *Silted by whitened bones,*
> *The washer of diamonds rolling from home.'*

'Who is there?' she calls out. 'Who else is there?'

'I am a Temne farmer standing
At a roadblock.
My wife, my sister, my baby are dead.
Who can tell me why?'

And a third voice adds:

'I am a young and first-time mother,
Eternally pounding yam,
And seducer of hot-pepper-loving palates . . .'

At these mingled cries, the colour of Adele's blood turns dark red, a colour that knows how to bide its time. She looks upon the lime-green weeds swimming in the depths of the River Rokel and calls back: 'I am your strong and ancient grandmother, let me wrap you in my arms.'

Then she closes her eyes and waits.

Ten

Freetown: the sight of the torn city upset me in a way it had not when I first headed for Uncle's house. My eyes panned slowly around the scene, followed a stream of military vehicles carrying soldiers in from Lungi airport. People passed in ones and twos, old and young. The evening was unusually cool. People were milling in the main streets and the back roads; some sat gossiping on verandas on old folding chairs; some had sidewalk counters to sell cigarettes, snacks and cans of drink. Lingering outside a house of corrugated iron with a half-completed roof, was a child with stick legs. He stretched out a hand, revealing some coins that others had obviously dropped there. I searched my pocket for something to add but it was empty so I left him there, alone. He might be young and physically weak but he would stand there, I knew. By the time I reached Uncle Moses' place, it was raining lightly: the yard was black and shiny in the drizzle.

'I would never have thought the city would come to this,' I said to him. 'I remember PZ, those lovely stores . . . it's heartbreaking.'

He stared at me for a long while then said, 'It is, but we will build again.'

I did know that too. He and I had both been able to travel in Europe and understood how landscapes and cityscapes change over the decades.

192

'I suppose London was not what you were expecting either, back in the sixties?'

'Too big. Countryside's better – the light in the morning in the countryside. If we had a car in those days we'd hit the road and head for the country.'

'It takes ages to get to the countryside from London now; you'd hit the road and get to the suburbs. Be stuck in a jam.'

'True. And we would stop and drink tea from a flask.'

'Now it would have to be a cappuccino.'

It wasn't his London any more. I said, hoping to impress him, 'I know London better than anywhere, even better than Paris which I loved.'

'You didn't stay there after all that?'

'No. My boyfriend and I travelled all over Europe eventually. Spent time in Italy and had an apartment in Berne for six months before returning to France. But Mummy fell ill and it was time to come home.'

'Best always to be with your family.' He had not been able to go to the funeral, which made him visibly sad. 'Look how things have changed,' he said.

'That's just what I was saying. Places change. And people. I did some photography.'

'Really?'

It was not his style of work. There were no photos of people in my portfolio. I had not needed to record England the way he did Sierra Leone.

'Let me see.'

I hurried to my room to collect what few prints were there among my things and spread them before him. I had never felt his interest so strongly.

'It's all a bit abstract, I know.'

I reached over to gather them together, thinking that he had already observed them closely and for long enough, but he stopped me. He was still studying them and, through them, me. The photographs flashed in the dim light. Scenes of London undressed, with a wild look, as though tawny tigers might roam Charing Cross or short-blade knives stalk Hampstead Heath.

'Not bad,' he said, 'not bad at all.'

I was delighted. Now I understood. A chance to be different and the same: two of a kind. Uncle Moses said that Adele was responsible for his setting up as a photographer.

'I was registered for medicine. They had already enrolled me in the second year, taking biochemistry and what else again? In the evenings I was earning extra money at the post office with some of the other boys. But she always saw me with my camera.' He waved away a thought. 'Waste of time medical school. When she saw that I was not studying medicine, she asked what I liked doing. I stared at her just as I'm looking at you now. "What kind of question is that?"'

Eventually he had put away the medical books and sold most of them to an enthusiastic Ghanaian, Etse, who read them into the night and quoted passages from them in letters home. 'Imagine his poor people sitting with some kerosene lamp reading about the myocardial this and the xeriphthalmia that, the poly this and the poly that.' We laughed together.

He left me in the studio and went to make some tea. I was topping mine with whisky when Anita came in and began to fry some plantain. Later that evening, at the kitchen table, Uncle Moses began telling me about the farm which Agnes and her husband Kole had run.

'It was not such a large farm, really a few fields. They grew cassava, rice, season millet, groundnuts, corn. The corn was at the back.' He remembered more: 'Also potatoes, sweet potatoes. You know we eat the leaves as well as the potatoes.'

I was thinking, *This is where Citizen was born, among such good wholesome grains and staples. Up-country where life was simple.*

'Kole, his father, had a farm before they married, so he was used to it before Agnes came. He hired some local boys to cut the bush and she looked after the big yard at the house.'

'I remember in the pictures you showed me.'

'Yes, after harvest we liked to visit. Everyone would be in celebratory mood, with special parties for children, naming ceremonies for the newborns and, well, a general feeling of plenty.'

Anita remembered how years ago this had indeed been the case. By selling rice and other produce Agnes and Kole had made things work. But the farm that had promised prosperity had finally become the scene of an execution.

'It was all for little George,' added Moses.

'George?'

'Citizen. George – that was his Christian name. But when they saw how he liked to run the place, be in charge of everybody . . .' He paused mid-sentence.

'So why "Citizen"?' I was still puzzled.

'You should have seen him at two, Julia. Thought he was in charge of the place. So Kole called him "First Citizen of the Farm", then we all copied and nicknamed him Citizen.'

Citizen, wear your name with pride. Be the country boy or be the city boy. You were never meant to be a soldier, just a boy-citizen first named George.

As though reading my mind, Uncle Moses said, 'It's funny, isn't it, the naming and renaming of people.'

Although travel was not easy, Auntie Adele had made the effort to go to them whenever she could, taking a bus part way, or poda-poda, and going part way by foot. On other occasions, Moses accompanied her and they stayed for a few days. Adele and Moses had invested some of their savings in the farm, in the form of cutters and tools. On the morning of Adele's last visit there she was up at five, making ready. Moses had woken late and Eddy, by her side with a bowl of cool water in his hands, struck him as oddly irritating. The monkey nodded to Adele's every statement. Moses made a bid for attention by washing the dishes; he filled the green plastic bowl with suds, plunged the knives in, examined their gleam as they re-emerged. The breakfast plates squelched into the bowl and were returned pristine, the glasses too, clinking against one another. As he pulled them from the water he saw that one was cracked. Slithers of glass lay at the bottom of the bowl. He tipped the water out to avoid cutting his fingers and went to empty the bowl in the yard. Returning, he wiped the bowl with a damp cloth and refilled it with cold water. He took two more glasses and buried their mouths in the soapy water. Just as he was withdrawing them, Adele had called out: 'Moses, Moses, come look . . .'

He dropped the glasses, cutting his finger, which released an angry shot of blood. 'Silly woman!' Outside, Adele was sitting in the yard holding a pink apple in the palm of her hand. It had an odd shape, with three protruding heads like a hydra. He looked and smiled. It was strange. Then he remembered his hand and he remembered his anger:

'What, you call me out here to look at fruit? Don't be so silly!'

'Don't be so cross,' she answered back and put the hydra apple in the pocket of her full apron to show to her grandson. When he saw the apple he would laugh. She would give it to him.

For an instant, Uncle Moses stopped, unable to go on with the story. He remembered life on the farm as it used to be. Often when Adele awoke at dawn at her daughter's house she went to the river to bathe. She would make pepper soup around four in the afternoon, when the tasks outside were completed: the clearing and burning of weeds; the clearing of a drain choked with debris, rotten leaves and muck, so that the water would flush through like a natural stream. Often she had bent down and allowed it to run over her fingers, clean and pure, like a necklace of glass.

And once, maybe once, she discarded her brassiere in the middle of this work, for it lay there where she died. We imagined how it might have been when Adele stood at the end of the field, furthest from the house, felt her wired brassiere cutting into her flesh, and reached inside the dress and around one breast to unhook it. Perhaps it would not budge. Perhaps she stretched up an arm, poked down from the collar of the dress, but still could not reach. Frustrated, she looked about and, confirming she was alone, slipped the dress from her shoulders, unfastened the bra and threw it to the ground. It fell on the shoots peeping through the soil. In half an hour or so, she would return to the house to begin the pepper soup. It was nearly four o'clock in the afternoon . . .

At around ten, I went up to my room and quickly fell asleep but four hours later I was wide awake, thinking about Citizen and Uncle Moses.

The rain had stopped. I turned over, desperate for sleep, but it would not come. I took two sleeping tablets and began to feel more sluggish. Uncle Moses and Citizen were in deep slumber in their beds. Back downstairs in the sitting room I drained the remains of the tea and poured a slug of whisky down my throat before taking up the lounger. Into its depths I sunk.

I dreamt of swimming in the river by Bemba G's home but it was bordered with rocks and boulders on one side. These caused the waters to spit and hurtle and I struggled to stay afloat. Citizen leapt into the river. His arms shoved back the waves and his legs kicked bravely. Intuitively, he knew how to master the waters, survey the bed and control what was before him. He turned back to me, his eyes giving permission for me to follow him. He was helping me: with each lunge forward he pulled weeds from before his face and hurled them to the river's bank. The spray from these glistened in honey sunlight. With every stroke forward he cleared the river, tossing aside stones, debris, the dark glutinous pods blocking our way. The water became soft and green, the slime yielding, then gradually it turned blue and luminescent as weeds and poisons shrivelled and died on its bank. Seeing him clear the river, I grew more assured and my muscles responded to the exhilarating challenge. As the water caressed, I could see the bottom of the River Rokel; hundreds of feet beneath us were diamonds encrusted in the mud, not glistening now but black and hard and stubborn as souls.

Arising from the water, I was on the journey from Freetown to the compound, walking with a model's gait, my hips swinging musically. There I go traipsing along, attired in a buba and lappa of African purples, that's me: cousin to Cleopatra! And look, what are those bleached white pyramids growing from the top of my head? A stack of sheets pinched from Adele's linen cupboard – on their way to being Roman togas for the child soldiers . . .

Eleven

So the rain forest has become an amateur stage
And
The trees have turned into a scenic frontier
Where
Cut
Free
Children
Act above
Uncut
Free
Diamonds.

They were all there. Behind Bemba G's hut, the company gathered to fit their togas, which Miriam, Thomas and I had hastily put together the night before. Corporal Kalashnikov, our solo drummer, was also there, arranging the drums in a circle, practising and occasionally singing along. He had been particularly helpful the previous night when, around 2 a.m., I realized we did not have a 'Green Room' for after the show. In the pitch black, we had cut down branches in every shade of green, from the lime-lemon of riverside weeds to bright emerald grasses to the black green of mango. We had also come across Bemba G still up, ruminating about the show and finishing off a second jug of the rainforest recipe he had served days before.

'What is that?'

'Kola drink.'

'My goodness, what will you serve for drinks?' Another oversight.

'This,' he had pointed to the almost empty jug.

'If people are coming from far and wide, we need more choice, a menu.'

'Let's keep it simple, just serve this.' He did not see my point.

It was too modest, too unambitious. We reached a compromise, and a sign was written in large print and pasted on a tree near the entrance of the compound:

KOLA SPRITZER

PALM WINE SPRITZER

OR RAINFOREST PUNCH

ONE POUND STERLING OR TWO DOLLARS (2$US)

Nervous laughter came from the group; they were excited and tense before the big show.

'Someone help me fit my toga?' Thomas was grinning over his shoulder because he couldn't drape the garment correctly. Bemba went to assist.

'Remember, when I make like so, you follow me,' K.T. was telling Citizen, gesturing with his left arm under the baggy toga. When I looked up, I saw Miriam coming towards me smiling:

'Julia, you looked beautiful when you came in last night.' Miriam stood by my side, her expression credulous.

'Did I?'

'Yes. So you have some *good* clothes.'

Bemba G joined in: 'Seems so. She decided to throw away those ragged old jeans and T-shirt then?'

'For full African dress!' chimed in Miriam. 'Well done, Julia.'

'How do I look today?'

'The best you've ever looked,' she assured me, walking round me for a better look.

'And how do I look?' Isata asked, patting down her recently brushed hair. Fine, everyone looked fine.

I peeked around to where people were coming in. The crowd was growing. A few meandered in, a little uncertain whether they had the correct compound. We had a sign up – THE CHILD SOLDIERS' *JULIOHS SIZA*: ALL WELCOME – though inevitably a few would have missed it. More people were arriving. Over the next half-hour, the compound was almost full. By the time we were ready to start, the numbers had swollen to over two hundred. The audience was a mixed bunch, a medley of ages, nationalities and types: British and American soldiers in uniform, village people from across the river, some of the Freetown elites with their own kerosene lamps in hand, and more child soldiers walking barefoot. A group of schoolgirls in fading cotton dresses placed themselves in front of the representatives from one of the international agencies. The press bench was occupied by a troupe of South African actors and musicians – all crowded into our compound home.

'What a good place for a play!' exclaimed a German-sounding man within my earshot.

'Have you come from far?' I was curious that so many Europeans had made it to the country place at such short notice.

'I was on my way back to Hamburg when I heard about it. Thought I would stop off and see what's new in African theatre.'

'Are you a theatre person – a professional, I mean?'

'I am director.'

I moved on. His response left me feeling intensely nervous. The child soldiers had been pumped up and excited all day. Now I was. Would we make fools of ourselves? Seem absurd? *Absurd! Absurd!* screamed in my head: lost souls hanging around a black rock, making bizarre comments. I began to wonder whether Peter had been right; perhaps people would laugh. But I stopped myself spiralling into self-doubt. We needed this international community with us and there was no going back. I should have welcomed the German director and ushered him to a seat, not left him to fend for himself, but I spotted him later leaning against halfway silk-cotton tree and talking animatedly to a South African group.

Bemba G was pacing up and down but keeping his distance from the child soldiers. Whatever happened now was in their hands. Then he caught sight of Isata and gave her the nod. Isata came forward and took her place.

'They're starting,' someone whispered. 'Shhh, they're starting.'

Out they came from behind the bushes, the entire company led by Hinga, Peter and Miriam. When they had all assembled on stage, they hurled their weapons and ammunition to the ground before forming a big circle. Offstage, I shouted, 'Playtime!' and they began their song.

> 'If you're happy and you know it, clap your hands,
> If you're happy and you know it, clap your hands,
> If you're happy and you know it and you really want
> to show it,
> If you're happy and you know it, clap your hands.'

Meanwhile the small boys and girls were playing a modest game of tag, waiting for their cue. Bemba G came on. 'Are you the child soldiers?'

'*Na we, na we!*' they all shouted back.

'Well, you don't have time for child's play. Let me show

you a story about people in this same forest who have been plotting to bring down our rulers.'

'True story or made-up story?' asked Isata.

'True story,' answered Bemba G.

Isata stood in the middle and raised the old gin bottle above her head. Among the audience were local people who recognized the sign: 'A true story is coming.'

'Oo, oo, true story, true, true story,' they said. The younger children joined the audience, encouraging them to leave their wooden seating and promenade.

Then once they were in costume, the play began. Peter strode on to the stage, a proud and victorious Caesar, calling for his wife:

'Calpurnia!'

Out came Sally. Our version of the play, with intercessions of drumming, dance and mime, was about to unfold. Appreciation was evident from the hushed audience.

'Beware the ides of March,' repeated Victor for all to hear.

The crowd was still growing. Next to me a couple were explaining, as room was made for them next to their friends, that they had been stopped at three different roadblocks.

'At the second one, a hysterical young man leapt out from the bush waving a gun at our heads, then the peacekeepers appeared from nowhere and calmed him down,' the woman said.

'Shhh,' said a voice from behind her, 'we can't hear.'

She continued in more hushed tones: 'We gave him some money.'

The play had reached the scene where Brutus and Cassius engage in a long dialogue about Caesar, drawing attention to his personal weaknesses and superhuman claims.

'Just like our little Caesars,' said a local man, nodding apparently in agreement with himself, since he was quite alone. The two actors retreated behind the hut and Caesar was on stage again with his followers.

Eyes turned to Miriam playing Portia, crazily pleading with husband Brutus to confide in her. Light from candles, lamps and the moon brilliantly illuminated her female form:

'If this were true, then should I know this secret.

I grant I am a woman.'

The audience had no notion of what was to come. Departing from the script, she lifted her toga, to reveal the cuts, bruises and lacerations from years of torture during the civil war:

'Here in the thigh; can I bear that with patience,

And not my husband's secrets.'

'Oh ye gods!'

Bemba G gasped. He had thought, as had the other child soldiers, that the pretty Miriam was the least tormented soul. He watched, sobered, as she lowered the toga again but the audience had not recovered from the sight. Nothing in the performance had prepared them for her parade in stony-faced elegance before them, pressing in close so that the cuts on her back, upper arms and wrists were seen for what they were. It was spontaneous, nothing contrived; no theatre game brought from rehearsal, Miriam gave all the clues she could of how the act of love and the acts of war had combined.

'Cowards die many time before their deaths;

The valiant never taste of death but once.'

The audience picked out, here, the dance around Caesar, there, the rich tapestry of adult games, deceits, omens spilling from the words of Artemidorus. The swirling of naked swords performed through a dance around Caesar, executed by a group of boys, kept the audience enthralled. Answering the drum, feverishly clamouring for the death, the boys circled Caesar. The candles and lamps of the compound flared, as if caught in a knowing draught. There was Caesar, vulnerable. Kill, kill, kill. Already almost lifeless, cold and pale, Caesar descended the stage floor to stand before the audience. Black Rock crashed. Among the spectators was the tingly recognition that what was passing in this compound was the horror of their own civil war. Black Rock crashed. The drum beat quickened. It sounded like the ritual music for a bloody death.

'*Et tu Brute?*' Peter said.

The audience leaned in and there was a sudden hush as the body fell to the ground. The drums had stopped. Child soldiers stood in frozen pose over the body.

> '*What drives such aggression?*
> *Such African brutality spilling out on the fields of Goro!*
> *What is this hate, ambition, greed?*'

A child in the audience, on the lookout for accomplices, coughed and suddenly all child soldiers left their benches and rushed out, screaming:

'Peace, Freedom, Liberty!'

'Peace, Freedom, Liberty!'

They stormed across the compound floor disrupting the performance. Lights flashed from the top of Black Rock, some adults too sprang to their feet, running, stumbling into the middle of the compound. They did not need to see the closing scenes of the play and dared not miss the chance to join the chanting:

'Peace, Freedom, Liberty!'

'Peace, Freedom, Liberty!'

Caesar lay on the ground, stabbed.

Older spectators began screeching, wailing and shouting: 'Peace, Freedom, Liberty!' Their voices penetrated the forest around us. Soundlessly, our company of child soldiers came out of their poses and dispersed among the crowds, willing them to continue the chanting, an involuntary impulse to go beyond the usually decorous audience participation. Their forefathers had lived on this coast for more than two centuries and what had they to show for this longevity? Murmuring to themselves, the spectators took their seats again. The players were moving in opposite directions among the audience and, without looking at one another, Hinga and Bemba – our Mark Anthony and Brutus – slid out of the group into a silent and mesmerizing dance.

'Friends, Romans, countrymen . . .' Hinga began and the crowds joined in with the words they knew: 'lend me your ears.'

Bemba G's direction was proving wholly original. Members of the audience had become involved good and proper. Adults now lay sprawled on the ground watching the action and many benches were left unoccupied.

It was at this point that Citizen, playing Brutus's servant, began to sing, his flute voice filling our ears. I wanted to call Uncle Moses to come and see, to witness what Citizen could do.

I heard a Krio woman ask her neighbour: 'Na Siza, Siza dem calling,' as the child soldiers shouted lines from among the spectators. 'Caesar, Caesar,' her neighbour answered. It did not matter; whatever languages poured into the compound that evening, Black Rock, utterly devout to our needs, offered simultaneous translation so that everyone could follow. We were all in this together and it did not matter what tongue was spoken on the forest stage that night. Be it: *'Padi dem, kohntri, una ohl wey dey,'* or: 'Friends, Romans, countrymen, lend me your ears,' everyone followed the action, understanding the words. Stage or no stage, 'gud' is good, 'want-want' is avarice, 'pickin' is child.

Now it was time for the Ghost scene in which Brutus's boy soldier Lucius falls asleep. Only now would we see how Citizen would play his part.

Bemba G spoke:

'This is a sleepy tune; O murderous slumber,

Layest thou thy leaden mace upon my boy

That plays thee music?'

Lucius the boy soldier prepares to rest and washes himself. He lies on the rug by Brutus's feet and takes up a string instrument. He mimes a tune, placing his fingers over imaginary strings. He sings. A clement moon hangs over the battlefield. Another young boy enters the tent, walks over to Brutus, pours from a jug of wine into a goblet. He bows and leaves.

The boy soldier sings. 'With you I'll share the joys that life brings . . .'

There is a caress in his voice, as though it understands. It is a child's voice but one that suggests a dark muscatel, as though it had been somewhere else before entering this world. He hears himself sing out loud. Then, clasping his instrument to him, he stops, looks about, curls up his legs and falls asleep. He dreams. He sees before him a ghost standing in the ground, lips pursed, arms outstretched. In his sleep, he rocks back and forth to comfort himself and just at the point he sees clearly, it is sliced away, guillotined. The ghost speaks:

'Thy evil spirit.'

In his dream, he crosses and recrosses the field: he watches the sun, a violent red, setting on the horizon. He hears a bird cawing above. He hears the ghost speak once more:

'To tell thee, thou shalt see me at Phillipi.'

He shivers and cries out – who is this ghost really? The glory of her voice, those assessing eyes, naked brown arms with flesh gently drooping. He thinks of tenderness and love – and joining hands. The ghost turns, revealing a back torn with wounds from a cruel death. He shivers. What is it he feels? An abnormal heartbeat, his blood running cold.

He feels a gun being pressed into his hands, another gun pressed to his head. He cannot respond: his hands are small. He cannot speak: this is not what he wants. He wants to play the instrument, to sing again and feel the sun on his face and limbs. He sleeps, but not for ever. His head is being lifted up . . . 'Lucius, Awake!'

Citizen lifted his head. He looked about, seeking out the living faces of the actors filling the tent. But his eyes said there was a dream, a dream of self-mortification. His face spoke of a heart softening from fossil to pearly shell. His open lips said the shell was ready to be broken.

I went to sit next to Corporal Kalashnikov who, at some distance from the ghost scene, was beating his drum, heralding that the end of the drama was drawing near. The child soldiers made ready to fight: this would be their last spectacular battle on the fields of Goro being broadcast to the world. They stood up proudly, and began moving in and out of position, hands raised, heads close: a wasteland of child flesh on show.

One, two: a kick in the air.

One body falls: a figure of youth thrown in the dust.

One, two: an arm is raised, a body falls.

It was like watching a ballet, a choreographed fight, leaping and strange.

Suddenly, in the distance, beyond our compound, noises intruded. The cackle of gunfire became a powerful chorus that I feared might unsettle the actors, but no. On they went with the final act until all of them bar Mark Anthony were lying on the ground. He strode out from among the bushes and spoke a few lines. Darkness fell in black beads of night. I heard a shout from my left. 'Bravo, bravo,' called out the peacekeeping troops, their enthusiasm spreading across the stage floor. 'Jolly good show,' came an English voice unlocked over the mêlée.

'Lord have mercy!' called some Freetown old ladies, clutching their bosoms more tightly to their hearts. 'Lord have mercy!'

As the war scene ended the audience breathed again, remembering this was only a play.

'It's only a play,' some woman reassured her friends.

She was right, it was only a play after all, performed in the open air here in the rainforest. It had started as a game, with a bunch of kids in the bush making noise, making fists, having fits, fighting it out among themselves. I thought of Decker, the playwright. Among the countless scenarios he had imagined, surely never this one with performers who knew what it was to see a throat being slit. From where I was standing, everything looked upside down, as though that night the diamonds had moved into the sky and the stars were queuing to dance in the compound. The world was being ruled according to reverse laws, with reverse atoms coming from above. There was just one distinct moment when things seemed clear, but a second later confusion again.

'Whatever happens,' I said to myself, 'this performance will not last for ever.'

The audience clapped and cheered. I caught sight of the German director who had talked to me earlier. He looked amazed, as if to say: 'Do you mean child soldiers are capable of this?' I joined him and the South African troupe and he immediately began to talk: 'I did this play using the political schism in the Eastern bloc post-nineteen-eighty-nine.'

'Oh, very interesting,' I answered, my eyes and thoughts still focused on our child soldiers, visibly pleased with their show.

'You could take this to other places,' he continued, 'plan a tour.'

'We could, I suppose.' A half-hearted response that failed to elicit a tour plan. Did he mean venues in Sierra Leone or other countries? Instead, I ran my hands over my plaited hair to remove the moisture from them, ready to clap and cheer the company who were coming forward for a third encore. They came out again, taking a bow in their muddy togas and regular 'battledress' underneath – torn T-shirts, ragged shorts, and some of them with Reebok feet.

'Well done, everyone, very well done!'

Corporal Kalashnikov was beating his drum in a fantastic rhythm, summoning everyone to dance and clap more loudly. The drumming grew louder and more insistent. The impression was of a pulse vivid enough to resuscitate cold and tired hearts. People responded. Women, children, soldiers began dancing around halfway silk-cotton tree in styles that were completely freeing of their bodies. The soldiers picked up the children, placing them on their shoulders so everyone could see. There was Peter waving from the podium of a UN officer and laughing with Hinga, who was also up in the air. 'What wonderful children!' people said, as the drum music bent subtly into another rich rhythm. When it stopped, the child soldiers gathered around Bemba G.

'Sing your song again,' he urged them, and to the audience, 'join in.' The forest skies lifted as hundreds of voices struck out:

> 'If you're happy and you know it, clap your hands,
> If you're happy and you know it, clap your hands,
> If you're happy and you know it and you really want
>   to show it,
> If you're happy and you know it, clap your hands.'

The audience was clapping. The child soldiers were clapping themselves and bowing to the audience.

Excited voices emerged from the Green Room. Our child soldiers had been 'discovered' by journalists.

'How did that happen to you?'

'Can I interview you here?'

'Let's get the lead actors in first. You, you and you.'

All company members, thirty-five child soldiers, prepared to have their pictures taken. They were talking about their scenes, their lines, the sayings, their games, their memories, their ideas. Like a fountain spurting into that difficult basin, the words poured. Whenever a journalist was free, they began telling their stories just as they had told each other in the afternoons on Black Rock. Since almost all had rehearsed using the beginning, middle and end technique, the journalists had no difficulty in keeping up. The line for the Green Room sported confidence. They stood close together and listened patiently to each other's telling. The lush Green Room with so many notebooks and cameras at the ready was filled with hushed tones, attentive ears.

I returned to Bemba G, who was talking with Citizen and Isata at Black Rock.

'The time has come for you children to move on. You can do it now. These men are safe and will carry you on their trucks.' Pointing to the UN and peacekeeper trucks lining one side of the compound, Bemba G encouraged the company to disband and move on.

Why did this ending seem so abrupt, so sad? We could hardly have expected to stay for ever it was true, and yet I felt disheartened. Bemba G made two exemptions: Peter was to stay to learn more in the rainforest and Victor must stay because of his injured head. The offer to shelter the most rambunctious and the most disturbed guests was surely an act of kindness. The others would have to find their way back to ordinary life with whatever means available.

The queue for interviews and photos was thinning. Some children preferred group shots, some not to tell their stories. At last it was time for Citizen to stand before the journalists. I could see he did not want to talk but every time a journalist leaned forward and pressed the play button on his tape recorder, Citizen followed the movement with his eyes. The journalists stayed for over an hour, sure that some resolution must come. Citizen and I felt this also. To help out, an Englishman named Paul took some shots of us standing together. 'It's digital: one of the latest models, five million pixels,' he said, and later: 'I'll show you the good ones.'

Paul stooped to bring himself to our level and show what he had taken. He sighed; there was so much work to be done here. He was scrolling through the images – the boys in togas, the eager eyes – when all of a sudden Citizen shouted out: 'Grandma!'

Citizen reached for the image of Adele standing between us. In her hand was the imperfectly formed fruit she had brought to show him. Around her waist was the patterned apron she wore to do chores.

In the Green Room, questions left unanswered: 'Is it his grandma?' 'Does he see his grandma?'

In the Green Room we hear her praying for her grandson as she did before:

> 'Lord, Lord, don't let more sin fall on his head.
> Lord, protect my grandchild,
> For Agnes's sake.
> Lord, look on Moses' line,
> Let him live . . .'

Death is upon her but the juices of the apple in her hand pour from her fingers; they sting and hurt like metal pincers. With chemical precision rehearsed over centuries the apple's juices are poured, becoming a deluge. They hurtle along Citizen's veins, starting with his index finger pressing the trigger, reducing his hands to the size of a helpless baby's. The gun falls from his hands, the spell of murder over. He will never kill again.

Twelve

The church bells of Freetown announced the start of another day, calling all good Christian women to doff their veiled straw hats, straighten their black stockings, and leave for church. Meanwhile, I was still resting on the lounger, a half-empty tumbler of tea and whisky balanced precariously on my stomach. I levered myself up and went to take a bath and change my clothes. After a while the familiar smell of plantains being fried wafted in my direction. I dressed in cotton jeans and a striped blue blouse, looking in the mirror to brush my hair. The mirror reflected back with gleaming clarity a thin drawn face, similar to mine but more of some other woman with tidy shoulder-length braids, not in need of brushing, and a confident smile. Her appearance seemed to confirm what I had long suspected: that night-walking, eavesdropping women are always reduced to immaculate plainness, eventually. Their fledgling wings are trimmed, their busy tongues stopped. There were two ways of responding to this realization. I took the easier route. I straightened my lips, applied some plum lipstick and went down for breakfast.

Sitting at the kitchen table, I felt self-conscious, as if the truth about my other life in Sierra Leone was still written on my face. But then Anita, smiling broadly, set a plate of fried plantains and black-eyed beans in front of me, dispelling my fears. She sat beside me, drinking tea.

'There are a few things I need to finish off in the studio,' I began.

'Today?'

'I'd like to do it this morning. What about you? Church?'

She looked alarmed, as though I were brandishing an infectious razor in her face.

'I could help you here, then I need to go out.'

She left me to finish in silence and went into the living room, where I could hear her tidying up. Breakfast over, I peered round the living-room door and saw her plumping up cushions, her duster licking the bookshelves and table.

'It's going to be all right, Anita; everything will be in order, I promise.'

'I believe you.'

I entered the cool darkness of the studio. My work was nearing completion. I looked down at my list of tasks and ticked every item under J. P. Decker, most of those under Alphonso Lisk-Carew and more than half under the late 1880s photographer, W. S. Johnston. As for Uncle Moses' work, there was no point. It was so comprehensive, offering a variety of styles and themes, numerous individual and group portraits, landscapes and seascapes that I felt both over-whelmed and exhilarated. I loved the very idea of hundreds of people, in Sunday best, at school celebrations, acting, farm-ing, or simply day-dreaming, being captured over the decades. He had also snapped at regular intervals the Cotton Tree, Freetown's most familiar landmark, in an attempt to safeguard each phase of the city's life.

'What's going on in here?' asked Elizabeth from the doorway.

'A bit of everything,' I said prevaricating, unable to divulge exactly what I was feeling.

'What *is* going on?'

'There is so much here. He could make an archive. Hun-dreds of portraits, so many faces.'

I nodded my head as the idea started to balloon. Elizabeth had a look in her eyes that I had not seen before, an expression of puzzlement.

'What is going on here?'

'Stuck record,' I hurled back.

Hearing the children shout outside, Elizabeth left to see if something was the matter. 'They are just playing,' she reported back. Citizen and Sara covered in dust were playing at the back of the house. He had set up a stove of loosely stacked stones with a gap in the middle on top of which were two rusty tins filled with mud and water. Each was stirring one of these supposed cooking pots with a wooden spoon.

'Have you two finished making my lunch?' Elizabeth teased.

'Your stew is burning,' Sara informed the kitchen assistant.

'Let's give them something real to cook.'

'Best not. Let them just make-believe. You know tonight they can help cook. Cut up the onions and tomatoes. Learn to make sauce.'

'It will be horrible.'

We both screamed with laughter. Eddy in competition, let out an ear-blasting sound, then gibbering to himself, went into the house and came out with a bowl of peanuts, which he offered to Citizen.

'Come to London sometime, Elizabeth. I'll introduce you to some people of your own age.'

She tilted her head all the way back, showing off her long neck, and from that swanlike position asked, 'You know young men of my age, Auntie?'

'You don't need help there, they'll come out in droves, you'll see.'

The midday sun was grilling the earth but my heart was seized with a terrible coldness, indistinguishable from doubt.

'Don't you see, Elizabeth, you could have it all.'

Everything about her style would intrigue and fascinate. She personified black grace without complications, exerting a powerful attraction wherever she chose to be. Armed with her natural qualities and with the wardrobe to match, who could resist?

'Just come and see.'

A couple of days later on my way back from a morning walk, I noticed a young man with his back to me, standing outside Anita's house. I went up to see what he wanted and Elizabeth came out just as I was about to speak with him. He was a boyfriend of hers I had not seen before, who was offering to take us into town in his car.

'Auntie, this is the Olu, who was nursing at the reception centre.'

I shook his warm hand while she returned briefly inside. He was an old flame but still hopeful. He had been up-country and back several times since they interrupted their affair. Twice he had tried to win her back, he told me, but she was stubborn. He waited patiently as she got ready, catching glimpses of her slender figure, wondering if her lips would be affectionate again.

Citizen and Sara came out as we were standing there and I asked if he remembered this charge who had been sneaked away.

'Very well.'

Citizen recognized him too.

'That time was so busy. The child soldiers were coming to us in trucks every day when they heard the war was over. Some of them came in helicopters, some by foot. Then the journalists came also from all over the place; radio and television came, people from England, America, different parts of Europe, from Sweden, Holland, they came too. And there was one Adam Hoekstra who was there that day. He was Dutch. The children were singing their song, you know it? "If you're happy and you know it, clap your hands . . ."'

'I've heard that one several times,' I replied.

'Children's songs were everywhere,' he said, 'and this one they all sang. And Adam took an interest in those small boys, like his own flesh and blood, so when the singing began he mouthed to me he wanted it on tape, then he turned and asked your small boy who was standing in the front: "What is your name?"

'"They call me Citizen."

'"How old are you?"

'"Eight years old, sir."

'"Why did you join the fighting?"

'The boy paused as though not knowing what to tell them. The tape was still running. He bent down towards the small machine and whispered into it that he had killed his grandmother, and he fell down on the ground. We thought: "Maybe this one will die," he was so thin and weak.'

All the time Olu was speaking, Citizen was paying close attention, longing to hear this story about himself since, it seemed, he had only had fragments. Here at last was someone who could help position the fragments, who could tie on the beginning and middle to the end.

'Go on,' I urged Olu as we all sat down to hear more.

'Do you follow Krio?' he asked me.

'Yes.' He was kind to ask.

'"He no dey talk," explained one other small boy who was there.

'"He does talk – he just spoke to me," said Adam. "He told me his name is Citizen and he is eight years old."'

Citizen nodded. This was as it had happened. Olu wiped his own brow before continuing to tell us of the effects on the children of stress, sleep deprivation and hunger, and drugs.

'Maybe the other small boy was Abu,' I suggested. Olu shrugged, but Citizen nodded:

'And one girl pickin too.'

'Sally, that must have been Sally,' I joined in.

Olu continued his account: '"Look at him han, tiny tiny han." Sally pointed out Citizen's baby-sized hands and fingers. Adam took the boy's hands into his own and examined them. The baby fingers wrapped determinedly around Adam's index finger. The features of the boy Citizen looked wonderfully calm, free of cares. But his fingers gripped tightly like an infant's.'

'We have fortified milk for the ones who are so sick,' Olu had explained, taking charge, as if to protect the new arrival with the curious hands from others' gaze. He bundled up Citizen and carried him into the office, placing him on a small chair while Sally, Adam and the others followed. In that office and for the first time in several years, Citizen received a cup of milk from the hands of a man who made small circular movements on his baby hands and over his forehead. Once he had fed him the milk each day, Olu would put Citizen to bed and sing him the lullaby:

'When shall I see my home again?

Oh, my home,

Oh, my home,

I shall never forget my home,

O sweet Sierra Leone.'

As he sang this Citizen, who was sitting next to Sara, began to smile. The song and the fortified milk had served him kindness in the way that a longed-for nipple is kind. Kindness had slipped into his body like heartsease, permitting his hands to grow. Over the next few weeks, changing like molten glass forged in fire, Citizen's hands grew big. Forgiveness came. Alive with pride, Olu invited Adam to come and see the charge whose little fingers were growing to the correct size. They paid him attention and in turn he would learn to pay attention to himself.

'Adam liked your boy. He came back to see him three or four times. Each time he looked at the little hands. Do you remember, Citizen?'

Citizen said, 'Yes.'

'Show me your hands?' asked Olu.

Citizen spread his fingers and raised both hands in the air to show that they were the right size for his age and stature. We all looked closely at his hands, delighted to meet the man who had cared for Citizen and allowed his hands to grow. The expression on Citizen's face showed that he too was delighted.

Olu said to him: 'Your hands began to grow. It was when your hands had grown again to the correct size, you told Adam how after you pulled the trigger on your grandma, the hands became small. So small after that, you could never pull a trigger again. You said you were so shamed of the small hands. They told you to raise a stick and beat a boy, but you could not lift a stick. They told you to carry weapons but they fell from your hands. Only small, small things could you carry.'

Citizen began to discover what his life story really was, or the pointers to it. People had come and helped him. They had taken care of him. Olu continued to address him directly, transferring the elements of story to layer upon layer of experience that could be excavated later, studied and labelled. 'Adam liked you so much, he picked you up and kissed your face.' Then Olu turned to me: 'You should have seen him, hugging the boy.'

What Olu could not see or maybe took for granted was how he himself had loved the boy; comfort had come to Citizen 439K like the white eye of a passing vehicle on a dark stretch: Olu, a stranger offering milk, Elizabeth, a neighbour, plucking him from chance.

His arm around her shoulder, Olu and Elizabeth swanned off to town. Trailing yards behind them like ducklings, Sara and Citizen went along for the ride.

'It's you and me now, Eddy.' He had come to keep company and was scratching enthusiastically. It had been a wildly passionate day. I remembered sitting with Sally at the Doria camp weeks before when she had told me about reading palms. I remembered her softness: how she must have cradled those baby-sized hands in hers. No wonder she had been unable to decipher lines. Images floated back to me like leaves billowing in the wind. Let them pass. Countless faces, countless scenes: let them pass. An eruption of sounds from my monkey companion. And then in an instant, as if I had been kicked out of a waking dream, I saw it. A RISK TO HAVE HANDS: HANDS CAN BE CUT OFF!

Two days later, Olu was back. Seeing him hanging about in the yard, Anita raised her eyebrows at me. Elizabeth was out, but he wanted to be there. She told him to make himself useful by helping me in the studio, which he did. He told me of his travels in Guinea, where he had found Guinea brocade, a kind of damask cloth, in an array of colours further enriched with pattern through tie-dye. He had bought several lengths. From then on I began to think how he might help Uncle Moses with building an archive. The images were all there: in his house and on the studio walls. For art was both serious and visibly a celebration of life.

We stopped for lunch. Everyone helped with the preparation, even the children. The conversation was about everyday things and about Uncle Moses' relationship with his daughter. He talked about missing her when she left home.

'But that's the way it has to be, Mister Moses,' Anita added. She was right; holding on to Agnes would never have prevented the loss.

That afternoon the very fine weather broke. Rain fell, sucking light from the sun. The rain drifted across the yard and slapped against the living-room windowpanes. I looked out and saw streamers of rain running off the tree on to the sodden earth. Eddy was sheltering under old palm leaves that he'd arranged in the shape of an umbrella. Inside we sat together quietly for most of that afternoon – Moses, Anita, Elizabeth, Olu, Citizen, Sara, and me.

Elizabeth began to sing. We listened. Citizen, seated on a low wooden stool with his back to her, swirled around when he recognized the love song. He slowly stood up and moved next to her so that she must have felt the warmth of his body. He opened his lips and joined her song.

Tiny currents of excitement ran around our circle, the same electric thrill that accompanies baby's first word, first step.

> *Such harmony is in immortal souls,*
> *But whilst this muddy vesture of decay*
> *Doth grossly close it in, we cannot hear it . . .*

Anita's mouth opened and shut. Afterwards, without discussing this we all returned to what we had been doing. We moved together like a family but without the drama. That evening Anita and I talked about the way Olu seemed to be taking a serious interest, the way Elizabeth was letting him in.

'Everyone reaches a time for letting things be,' Anita said wisely. She liked Olu. She could not explain what it was, but I felt that it was because certainty was in charge again, when everything had been left to chance for so long.

One day Olu came early, before Elizabeth had laid plans for the day. He invited us out to Lumley beach where we spent several pleasant hours. On the way back, we stopped at the garage where his car had been fixed a week before. The open courtyard was full of half-repaired cars, motorbikes and trucks, most of which would have been abandoned for scrap in other countries. Olu tooted. Then we heard children's raised voices and laughter coming to greet us.

'Mornin, sir,' said one of the mechanics, recognizing Olu.

'Mornin, ma,' a second boy peered at me, 'Hinga at your service!'

'Well, hello,' I acknowledged the smiling teenager, 'I'm just the passenger today.'

'No, come and look at what we have,' he persisted, no doubt catching the English accent.

'Don't you want a new car?' asked another.

I shook my head, but my actions betrayed my curiosity. 'Let me look then.'

A patch of sun on my back, then in a moment I was standing in the shed with corrugated-iron roof surrounded by engine parts, fenders, spare wheels, plugs, dashboards, clocks, panels and tools stored and waiting. 'Could you make me a car then, if I wanted one?' I asked, bemused.

'Look here!' The taller boy gestured to me to enter the shed. With the others following, I walked to the back, where I saw the wreck of an ageless cream-coloured Bentley. The paint was scraped off in ugly patches, the fenders bent and twisted as though this car had been driven into battle, but with some work no doubt it could be put on the road. 'Not there,' said one boy, directing my attention to a pristine dark blue truck. 'We rebuilt that one!'

'Fantastic!' I said. Four heads of black curls followed my gaze, watched me clamber into the car and returned my wave as we left. As soon as they were out of sight, I wanted to go back.

'I always come here,' Olu was explaining, 'to help our boys. Ex-child soldiers, you know.'

'Ahh!'

'They know about good service. Even the UN people come here.'

'I'm glad, really glad,' I told him, a patch of sun along my arm as I waved goodbye.

We came home at around three. Citizen was in the studio with Uncle Moses, helping him to hook up a thickly woven brown curtain to replace the old blue lappa. Citizen was on the stepladder while Uncle Moses fed the fabric up to him a few hooks at a time. I left them to find Elizabeth. She had begun to wash up and prepare some snacks in the kitchen.

'Do you like to cook?' she asked. I wondered whether she was starting to warm to the idea of visiting me, trying to visualize herself in a different life. 'I can do French cuisine, Italian, some Indian and even West African if you like.' She laughed.

When we had enough prepared vegetables, we put on a pot of rice and retreated into the lounge with our drinks. Citizen and Sara were playing outside, exchanging stories. She was telling him one of many in which she was the heroine and he presumably the hero:

'Cry? I cried till the water done in my eyes,' she recounted dramatically, 'then he leapt into the water and said, "Sara, is that you? Don't worry, I'm coming for you!" The whirlwind was blowing up, threatening to carry me away, so I shouted out, "Help me, help me!" and finally he grabbed me, pulled me off the rock and saved me.'

We exchanged glances and sipped our drinks. 'Children, huh!'

'Ask them to come in, Auntie, I'm going to check the rice. Have you seen Mummy and Mister Moses?' She was halfway out of the door before I could answer: 'Yes, they are outside, cutting back the hedge to our entrance.'

I smiled to myself: this was becoming a most pleasant day.

Not for a moment had I thought this would happen. Not for a moment had I imagined that the rhythm of our days, the piecing together of our lives could be so satisfying. The bare walls upstairs needed a lick of paint. We could fix the place up a bit and display the photographs. We could build the photography archive here and set aside space for visitors to come and look at those lovely mysterious images of Alphonso Lisk-Carew, and the photographs of people up-country by Decker and so much more by Uncle Moses. We could do this together. And we should add those shameless scenes from which we always want to shield our eyes.

Here was the gift of a daydream that could shape our lives. Follow it and there would be a home for Moses, Citizen and me, and the night dreams could be surrendered. Follow it and see how the veil thins between one world and another, one person and another.

I leaned my head back on the lounger, balancing my glass on my stomach, and closed my eyes, an interlude before dinner.

Adele, the last-night dream I had was about your grandson Citizen and me.

We were in London and I was taking him to a swimming competition. It was a chilly morning, but I had left the flat without realizing how cold it was. After ten minutes or more, my fingers began to feel numb. Citizen was wearing his grey woollen gloves. I was rubbing my hands together to thaw them when quite suddenly he removed the left glove, folded it and put it in his pocket. Then he reached out and held my hand. I can feel it now, that small warm hand in mine.

At the pool-side was my friend Clare, watching over her three-year-old, Chloe, who flapped like a tadpole in the shallow water. The whistle was blown for Citizen's race and he was off, weaving through the water. He turned a little clumsily but started back in good time. Only two swimmers were before him; he dug in and swam hard. Clare, Chloe and I were on our feet:

'Come on, Citizen, swim – come on, Citizen.'

He would not be able to hear us, though our voices were so strident they would not be hindered by the roughness of the Bay of Biscay, nor the weeds of the River Rokel.

'Swim for you, Citizen, swim for you, my boy, swim for me!'

We all triumphed that day, Adele. Clare and Chloe, Citizen and me; we jumped into the car and headed for a café off Lavender Hill. We had burgers with extra cheese, followed by apple pie. Perfectly made with English apples.

Apples green and red and unashamed, like everything in primary school.

Apple trees in the garden.

Apple blossom – pink and fulsome – springing.

Apple pies made with nutmeg and cream that runs on to the sugar and curdles.

Cox's Orange Pippins that sound like an up-and-coming couple in a Dickens novel.

Apples – Sierra Leone apples – pink plentiful soft fruits – no biting required – surrender to the light juices trickling down your throat.

Surrender

Surrender

Acknowledgements

It is important to stress that this story is a work of fiction. While Thomas Decker, the translator who appears in this book, is a historical figure and the geographical areas described, such as the Upper Guinean rainforest, do exist, the portrait of Decker and the events and most 'journeys' are fictional.

Several books were important to me in my research. The groundbreaking *History of Sierra Leone* by Christopher Fyfe, along with *Creoledom* by Arthur Porter and *A New History of Sierra Leone* by Joe A. D. Alie have helped me to understand the political and social history of the country. *Fighting for the Rainforest: War, Youth and Resources in Sierra Leone* by Paul Richards was especially useful, in particular his reading of the war as a 'crisis in modernity', which assisted my own thinking and Bemba Gogbua's story (pp. 98–100) inspired my own Bemba G.

Juliohs Siza by Thomas Decker, edited by Neville Shrimpton and Njie Sulayman and published by the University of Umea (Sweden), proved valuable as a primary source and enabled me to visualize Shakespeare in Sierra Leone. Neville Shrimpton's essay 'Thomas Decker and the Death of Boss Coker' enhanced my understanding of the translator and his times.

Factual information on the Sierra Leonean photographers has been drawn mainly from the work of American scholar

Vera Viditz Ward, whose essays include: 'Studio Photography in Freetown', in *Anthology of African and Indian Ocean Photography*, Revue Noire, 1998; 'Alphonso Lisk-Carew: Creole Photographer', *African Arts*, November 1985 (Vol. 19, no. 1, pp. 46–51); 'Paramount Chiefs of Sierra Leone' for National Museum of African Art, Smithsonian Institution, 21 November 1990–2 September 1991. Thanks in particular to the Schomburg Library of New York Public Library for assisting with this research.

Contemporary imagery of Sierra Leone had to follow the threads of the photography pioneers Alphonso Lisk-Carew and J. P. Decker, both of whom recorded the lives of ordinary Sierra Leoneans from 1870s onwards. I would like to acknowledge the work of documentary film-maker Philippe Diaz, whose *Nouvel Ordre Mondial,* premiered in Paris, April 2001, fearlessly portrayed many of the 'atrocities' and included the work of the brave Sierra Leonean film-maker Sorious Samura. In addition, extensive BBC radio and television coverage of the war gave me much important information. Thanks too to Radio Netherlands for their fantastic CD-ROM: *Sierra Leone, the Scars of Brutality,* presented by Eric Beauchemin and including the work of Corinne Dufka of Human Rights Watch.

Non-governmental organizations were very generous in sharing information about their work in Sierra Leone and I am indebted to Antonio Cabrol of CAFOD, Jill Clark of Save the Children (Sierra Leone) and staff at Monde Contre Faim (France). Rachel Brett and Margaret McCallin, co-authors of *Children: The Invisible Soldiers* for Swedish Save the Children, greatly assisted my research. Finally, I was fortunate to see the Royal Shakespeare Company's wonderful production of *Julius Caesar* directed by Edward Hall in Stratford (August 2001), which turned Caesar's Rome into a fascist city-state and explored the link between private flaws and public actions.

This book is a tribute to the children of Sierra Leone whose indomitable spirit inspired the work. A most special thank you to all of those who shared their experiences about the war in Sierra Leone whether directly or not, especially to Elizabeth Mensah and Umu-Jalloh.

Many thanks to Margaret Busby who has proved to be an exceptionally fine big sister.

Thank you to Sara Holloway and all at Granta, Patrick Walsh and all at Conville and Walsh for their invaluable support.

Thank you to Debbie Licorish, Catherine Hall, Virginia Crompton, Barbara Heinzen, Elsbeth Lindner, Susan Pennybacker and Sarah Tyrer for advice and encouragement; thanks to my family and other friends for their kindness and love.

I am grateful to numerous poets, novelists, artists and musicians whose works have inspired my own. In particular, the words 'bougainvillea in mauve passion' on page 77 are by Sierra Leone poet Abioseh Nicol. The words 'some nice boonoonoonous lady' on page 136 are by Jamaican poet Louise Bennett and the lines in italics on page 138 are by Kum Kum Sangari.